THE CURSE OF THE
BIG WATER

PETER
GEORGAS

ALSO BY PETER GEORGAS:

DARK BLUES
THE EMPTY CANOE
THE FIFTH SLUG

For Martin

Prologue

"Where are you, Beth?" Damon asked aloud, his words spilling out of the boathouse and into the lake. The burgeoning dawn was insinuating itself anew. After a slow beginning the sun swiftly, silently invested light in another day, and color returned as a dividend to brighten the earth.

Water lapped gently against the concrete apron. He waded out in his bare feet, the cool water a soothing counterpoint to his hot nerves. He stared down, his mind awash with disturbing scenarios, his eyes focusing not on the water's surface but in its depth, and he spotted a dark mass on the sandy bottom where the boathouse met the dock. He dropped to his haunches for a better look. The water was about four feet deep. In spite of the shadows not yet cleared by the spreading daylight, he was able to read the outline of what appeared to be a rolled-up canvas or some other waterlogged material. Maybe one of the storage bags on the Chris-Craft had fallen overboard and sank. That would explain the splash that had awakened him in the first place.

But everything was so neatly secured it didn't seem likely anything could have fallen into the water unless it was knocked in, or thrown in. Whatever the case, he better retrieve it.

Damon grabbed an oar leaning against the boathouse wall and fed the blade into the water ahead of the object, pulling it toward him. It rolled along the flat, smooth bottom easily, nearly weightless in the water, and maneuvered it toward the concrete apron.

He was more intrigued with removal than identification and only after he actually had his hands on the form could he no longer deny the truth.

He had found Beth.

Quickly, with nervous energy as though he might still change the calculus from death to life, he dragged her onto the floor of the boathouse by the bathrobe clinging to her shoulders, exposing blanched nakedness, lake water making a small rivulet to her naval. He tried chest compression, pushing and pushing on her sternum till he exhausted himself. He felt for a pulse but there was none.

He lowered his head to her breasts, dropping tears of remorse, regret, fear...

1

The funeral was private—Sarah Rand insisted on that. It was bad enough to have the Minnetonka Police and the Hennepin County Sheriff involved, men in uniform crawling around, using that awful yellow tape to cordon off the boathouse. And the nosy reporters and cameramen from the local television channels using long lenses from the main road trying to catch someone in a moment of grief, anything to feed the endless fascination with the Fischers, one of Minnetonka's oldest and richest families.

The service was at St. Martin's by the Lake. The Episcopal Church overlooked Lake Minnetonka on prime real estate, minutes from the Fischer estate. The edifice had a country look with a bell tower extending upward from a sharply peaked roof, and gray clapboard siding—modest by Lake Minnetonka standards, but maybe this was God's way of setting a temporal example for those parishioners who embraced Thorstein Veblen's concept of conspicuous consumption.

A row of black and white squad cars blocked Westwood Road from passing traffic while a cortege consisting of a hearse and three Cadillac limousines sat respectfully in the parking lot next to the church.

But inside the church was another matter. Orderliness was not a virtue of the Fischer clan. The last time the entire family was forced to gather in one room was a dreary November morning four decades ago when the will of Christopher Thomas Fischer was read aloud in the law offices of Wallace Wallace Custer and Madden. Even if she weren't executrix, Sarah Rand, CT's eldest, maintained control simply by her commanding presence, not unlike the flyball on a steam engine, allowing CT to rest in peace in his tomb at Greenlawn Cemetery.

He had a full life, nothing to complain about. In May of 1865 when he was 22, CT boarded the Akron Maiden, a sternwheeler, at Berea, his hometown, traveled down the Ohio and up the Mississippi to St. Paul, the northern terminus of riverboat transport. His destination was further upstream, St. Anthony Falls, where opportunity lay for an enterprising and, to some extent, unscrupulous young man. The Village of St. Anthony, soon to be incorporated as the City of Minneapolis, was on the verge of a building boom, and white pine forests lay just two hundred miles north ready for plucking or, should one say, axing. CT bought up Chippewa land scrip and obtained title to vast areas of virgin timber, which prompted the federal government to determine if he violated the 1855 Treaty with the Chippewa of the Mississippi. Although he was never charged, CT's transactions were considered egregious if not illegal.

While accumulating acreage, he lived in a boarding house in Nisswa where he met Anna Spencer, the daughter of the landlady. They married after a short courtship and moved to Minneapolis. She bore him five children—one too many, alas, because during the birth of her fifth, a second daughter, the infant survived but Anna did not. CT remained a widower the rest of his life.

By the first decade of the twentieth century, half the buildings and most of the homes in Minneapolis were built with Fischer lumber. This not only made CT one of the richest men in America, it also gave him the resources to amass one of the largest private art collections in the country. In the late-1920s he repaid the community that enriched him by erecting, on Lowry Hill overlooking downtown Minneapolis, a public museum. The popularity of Rudolph Valentino convinced him that the style of the Arabian Nights was an enduring fashion and he hired Thorsov & Cerny, the city's pre-eminent architectural firm, to design a replica of a Moorish palace complete with minarets and half moons.

Even the Fischer fortune was not immune to the Great Depression and the museum closed for several years. All was not lost, however, because the Depression, paradoxically, provided an opportunity to rethink the museum's mission. CT was dead after all and attendance, when the Closed Until Further Notice sign went up, was only a few dozen a month. A new direction was needed and the inspiration behind it was Irene Campbell, Sarah's younger sister. Much of CT's eclectic art was auctioned off, except for a nonpareil collection of jade carvings and a group of 19th century Romantic landscapes, to finance a new direction: contemporary art and design. With a modernized façade and a new mission, the Fischer Museum reopened in 1940 as the Fischer Art Center.

Fast forward twenty-eight years. The Art Center is now a driving force in contemporary art, its programs recognized nationwide, its annual attendance in the hundreds of thousands. The administration wing of the Art Center is an open plan of cubicles, a layout ahead of its time, whose epicenter is the office of the Director, Troy Adamson. "Open Access" he named it, where he can keep an eye on things.

Troy stood in the doorway of his office. "Damon," he called to his publicist, "drop whatever you are doing. I have something I want to discuss with you."

Troy returned to his spare Herman Miller desk, a glass-topped worktable, exuding an air of self-confidence that was his trademark.

"Sit down," he said as Damon entered his office.

11

He pointed at a pair of identical Corbusier chairs of opulent black leather and chrome tubular construction.

"Take your choice."

Damon smiled at Troy's stab at humor—as if it made any difference. Besides, Damon had never seen a lone Corbu chair. They came in pairs, one to sit in and one to look at.

"I have a new assignment for you," Troy said. His eyes dominated his face—they honed in deep enough to read your mind.

"New?" Damon asked, choosing the left chair because he was left-handed. He had the schedule for the year: exhibitions, performing arts, lectures, films, coming issues of the *Design Quarterly*. What else was there?

"This is outside the museum."

Oh, that was it, pro bono. Troy had earlier asked Damon if he would devote some hours to CUE, the Committee on Urban Environment, whose efforts were to make Minneapolitans tidier by using, for example, bright-white trash containers silk-screened with evergreen trees and the legend "Spruce Up Your City."

"I'll cram it into everything else I have to do."

"Don't use the word cram. This is something that will involve you for some time."

Damon stared quizzically. "For some time?"

Troy nodded. "Three months, maybe longer."

"Who needs three months to help CUE?"

"I'm not talking about CUE. Let The Art Institute handle that. This assignment is more important, and more personal. Henry Fischer wants help in writing a family history, like one of those as-told-to yarns. He is looking for someone with discretion and a good writing style, not a freelance hack. You are the man."

"Me?" Damon said, now truly surprised. Henry, the younger brother of Sarah Rand, was a reclusive bachelor whose passion was polishing rare stones. "The only time I see him is when he visits the museum and drops one of his stones on my desk, like his version of a raise. He doesn't even know who I am."

"Henry may be shy but he knows the whole staff by name."

"Well, he never uses mine. He never even says hello, unless a nod of the head means the same thing. Besides I'm busy. I have a stack of ASAP notes from you, or have you forgotten?"

"This is not a nine to five assignment, more like evenings and weekends."

"I do have a social life."

"Socialize with the Fischers." Troy leaned forward, his steely eyes getting steelier. "Look, Damon, this is non-negotiable. Our benefactors have extended an invitation to share their private lives and write about them as well. This is the most important PR job you will ever have, working with the family that pays our salaries and funds this museum."

"Did you have anything to do with this, Troy?"

Troy smiled enigmatically. "Henry asked me who was the person I trusted most, and I told him, Damon Petroulis."

Damon sat in the back pew of St. Martins like a disowned relative. Sarah did not invite him, nor did he think it was his place to ask. Regardless, he could not miss Beth's funeral. Even though he was not a member of the family, per se, neither was he a stranger.

It was Henry, or rather his absence, that brought Damon and Beth together. Henry's work method was to leave a pile of folders, ledgers, letters, newspaper clippings and photographs on a table in the library and then retreat to his lair on the top floor, leaving Damon alone to sort through the material and make notes, which Henry would later review. Into this void stepped Beth who came to the library, first out of curiosity and then with growing interest. Before long she was helping him sort through the dusty records, including crackly Kodak snapshots whose ghostly images she helped identify.

Working side-by-side, fingers touching, shoulders bumping, the two inevitably sparked a relationship, so unlikely, so antithetical to his Greek immigrant roots that, even now as he thought back on it, their affair was more a dream than reality. How could anyone take it seriously, especially the Fischers who saw it for what it was, an improbable fling, nothing more, with a young man sent from the Art Center by Troy Adamson. Beth had eligible suitors galore whose family names were listed in Mrs. Astor's Four Hundred, and one day she would marry one of them.

But until that day came, there was this dark-haired man with an exotic handsomeness who occasionally stayed over the weekend to work on his research, sleeping in the guest bedroom so he would not have to commute from his apartment at Franklin and Lyndale on the south edge of downtown Minneapolis. Occasionally, Beth would sneak into his room in the middle of the night. Everyone knew what was going on, including the help, but they looked the other way as long as the two were sharing his bedroom, not hers.

And so Damon felt justified attending the funeral—as long as he parked himself in a back pew. However, this also had the unintended consequence of making him stand out by sitting alone, if one may use a play on words to describe a solemn occasion.

The family was still in the prayer room adjacent to the sanctuary when he entered the nave. It was not very large, but the emptiness made it seem so—no acolyte or assistant pastor for company, only Beth inside her closed casket resting on a catafalque.

Staring at the ornately carved, golden-oak coffin, he thought about his own reaction to her death. He was in mourning, of course, how could he not be—he was her lover—yet it was not the soul-searing reaction of her family. Maybe guilt was more appropriate. Had he behaved differently, been more alert to troubling signs, he might have saved her. If only, if only...

Trapped by uncertainty, which was to grow as time went on, he failed initially to sense the presence of someone moving into his pew.

"Great hat," came a whisper that echoed in the empty chamber. Only one person talked that way, Jon Love. He sat down next to Damon, his heaviness squeaking the pew's wood seat. Damon was surprised that Jon turned up. He was not a family member, rather a family retainer, Sarah's personal lawyer and financial advisor to be precise. Showing up at Beth's funeral was a bit brassy, Damon thought—but then, still thinking about it, maybe not so different from his own presence.

Jon had an ego that matched his last name. He wanted to say he "loved" his name but that would be gilding the lily, and Jon was already gilded enough. He wore his name proudly, even as a lad when he was teased by his peers, according to what he once told Damon over cocktails at the Minneapolis Club.

"Thank God my father was a Love," he said, "rather than my mother who was a Hanson. How could I have been successful if my last name was *Han*son?"

Love was a successful barrister, as he liked to call himself, using his last name to great advantage, especially with older women, widows and spinsters who romanticized their amours because they no longer had them. Jon was a bit rotund, not roly-poly as his detractors described him, in the mid-range of Weight Watchers' client list, and he used his soft roundness, or was it round softness, to distinct advantage. To his female clients he was cuddly, a substitute for the teddy bears of their childhood. He provided a nostalgic symbol of security in the securities business.

Jon's most important client was also his oldest, Sarah Rand who at 92 was the doyenne of the first family to settle on Breckett's Point after the Dakotah Sioux. She married Alfred Rand in 1898 and lived in stately splendor in Kenwood. When Alfred died Sarah resettled with her two children in her father's mansion where CT, from his office overlooking the lake, taught his widowed daughter all about the lumber business.

Jon Love's timing was immaculate. Just as he sat down, the door to the prayer room opened and the family began filing in, a lugubrious procession of black suits and black dresses.

First to enter was Sarah, short in stature but long on power with her proud bearing and high Elizabethan forehead. A delicate black lace shawl covered white hair of permanent waves fashionable in the 1930s, a style she still wore because to her, permanent meant permanent. Sarah's creased face showed no emotion but she had to be devastated that Beth, the granddaughter upon whom she showered all of her attention, was dead.

Holding Sarah's arm, although she resented help, was her brother, Henry, the stone polisher, younger than Sarah by five years. The only difference between Henry visiting the Art Center and Henry in the present moment was that he was not at all his usual rumpled self. The suit he was wearing was as wrinkle-free as a horse's hide. His head was lowered almost to the breaking point of his spine—a man barely managing his grief. They took their place in the front pew on the aisle.

Behind them came Dolores, the widow of Sarah's son, Harrison, who died in an air crash. Dolores was Beth's mother. Damon learned, not from his research but from Beth letting him in on a family secret, that Dolores was plucked from the chorus line of "No No Nanette" in 1927 by Harrison, a graduate student at NYU. Her fading good looks belied her age, relentlessly held at bay by cosmetic surgery.

Sarah's only daughter, Elizabeth, after whom Beth was named, died at a young age. Her memory was like a shadow in a family photograph, undefined but still there.

A step behind was Richard, Beth's twin, the playboy of the family who spent most days on the tennis court of the Wayzata Country Club. Athletically trim and tan, he was friendly to Damon the way he was friendly to the Club's locker room attendant. Damon got back at him in a small way by calling him Poor Richard, but not to his face.

CT II, Beth and Richard's older brother, came in next with his family in tow—wife Ruth and their two teenage sons, Rolf and Clarence. The quartet evoked an air of superiority even though none of them had ever done anything to earn it. CT II was known in his family as CT-Two. Carrying his grandfather's name also carried with it the title of presumptive heir to the family business after Sarah passed away. Ruth's father owned a steel foundry in Spokane, the largest west of the Mississippi. Once Sarah passed on, CT-Two hoped to orchestrate a merger of the two privately held companies, lumber and steel, and create a conglomerate capable of competing anywhere in the world. This ambition weighed so heavily on his shoulders it made him seem even shorter than he really was, perhaps the main reason why he was always defensive around Damon, who at six-two could not help but look down on the diminutive Fischer, barely five-nine in his elevator shoes.

Next to enter were Sarah's middle brother, Edmond, and his daughter Ellen, pushing him in his wheelchair. He wore a scarf around his neck even though it was a warm day. Edmond had suffered a stroke and was taken care of by Ellen, for whom life did not begin at 40 but rather ended, metaphorically speaking. She played the role of spinster all too well: hair wound in a bun, looking down to avoid eye contact. Ellen parked Edmond in the aisle across from Sarah and sat in the pew next to him. Staring at her curved back Damon thought she would be very striking if she just loosened her hair and put on makeup.

Following Ellen and Edmond was Irene Campbell, Sarah's younger sister, who chaired the Art Center's Board of Directors. It was her determination that turned the museum from a stuffy repository of CT's art to a vibrant modern art center. She seemed to lurk in Sarah's shadow except when she visited the Art Center where she shined like a Brancusi bronze. A dutiful step behind walked Arvid, Irene's enigmatic son, and his wife Crystal. Arvid moved away in his early twenties only to return the day of Beth's funeral, which prompted Jon to lean over and whisper in Damon's ear, "The prodigal son has returned."

The last to enter the nave were Madie and her companion, Mrs. Stockton. A child in a woman's body, Madie was dressed like a schoolgirl. All she needed was a lunch box to complete the ensemble. Withdrawn and plain, Madie was the Fischer's version of a skeleton in the closet. Damon did not know where she fit in the family hierarchy. He did not even know she existed until he came upon a photograph of a birthday party on the terrace. Members of the family were beaming at a woman in a distinctly little-girl party dress blowing out the candles on her cake.

Ramrod erect with a face that might crack if she smiled, Mrs. Stockton directed her charge, whose benumbed features made Damon wonder if Madie was sedated. They sat in the second row near the door they came through so that, Damon assumed, they could make a hasty exit in case the walls started pressing in on Madie.

Even though the family was aware of Damon and Jon sitting in back, no one looked their way or acknowledged their presence with even a nod or the lift of a finger—nothing to indicate there was anyone present but themselves.

Now that they were settled in their pews, the priest entered the sanctuary from a private access and the funeral began. Wearing white vestments, he conducted a brief service, concluding it with a short tribute to Beth, delicately touching on the untimely loss of so fine and fresh a person who left a void that would be difficult if not impossible to fill. There were no sobs or tears. The Fischers were brought up to be stoical and expressing grief was a sign of weakness.

After the service they filed out the way they had

come in, marshaling in the parking lot so that the funeral attendants could usher them to their respective limos. Two of the undertakers, so proper and well-rehearsed they appeared like automatons, entered the church and rolled the catafalque outside to the waiting hearse. A private funeral, Damon realized while watching the drill, meant no pallbearers.

He and Jon Love stayed where they were until the cortege left for the cemetery.

"Well, old bean," Love said in a loud voice now that they alone, "what did you think of the line-up?"

"Line-up?"

"You know, as in police line-up."

"You make them sound like criminals."

"Well, one of them is. Someone did that poor girl in."

"Come on, Jon. The coroner hasn't yet said how she died."

"You found her. What do you think?"

"I want to think she drowned."

"As do all of us, but she was young and strong. Doesn't make sense."

"So who has the most to gain with Beth dead?" Damon asked.

"You are researching a family history aren't you?"

"Yes, you know I am."

"Well, then, keep digging. Find out who has the most to *lose* and you will find the person who did her in."

2

Damon arrived at work and found six ASAP notes from Troy, not bad for a Monday morning. He wasn't that pressed for time anyway. Ever since Beth's passing, the history project at the Fischers was more or less on hold. It was too tough for Henry to sit down with Damon in a room whose black curtains were still drawn against the optimistic sunlight. The family was still in mourning.

Under the pile of notes was one from Donna the switchboard operator: 8:30 a.m. Call from a Lieutenant Harris, Hennepin County Sheriff's Office, number 773-1200.

Curious as well as apprehensive, Damon dialed and got the lieutenant directly, no central operator intercepting calls—evidently his direct line.

"Lieutenant Harris."

"Damon Petroulis."

"Thanks for getting back to me so promptly. I need to talk to you. When would be a good time?"

*****

They met that afternoon in the Sculpture Court, the centerpiece of the Art Center, domed by a skylight that let in natural illumination. They sat on a bench next to a bronze horse and rider by the Italian sculptor Marino Marini, one of a dozen 20th century sculptures in evolving states of abstraction. The works were situated between clusters of flowers and shrubs in square cast-concrete tubs.

Harris was middle-aged, graying but not balding, in plain clothes, and plain they were—out of style too. The current *de rigueur* for men was narrow trousers and jackets with deep vents. He could have been an insurance agent or a process server or a cop—which is what he was—and it showed in his discomfort.

"What's that statue all about?" he asked, pointing to the Marini. "The rider is missing his hands and the horse looks like it's starving."

"Marini is expressing the futility of war," Damon said, "unlike those sculptures you see in public parks where the horse is rearing in victory and the rider is flashing his sword like a conqueror. The subject matter is not too different from a famous painting by Picasso called Guernica, named for a village bombed by the Fascists in the Spanish Civil War. Picasso's horse is looking skyward like Marini's, not in victory but in agony and death."

"Spare me the details," Harris said, shaking his head. He pulled a small notepad and a pencil stub from his shirt pocket. "I want to ask you a few questions, and they ain't about art." He wet the tip of the pencil with his tongue. "I'd like to know about your relationship with Beth Rand."

Damon tensed. This was not a subject he talked about, least of all to a cop. But Damon was not surprised. He was the one who found Beth, perhaps the last person to see her alive. He was now the center of attention, but it was a center stained at the edges with suspicion. Though family members were polite, Damon had the uncomfortable feeling that he was now looked upon as a "person of interest." Everyone knew that he and Beth were more than casual acquaintances, but in the lofty air of propriety that old money inhales, he was still an outsider— the Publicity Director of the Fischer Art Center assigned to write a family history, that's all. This gave him unique access to a very private dynasty whose namesake was known to the public as the eccentric founder of a modern art museum—but it did not provide entitlement.

Beth's death was not only big news locally, it even made the New York Times. Her death, at 29, according to the obituary, was a devastating blow to the Fischers who hid their sorrow, grief and pain behind a wall of stoicism. And inside that wall, the family drew within itself even further—a black shroud, and it was shrinking around Damon.

"So what do you want to know?" Damon asked as innocently as possible.

"Well, first of all, to put it bluntly, were you sleeping with her?"

Damon looked at the Marini rider with renewed sympathy knowing now what it felt like to be under attack.

"We had a relationship."

"Can the bullshit. You had a guest room at the mansion, I was told, where you could stay overnight when you went out there to work on the family history, right? And you didn't always spend it all by your lonesome."

Damon could not imagine anyone in the family providing this information. "Where did you hear that?"

"The help, including the stiff broad who's the nursemaid to that goofy girl..."

"Mrs. Stockton?"

"Yeah."

Damon lowered his head.

Harris waited a moment and then said, "You want to talk about it?"

"Never in her room."

"I didn't figure you would be that dumb." Harris wrote some words in his notebook. "Ok. She was with you the night she died?"

Damon nodded.

"Tell me what happened."

And so Damon described that night—his waking

up to the sound of a splash coming through the open windows, his growing concern about her absence, getting dressed, stepping into the hall, peeking in Madie's room to see if Beth was there, and finally walking out to the boat house where he found her in the water.

Harris wrote rapidly. "Why did you look in Madie's room?"

"Sometimes Beth stayed with her. They were very close and it was not unusual for Beth to lie down with Madie if she was agitated about something."

Harris looked up from his pad. "Why did you go to the boathouse?"

"Like I said, I heard a splash."

"Could have been a fish, maybe a muskie. They make a big noise."

"You think I'm making this up?" Damon asked with growing frustration.

"I don't think, I question." Harris folded the pencil stub into his notebook and laid them on the bench. He became thoughtful as though weighing his options. "Mind if I call you by your first name?"

Damon settled back. "Go ahead if it makes it easier for you to believe me."

"A cop is dubious by nature—no one is above suspicion."

"Sounds like the title of a movie."

This time Harris did smile. "I know that one. Fred MacMurray and Joan Crawford, one of Hitchcock's early films."

"Right," Damon said returning the smile.

"I'm a fan of old movies."

"So am I."

Harris leaned forward. "I also came to see you because I need your help."

"You need *my* help?" Damon asked in surprise.

"First, I want you to read this."

Harris pulled a buff colored envelope from the wide pocket of his jacket and handed it over.

Damon stared at the inscription in the upper left corner: Hennepin County Medical Examiner & Coroner, 530 Chicago Avenue, Minneapolis, Minnesota.

"Open it."

He did so gingerly and unfolded a form titled Summary Autopsy Report.

"I'm not sure I want to look at this," he said but began reading anyway, curiosity getting the upper hand.

At the top were boxes filled in with typewritten lines identifying the deceased as

Elizabeth Fischer Rand

Age 29

Followed by:

Case number 001294-23E-2003,

Investigating Agency Hennepin County Sheriff

The clinical reportage, with as much compassion as describing a side of beef, sent a shudder through Damon:

The body is presented in a black body bag—the report began—the victim is wearing a gray sweatshirt and navy blue sweatpants. The body is that of a normally developed white female measuring 67 inches and weighing 122 pounds, and appearing generally consistent with the stated age of twenty-nine years.

The genital system is that of an adult female. The structures are within normal limits. There is evidence of recent sexual activity but no indications that sexual contact was forcible.

The body is cold and unembalmed. Lividity is fixed in the distal portions of the limbs. The eyes are open, irises are brown and corneas are cloudy. Petechial hemorrhaging is present in the conjunctival surface of the eyes. There is a dark red ligature mark on the neck below the mandible.

Damon looked up from his reading. "What does ligature mean?"

"As it applies to forensics," Harris said, "it means a rope or a belt or a garrott—anything consistent with strangulation."

"Strangulation?"

"Your sweetheart," Harris said, making a fist by his neck and yanking it upward, "was strangled before she was dumped in the lake."

"But it says here Manner of Death: Accidental Drowning."

"That's what the Fischers want you to believe."

"I don't get it."

"Someone murdered Beth Rand and the family is covering it up."

"But why?"

"You think the Fischers want a killer in their midst? Unless they try to pin it on you."

"Me?" Damon asked, incredulous.

"You have a lot to answer for. You found her and, as far as anyone knows, you were the last one to see her alive."

"Why would I do anything that awful?" Damon pointed at his chest. "Is this what a killer looks like? Besides what possible motive would I have to kill Beth?"

"In a murder case everyone is a suspect and, if you study them like I do, it's the lover nine times out of ten."

Damon glanced around to see if anyone had joined them in the courtyard. They were alone. He leaned into Harris as if he were trying to tip him over. "Well, for your information, detective, I'm the one in ten."

Harris smiled, it was grudging but his lips did widen.

Damon replaced the report in the envelope and handed it back to the detective. "This is what you deal with all the time?"

"You get used to it."

"I'm not so sure," he replied, unable to personalize the fact that the cadaver in the report was once a living, breathing Beth. And now that she was no longer alive, guilt began to gnaw at him. He was her lover, yes, but was he in love with her?

Harris studied Damon's face as if he was reading his mind. "You knew her pretty well, damned well, in fact, if you were sleeping with her. Was she depressed at all?"

"Beth? Depressed?"

"Enough to take her own life, I mean."

"Absolutely not."

"Nothing in your relationship with her…"

Damon didn't let him finish. "There was nothing wrong between us!"

Harris shrugged noncommittally. "Just asking, that's my job, looking for motive. Regardless how she died, the Fischers don't want a scandal and will go to any length to avoid one. They have contacts in high places and are using a great deal of pressure to keep a lid on the investigation. Protecting the family is their top priority. They'd rather let the murderer go unpunished than let the outside world find out who it is. And that's why I need your help."

"What can I do?"

"You're on the inside, I'm on the outside, and I'll stay that way because there is no way in hell any of those swells will give me the time of day."

"And you are convinced someone in the family killed her?"

"Unless you were involved."

"Why do you keep bringing me up?"

"Because the Fischers would go to any length to protect their name including making you the fall guy. So you have a stake in this investigation, too."

Damon could not believe what he was hearing. What started out as a routine assignment, writing a family history, was now a factor in his very survival.

"Have you some kind of vendetta against the Fischers?" Damon asked.

"No, it just pisses me off that they think they can push me around."

"But I don't see how I can help you."

"You have the perfect cover. The methods you use to get material for the history are not any different from the way I do my investigations. Ask questions, study reactions, listen to conversations, look at files, records, diaries, letters, keep notes—the same things you do when researching a family history."

"But what am I supposed to be looking for?"

"Motive."

Damon threw up his arms in frustration. "Where in hell am I supposed to look for that?"

"Think of it as a puzzle, Damon, that's what investigative work is—solving a puzzle. Let's set up a schedule of meetings, say once a week, like right here in this courtyard to go over what you've come up with. In the meantime call me if you have any questions." Harris handed Damon his card.

"I feel like a piece of dirty laundry."

"Don't you want to nail the killer of your girlfriend? Help me dig up something incriminating, something out of kilter, something I can build a case on."

"I'll be betraying their trust."

Harris stared. "They don't give a shit about you, Damon. They won't hesitate to incriminate you to save themselves. That could even cost you your job in this…" Harris made a sweeping gesture of everything holy to Damon "… this pretty museum of yours."

"You play hardball."

"That is my job description."

3

They don't give a shit about you.

The words kept swirling in Damon's head as he spent the rest of the day trying to concentrate on a PR campaign he was developing for a new exhibition Troy had been planning for more than two years, The Industrial Edge, featuring newcomer sculptors, among them Larry Bell and Don Judd, who worked in non-traditional materials such as tinted glass and sheet metal. It was the process more than the materials that fascinated Damon— these artists were using commercial fabricators to make their art. They, the artists, provided the idea. But the idea was not fascinating enough right now to keep his mind from reverting back to his meeting with Lieutenant Harris.

If the Fischers didn't give a shit about him, he was arguing with himself, why should he give a shit about them, even if they did sign his paycheck. Didn't he owe more to Beth? Someone in the family was evil enough to kill her, according to Harris anyway, and so wasn't he obliged to help find out who that is? To hell with loyalty. He wished he could talk to Troy about this but no one, not even his boss, must know anything about what he had agreed to. This was his dilemma. How can he remain loyal to the Fischers when he had agreed to spy on them. But, he continued to argue, struggling for a rationale, wasn't he already a spy—isn't that what family research is anyway—digging into personal backgrounds, snooping through files, looking for secrets? When he was assigned to this project, he had decided to write an honest history, not pap to satisfy the whim of an egocentric family. Even before meeting Harris, he was committed to a course antithetical to the expectations of the family, the only wrinkle: he would now report to Lieutenant Harris as well as Henry Fischer. Damon had to laugh thinking about it: he was a double agent, like a character in a John La Carre novel.

He was ready to wrap up his day when Donna called him. As switchboard operator she occupied a cubbyhole next to the cloakroom by the main entrance, and it was her voice that defined her since she was largely hidden from view. That commanding voice more than made up for the lack of her physical presence—which was Native American, dark-haired and bony—especially at the end of the day when the museum was cleared of visitors and she bellowed over the PA system: "Head 'em up and move 'em out!"

"What is it, Donna?"

"Some guy in a uniform dropped off a note for you."

Damon was alert, apprehensive. Now what? "A cop?"

"No, a chauffeur—what do you call what they wear? Livery? He was all in gray except for black boots and a black visor on his cap. His pants were flared out, like you see at fancy horse shows."

"Jodhpurs," Damon said, realizing now that the person Donna was talking about was Delmar, the Fischer's chauffeur.

"Is that what they are called?" Donna replied. "Anyway he dropped off an envelope. I smelled it for perfume but I didn't detect anything."

"Please, Donna, spare me your asides. It was just Sarah Rand's driver."

"To you he's just a driver?" she shot back. "Sounds like you are getting too big for your own jodhpurs."

"That's breeches, Donna. I'll pick up the note on my way out."

*****

Damon sat outside on the granite steps leading up to the entrance of the museum, the snarl of traffic on the Hennepin-Lyndale bottleneck providing counterpoint to his troubled mind. Behind him on a pedestal, looming like a giant predator, was the Lipschitz bronze, Prometheus Strangling the Vulture, depicting in Expressionistic terms, the eternal struggle between good and evil—a metaphor if there ever was one for Damon's own mixed feelings. He opened the envelope with Sarah's neat script and withdrew a crisp square of linen paper folded in half. He unfolded it. At the top in embossed lettering were the words: Schloss Fischer Breckett's Point Lake Minnetonka. Below was a handwritten note:

> Damon
> Would you be so kind as to join me in the library this Saturday evening at 6 o'clock. There are some matters I would like to discuss with you in private. Afterward you are welcome to dinner. Thank you.
>
> S. R.

*****

CT Fischer had strong Austrian roots and chose an architect, long since forgotten, to design a rococo-inspired

31

mansion patterned after Schloss Leopoldskron in Salzburg, an 18th century private residence of Archbishop Leopold Firmian. CT went so far as to call his own version a Schloss. Sarah, however, was more reserved and preferred calling the conspicuous construction "the house by the lake." By any stretch of the imagination, this was not a house unless one attached the adjective "country" behind it, but even that stretched credulity.

The granite structure rose three stories, hidden from public view on ten acres of woodland and a thousand feet of pristine shoreline. When CT moved there, in 1894, his new home was written up in the Minnetonka Gazette as "a striking and bold interpretation of 18th century rococo, a period not sufficiently appreciated by American architects who seem too dependent on the classicism of ancient Greece and ancient Rome for their 'neo' concepts."

Damon was a few minutes early, as it was not proper to keep Sarah waiting, and so he occupied himself by walking around the library, the second time he'd seen this impressive space—another marvel of borrowed European tradition. The long room, running the width of the Schloss, some seventy-five feet in length, was a half-scale replica of the library in the Abbey Cathedral at St. Gallen, the idea of Anna, CT's wife, who spent a summer in the Alpine country and fell in love with the monastery. She hired a designer to remodel the Schloss library in the Baroque style, including wood-carved putti who looked down from a curvilinear balcony. Hundreds of antique books were stored in tall bookcases of curved glass, alternating between concave and convex so that the overall effect was an undulating wall of reflected images not unlike a fun house. But the glass, meant to protect the rare volumes, also had the unintended consequence of making the books appear hermetically sealed and therefore not to be taken out and read.

Damon was busy looking at titles, bending close so he could see through the glass, when he heard an unexpected sound behind him. He turned to see one of the curved bookcases open like a door, and from it emerged Sarah who appeared to Damon as an apparition.

She smiled at him as she closed the bookcase. "Surprised are you?" she asked, reading the expression on his face. "This is a secret door leading to my apartment on the second floor. The private access was originally built with a spiral staircase but after I could no longer climb stairs I had a private elevator installed. I even have a one-way mirror so I can see who is in the library before I enter it."

Damon examined the fake bookcase and discovered that what he thought were actual books were instead book spines glued to a panel, and above these, at eye level, was a mirror coated with a nearly transparent layer of aluminum to make it reflective and therefore difficult to see through from the opposite side.

"The library was my mother's inspiration but the secret staircase was my father's."

"A man of mystery," he said.

"CT was indeed that. There may be other secrets we don't know about."

Damon wondered why Sarah was revealing this private bit of family lore. He even entertained the notion that she wanted to confide in him. Maybe this will be his first opportunity to be Harris's eyes and ears.

She was wearing one of her standard outfits: a kaftan, this one hand-embroidered and patterned with delicate tropical flowers. It reached to the floor and was tied around her ample middle with a wide silk sash. This was the way she always dressed. Damon had come to realize her identity was wrapped up in the kaftans that wrapped around her.

She led him to one of the large reading tables, with a two-way brass lamp. The table was an antique, probably Biedermeier.

"Sit next to me," she directed, "not across."

Damon drew back a chair for her, then dragged another one over, and sat down.

She folded her hands in her lap and stared down at them. Then she looked up, sighing deeply. "We buried Beth next to CT. That was to be my place but since she preceded me in death, I decided that's where she should go. I think my father would have approved because Beth was very special to all of us." She obviously was including Damon as well.

"Beth was my life, my light. She meant everything to me. She represented the future of this family and her loss is incalculable. Let me be quite frank with you, Damon. People call the Fischers a dynasty, in the pejorative sense mind you, and that is fine with me. I am proud of it. My father had nothing but a transit and a tripod when he started out surveying the virgin forests of northern Minnesota, and from that humble beginning he created—yes, I admit it—a dynasty.

"There is much that you don't know about Fischer holdings in spite of the fact you have been working on a family history. You know about the Art Center, of course, and CT's art collection, but you do not know about the thousands of acres of forests owned by the family that supply The Star and Tribune and The Pioneer Press, among other major dailies, with newsprint. Nor do you know about the pulp mills that turn the wood into paper, or the shipping lines—the railroads and trucks—that deliver the huge roles of newsprint, each weighing three tons by the way. CT built his business literally from the ground up and left his heirs not only a huge enterprise but also the responsibility to manage it. That responsibility fell primarily on my shoulders after he died. Maybe father had these expectations for me, although he never expressed them. He even chose my name—Sarah, an Old Testament name meaning Princess.

"I succeeded well enough so that my father would have been proud, but not without the support and counsel of my husband, Alfred Rand. Women of my generation were not expected to be leaders, only followers to put it politely, and so Alfred got the credit.

34

"I was fine with that. I had no one else to turn to, no one else in the family I could really depend on. Henry, bless him, has his stones to polish and the best will in the world, but no business acumen. Edmond suffered a debilitating stroke and Irene has devoted her life to the Museum. James, my third brother, was killed in the first American engagement of World War I—the battle of Cantigny—on May 28, 1918. He barely got his uniform dirty. Had he survived he would have carried the family banner with the pride and success CT expected of a male heir. My son Harrison showed promise but he loved flying more than running a business." Sarah stopped talking no doubt recalling the time Harrison was killed in an air crash.

Damon nodded letting Sarah know this was one of the stories about the Fischer family he knew, everyone for that matter, as it was big news when Harrison Rand's vintage World War II Mustang fighter plane nicked the pylon at the Oshkosh Air Show Race a few years back.

"And so," she said, starting in again, "the responsibility to run the business fell on my shoulders. My father truly believed that our family had a destiny for greatness but after losing Harrison, and now Beth that promised destiny also died. She would have represented a new generation of Fischers. My goal was to live long enough to reconnect with the greatness that my father started. I could see in Beth the kind of vision that her grandfather and I shared."

Damon thought it was time to break in. "What about CT-Two?"

"What about him?" Sarah repeated.

"Well, he bears his great grandfather's name."

"That is all he bears," she said dismissively. "And his brother, Richard, inherited good looks but little else."

"Mrs. Rand, are you sure you should be speaking to me like this about your own grandchildren?"

"I have things to say and time is not on my side. I also trust your judgment and your discretion. It was fortuitous you entered our lives when you did because none in Beth's circle of gentlemen friends, and there was a stable-full believe me, had what I perceive in you."

"She told me about Harvey Wilson."

Sarah became attentive. "What did she say?"

"That they were almost engaged."

Sarah smiled, pleased. "I'm glad she was frank with you. Harvey comes from an old-line Minnetonka family, old-line like ours, subject to arteriosclerosis…such a union would have spelled doom, like rotting from within."

That sounded a bit melodramatic to Damon. "He would have been a lot better for Beth."

"You never met him."

"No."

Sarah raised her eyebrows. "Then how can you say that?"

Damon felt awkward having to explain the great social chasm between her world and his. If he tried would she even understand?

"It's not about him, Mrs. Rand, it's about me. I come from a very different background. My parents were immigrants. My father owned a Coney Island on Lake Street. I think Beth found all that…different." He almost said, quaint, because he was convinced that's the way she thought of him, like a plaything.

"Opposites attract," he added, "and that's what happened to Beth and me."

"You underestimate yourself, Damon. I've been watching the way you have interacted with Henry working on the family history. You and he get along very well and Henry is a very private person, hard to get to know. You bring something new and refreshing to the family—I don't like the word outsider but it fits because you can bring a new perspective that we sorely need. If I had thought for a moment that you were not good enough for Beth I would have put a stop to your relationship in an instant."

As flattering as her comments were, they

reminded Damon of the ill-fated relationship between a rich girl and a working class man in Theodore Dreiser's novel An American Tragedy, and it made him realize how unrealistic were Sarah's expectations of him.

She stopped to collect herself. "Did you two ever talk about...well...about the future?"

As you would have written it? Damon wanted to ask.

"No."

"Beth was very attached to you, Damon, so much so that in my mind I saw a union that would have assured an exceptional generation, even succeeding generations with the children you two would have produced. And now without Beth there is no legacy, none at all." She shifted in her chair. "Life offers no guarantees except death."

"Please," Damon said, wanting to make her feel better but not quite knowing how.

"There is something else, Damon, something so terrible that I am not sure I will survive it." She folded her caftan tightly around her body as though fending off something evil. "A policeman came to see me the other day, a Lieutenant with the Sheriff's office. He looked like a vagrant the way he dressed." She made a face of displeasure. "We talked in this very room but not at this table. Over there," she pointed, "standing by the window. I refused to sit down with him."

While it was fascinating to listen to Sarah air her dirty linen—maybe not so much dirty as soiled—Damon had learned nothing special that the Lieutenant would consider useful. Maybe now he will. In spite of the serious nature of their conversation, it still amused him that Sarah thought Harris looked like a vagrant.

"This is difficult to talk about because it is so abhorrent." She sighed deeply, and then dove in. "The investigator is questioning the coroner's conclusion that Beth drowned accidentally. He claims that Beth was murdered."

The abruptness of her comment threw him off

guard and he had to think quickly: how do I respond—
with anger, confusion, surprise?

He chose none of the above. "Did he tell you why,
Mrs. Rand?"

She waved her hand as if being bothered by a
pesky fly. "Something about a ligature, whatever that
means. He says that she was strangled before going in the
water." Sarah hesitated. "But I took care of that."

"How?"

"We are not without influence in our community.
A discrete telephone call to the city attorney from my
lawyer Jon Love with the understanding that nothing
would be gained by dragging our name into the
newspapers convinced the coroner that Beth's death was
accidental. Can you imagine the spectacle if it came out
that Beth, god forbid, was murdered?"

"Mrs. Rand, if it came out that you were using
your influence to suppress evidence there would be an
even bigger scandal, maybe people going to jail like your
lawyer and the city attorney…perhaps you."

"It's not as dire as all that, Damon," Sarah said
patting his hand. "The city attorney, his name is Frederick
Benson by the way, is delaying the investigation long
enough to give me time to sort things out. The Fischers
will not be dragged though the mud. We must not allow
events to dictate. We have to take charge."

"But how?"

"That's where you come in. You have heard of
damage control."

"Of course—Public Relations 101 in J-School at
the University of Minnesota." He meant to be humorous

"That's precisely what I need you to do."

Sarah came alive, re-energized, because now she
was planning the future, not wallowing in the past. "Yes—
damage control for the Fischer family. I cannot think of a
better-qualified person than you to help us through this
difficult time. I want you to be my spokesman, my advisor,
my eyes and ears, devise counter-attacks against bad

publicity, respond quickly to what the media says about us."

Sarah was throwing out too much too fast for him to absorb. "But, Mrs. Rand, I already have a job..."

"I talked to Troy. He's willing to give you a leave of absence. In the meantime, keep working with Henry. I want you to be as much a part of the family as if you were my own grandson. In fact I'd like to have you stay here, in the Schloss."

Damon was so stunned he almost stuttered. "You are asking an awful lot," he said.

"I will make it up to you," she promised, "financially and otherwise."

Damon did not know what otherwise meant, but he was not happy about living in the bosom of the Fischer family.

"Let me think about it." He was already thinking about it, particularly as it related to Lieutenant Harris, who would be overjoyed to learn that his spy was invited to live in Schloss Fischer.

4

Mrs. Rand gently chided Damon for being in his business attire: suit and tie. "If you decide to move in with us, and I sincerely hope you will, you quickly learn that casual is the dress code here. We are a lake family and that means, during the summer months, shorts, t-shirts and sneakers. The only caveat is dinner: a collared shirt, long trousers and dress shoes. Aloha shirts are acceptable."

Jesus, Damon thought to himself, I have to buy a whole new wardrobe.

They entered the Venetian Room where the family gathered for cocktails: Henry and Irene; CT-Two and his wife, Ruth; Richard, Beth's twin, so much a look-a-like of Beth that it always jarred Damon; Dolores, Harrison's widow; and Crystal and Arvid Campbell. Ellen was absent. Maybe she skipped the cocktail hour because she didn't touch alcohol.

The room they occupied was one of four fashioned after the rococo design of the late 18th century when it was the style of grand buildings to have distinctly decorated rooms: Venetian, Chinese, White and Red. The one Damon just entered, the Venetian Room, had walls adorned with Commedia dell'Arte paintings of harlequins CT had acquired from the estate of Max Reinhardt, the

Austrian theatre impresario who fled Europe with the paintings rolled up in his steamer trunk when the Nazis came to power. CT liked them so much he decided to have them installed in the Schloss rather than be part of the museum's collection.

CT-Two and Ruth had their own home in Medina and so it surprised Damon to see them there. He began to wonder if Sarah had invited them in order to tell everyone at one time about her plans for Damon.

That should be interesting.

A sideboard by the window held the usual array of what old money drinks—50-year-old single malt scotch, 24-year-old Kentucky bourbon, and triple-distilled vodka. CT-Two was mixing drinks and, when he saw Sarah arrive with Damon, he quickly swallowed his surprise along with some scotch and then poured Sarah's favorite, a French cognac. Damon failed to catch the brand name etched on the bottle, but he could not help but notice the elaborate silver stopper in the shape of the spreading branches of a tree.

CT-Two handed his grandmother the snifter glass and said to Damon: "Unless you are a woman it's every man for himself at the bar."

Damon mixed a light gin and tonic and tossed in a wedge of lime. He sipped and looked around, never having been invited to dinner before, despite his relationship with Beth. They both had decided that discretion was the better part of valor and not expose themselves to the stares and innuendos of her brothers who were none too keen about Damon behaving as an equal. He wondered what they will think when they learn he might move in with them. He smiled to himself, maybe he should do that just to get their goat.

"So," CT said to Damon, over his Glenfiddich on the rocks, "what brings you to Schloss Fischer?"

"Sarah invited me," Damon replied, and took a swallow of his drink. He needed it.

Sarah had gone off to talk to Henry on the other

side of the room, leaving Damon alone with CT. Maybe she meant to do that because it was no secret that CT did not get along with Damon—found him too tall, too well built and too handsome, among other reasons—and left them to fight it out.

CT was a good three inches shorter than Damon and he had to look up when he spoke, clearly agitating him. He also had a receding hairline and a curious way of cocking his head when he looked at you, like a robin listening for a worm.

"I hope she is not up to one of her tricks."

"Tricks?"

"She's full of them. One of these days she is going to go too far."

Like tonight Damon thought.

"Did she invite you for dinner or do you leave after you finish that drink?"

"Dinner," he said, ignoring the barb.

"Then she is up to something. What is it? You know, don't you?"

"And if I do?"

"Look, Soldier…" CT-Two began in a threatening voice, but he didn't get a chance to finish because Richard joined them. Not pleased to be interrupted CT walked away to join his wife.

When he was out of earshot, Richard said to Damon, "You don't like being called Soldier, do you?"

"No, I don't," Damon replied. Richard had the smooth features of someone who needed toughening up. Damon got along with him—he felt an obligation being Beth's twin brother—but Richard exuded an aura of irresponsibility that made Damon uneasy.

"Well," Richard said, "*I* won't call you that."

"Thanks."

"Saw you at the funeral," he said abruptly." I wasn't sure you would show up."

"I wouldn't have missed it."

"Three weeks already." Richard mused a moment,

holding his glass to his lips but not drinking from it. "I wonder if the time will come when I no longer think of Beth."

"I can't imagine that happening."

"Twins are very close you know. We could read each other's minds."

The comment jarred Damon, wondering if Beth's thoughts during their lovemaking had been transmitted to Richard via that twins grapevine he was talking about. It was like being spied on by a voyeur.

"Do you still think of her?" Richard asked.

"Of course."

"As much as I do?"

Damon did not answer.

Richard lowered his voice. "I was jealous of the attention my sister gave you. Is that normal?"

Jesus, Damon thought, the whole family is nuts.

He needed to mingle and spotted Arvid with his wife Crystal, just the two of them standing alone under one of CT's harlequin paintings, cocktails in hand, seemingly out of place. Damon decided to join them. From his peripheral vision he caught Sarah watching. He wondered if any move he made would be monitored by her, or someone reporting to her. Well, he thought, wade in—he might learn something he can pass on to Lieutenant Harris. Arvid and Crystal were the ones who intrigued Damon the most but knew the least. As he approached he lifted his glass in greeting.

"We really haven't met formally. I'm Damon Petroulis."

Arvid seemed relieved to have someone to talk to. He had sharp features as though carved by a chisel—cheek bones and Adam's apple, knuckles and elbows—but his manner was the opposite, tentative and uncertain.

Arvid raised his glass in return. "Cheers," he said even though his eyes were unhappy.

Crystal would have made a perfect model for a Sears housedress, her plainness was her virtue.

44

Nevertheless there was a steely look in her eyes that said, don't take me for granted.

The couple had flown in from California for Beth's funeral and stayed on at the sufferance of Sarah.

"Will Madie join us?" Damon asked, even though he knew that she took her meals in her room. He decided that if he was going to be of any help to Harris he might as well push the envelope. "She and Beth were very close," he ventured, "I wonder how Madie is doing without her."

"As best as can be expected," was Crystal's noncommittal reply.

"Beth acted like a mother to Madie," Damon continued. "I was happy to see her at the funeral. She seemed so calm."

"They sedated her," Arvid said suddenly. "They were afraid she might act up and embarrass them."

Crystal nudged him with her hip, the equivalent of poking his leg under the table.

"Well, it's true," he snapped. "Madie would be a lot better off if she was not treated like a hothouse lily constantly watered by Mrs. Stockton." His voice rose in frustration as he spoke and his comment carried across the room, causing everyone to stop talking, their cocktail glasses in mid-air, their bodies rigid, like a stop-motion photograph.

Sarah cleared her throat forcefully to put a lid on the tense moment and then said in a commanding voice unmistakable in its authority, "Shall we have dinner?"

Her announcement caught the serving staff in the dining room off-guard—Phillip, the butler, assisted by Karl and Hettie Schranz, an Austrian couple who prepared the food and helped Phillip serve it. The trio were like a family within the larger Fischer family, working together for nearly three decades, and living in their own apartments over the garage that housed the family's fleet of cars.

Sarah was seated first, at the head of the table. She directed Damon to sit to her right, normally CT's place, leaving CT to fend for himself. This pre-emption did not sit well with him, in a manner of speaking, and he did not care who knew it.

Sarah was having none of his ill humor. "Sit somewhere CT, will you please?" She looked around taking inventory of those present. "Where is Ellen?" she snapped. "She is late."

"Ellen expected dinner at the usual time," Crystal said.

"Well, someone fetch her," she replied testily, "before this evening gets completely out of hand."

Crystal started to get up when Ellen appeared in the entryway. "Why are we eating early?" she asked, walking to a chair and sitting down. Her father, Edmond, confined to his wheelchair, ate his meals alone, served later by Phillip.

Everyone deferred to Sarah's prickly mood, making small talk while being served roast lamb, small potatoes, green beans and mint jelly. Most ate staring down at their plates, giving Damon an opportunity to observe them without being noticed. He focused on Ellen with whom he had still not exchanged a word, she was that shy. She lacked the social presence of a woman in her late forties, frozen in time as though from arrested development. Once she glanced up at Irene who sat across from her, as if wanting to say something but then changing her mind.

After Karl and Hettie cleared the dinner dishes and poured coffee, Sarah took her spoon and banged it against her water glass with more force than needed as everyone was already paying attention.

"I have an announcement to make." She looked down the line of staring faces, and then without further adieu dropped her bombshell.

"I asked Damon to join us for dinner for a special reason. You all know of course that he has been working with Henry these past months on a history of our family. Because of the untimely death of our beloved Beth and the prurient interest this has created in the news media, I have asked him to represent the family in all things public. Damon is experienced in the field of public relations, of course, and all of us can point with pride to the great job he is doing, publicizing the Art Center's programs. Our family needs this kind of professional expertize, I think we can all agree on that."

Except for CT who stared glumly down at his empty coffee cup.

"Heretofore, any contact with the news media will be through Damon. None of you and, I repeat, none of you will speak to any newspaperman or television reporter. To make sure there is no chance for miscommunication and to make sure you understand clearly that I mean business, Damon will be relocating in Schloss Fischer for the foreseeable future."

Damon started to object. This is not what he had agreed to, he *told* Sarah that he would think it over, and now she had undercut him, but it was CT-Two who spoke first.

"Relocating?" he blurted out. "You mean *live* here?"

"That is exactly what I mean. And I have also decided that he should use CT's office upstairs."

There was shocked silence. Several exchanged glances of sheer panic. Sarah had lost her mind. It was bad enough to invite an outsider to live in the Schloss but actually *use* CT's former office—unoccupied since he died, more like a period room in a museum bespeaking a time long past. Rather than an interloper sitting at CT's roll-top desk there should be a velvet rope protecting it, as well as the brown leather desk chair, the bookshelves, the faded oriental rug, the heavy drapes…

"But Sarah," Henry implored, "Why can't Damon use the library, anywhere but CT's office. Sheets still cover the furniture…"

"Uncover the furniture, pull back the drapes, bring some life into the room!"

5

Donna hailed Damon from behind her switchboard. "I didn't think you were coming in."

"Staff meeting." This was his first time at the Art Center since Sarah shanghaied him into being her toady, the only word he could think of to describe how manipulated he felt. Nothing had gone his way since dinner at the Schloss except that Sarah accepted his request that he have time to visit the Art Center. This not only gave him a chance to keep an eye on things, but also to meet with Lieutenant Harris by the Horse and Rider sculpture.

"Got three messages for you."

Donna handed over the small stack of notes he carried back to his desk, soon to be occupied by someone else, he realized with bitterness and regret. It had been decided that Troy bring in a replacement to cover the bases while Damon shifted his focus, and his entire life the way he felt right now, from the Fischer Art Center to the Fischer Estate, aka Schloss. Troy was interviewing applicants, two Damon knew about: a man nearing retirement from Padilla and Sargent, a local PR firm, and another, a young assistant at the University of Minnesota Art Gallery

"Shit," Damon mumbled to himself, "pure shit" as he looked through the notes. One was from Harris to set up a meeting, another from Margaret Martin who wrote a society column for the Morning Tribune titled *Being There*—exhibit A of the PR pleasure-pain principle: I don't care what you say about me as long as you spell my name right—and a third call from someone Damon did not know, someone named Jacob Ratner.

He dialed Margaret's number—get the most distasteful one out of the way first was his own pleasure-pain principle.

"Margaret, this is Damon Petroulis returning your call."

"*Daaa*-mon," Margaret said, stretching the first syllable of his name till he thought it would snap, "so nice to hear from you. There is something on the grapevine I'm just dying to know about."

Dying was what Damon hoped Margaret would do right now.

"Word has it that Troy Adamson is looking for your replacement."

"Not replacement," Damon replied, carefully measuring the spacing between his words so as not to sound too anxious. "Assistant."

"So you are not permanently leaving the Art Center?" He could hear her hitting typewriter keys. She was taking everything down.

"Of course not."

"Are you getting an assistant because you are spending so much time at Schloss Fischer working on the family history?"

"It's not news that I am working on a family history."

"But having an assistant is. Know who she is yet?"

"She?"

"I hear it is Maggie Bovin."

"Maggie Bovin?" Damon repeated in surprise. She worked at Gallery 28, an avant garde wannabe that represented a pocketful of local artists whose work was more derivative than original. Maggie's ambition knew no bounds. If she sank her talons into his job, Damon was through at Fischer Art Center.

"This can't be happening," he said and then bit his lip.

"What did you say, Damon?" Margaret asked, typewriter keys banging away. "This can't be happening? Can I quote you?"

He knew she would regardless what he said and hung up in defeat. Could Troy really be considering Maggie Bovin? Well, he was going to get an earful. Damon checked his watch. Still ten minutes till the staff meeting. He dialed the number belonging to the strange name.

A male voice answered, "Ratner."

"This is Damon Petroulis. You left a message for me."

"Oh yeah," he said. His voice was gnarly as though he was talking around a cigar stuck in his mouth. "Arvid Campbell told me to call you."

Damon tensed. "Who are you?"

"Private dick if you read detective fiction, but in normal parlance I am an investigator specializing in missing persons."

Completely puzzled, Damon asked, "What is it you want to see me about?"

"Can't tell you over the phone. Got to meet you personally."

"Where?"

"Whitey's Saloon, East Hennepin and Fourth Street, back booth in the corner. Meet me there at noon."

"Will Arvid be there?"

"He shouldn't be seen with me."

"But it's ok for me to see you?"

"Look, this is no skin off my nose. I'm on retainer for Campbell. He wants me to bring you up to date on some information I got. If you want to clear it with him first it's ok with me."

"Never mind. I'll met you at Whitey's at noon."

Damon just had time to telephone Harris that he would meet him tomorrow at two in the Sculpture Court.

The Art Center's senior staff was intentionally lean—Director, Curatorial staff of three, Performing Arts and Film Coordinators, Graphic Designer, Business Manager, Registrar and PR Director—to meet around a circular glass table in the conference room that measured eight feet in diameter. Like King Arthur, Troy wanted to create the impression that he was one of ten sitting in the round, presenting ostensibly the appearance of equality. The staff was a team, a team with equal voice, unless that voice happened to be naming Damon's "assistant," according to the gospel of St. Margaret.

The meeting dealt with the coming exhibition, The Industrial Edge. It was a full agenda: installation, lectures, invitations, exhibition catalog, housing visiting artists, opening gala, ancillary programs of dance and film. There was a lot to do and everyone was expected to put in long hours. There was no such luxury as a forty-hour workweek at Fischer Art Center.

The final topic on the agenda completed, the staff gathered up pads and coffee cups to return to work when Troy said, "One more thing I'd like to discuss." Chairs slid back under the table and expectant eyes locked on the PR man. The staff knew what Troy was going to talk about. It was on everyone's mind.

"I want to discuss Damon's situation."

Situation? Damon thought. What the hell does that mean, that I'm cooked meat?

Troy then outlined the new arrangement with the Fischer family as though it were news, a temporary shift in responsibilities for Damon who was being lent out, as it were, to the Fischers (after all, they *do* pay our salaries, let's not forget that) in order to manage the bad publicity surrounding Beth Rand's untimely death.

"How can we publicize a major exhibition like The Industrial Edge without Damon?" asked Jan van der Mark, Chief Curator.

"Good question, Jan," Troy replied, as if he were still giving this a lot of thought. "The timing could not be worse, but the family is in crisis. If the situation at the Schloss is not resolved, it could jeopardize the Art Center as well. The greater priority is to help Sarah Rand. We can manage The Industrial Edge with outside help. Remember, Damon has developed the PR plan. All we need is someone to execute it." Troy gave Damon a quick glance. "I haven't made a final decision but I think the best person for the job is Maggie Bovin."

Damon winced. Margaret was right. "You've talked to her?" he asked.

Troy nodded. "I described the situation (there was that word again) and she understands that eventually you will return as head of PR."

Head of PR? What did he mean by that? Damon was not head of anything. He was the whole department. He smelled a rat. "Will she get the ax when I come back?"

"You have a big load, Damon, and I know how hard it is to cover all the projects we have going year 'round—it's too much for one person. I made a deal with Sarah, a quid pro quo you could say. She has agreed to fund a new, permanent position, Assistant Public Relations Coordinator, someone to work under you."

Damon groaned. He didn't care who heard him. "And you think Maggie is that person?"

"We don't have much time, Damon. We have to move fast. Maggie knows the media, she is available, and she is eager to join the team. She can hit the ground running with your campaign for The Industrial Edge, and when you return you'll have a seasoned partner to work with. I want to call her after the meeting and make it official—if that's ok with you."

It wasn't ok with Damon but he was not in a position to argue with Troy. Oh, he could argue all right but what good would that do?

"When does she start?" he asked, his voice hollow, listless.

"Monday."

Whitey's was crowded and noisy. Damon had to work his way past a logjam of customers standing inside the entrance waiting for a booth. The bar comfortably evoked the past, feeling much like a speakeasy with its dark-stained wood, white-and-black hexagon tiles and a waffled tin ceiling.

He was glad to be here. After the staff meeting he really needed a drink. He made it to the bar and ordered a gin and tonic, paid for it, and carried it with him.

The bar was long and narrow with two aisles, tables down the middle and booths along either wall. Damon followed an aisle to the rear. One of the two corner booths was occupied by a threesome, professionals who appeared to Damon as architects. They had that look— casual but trendy, long hair, round glasses. In offices above the bar, Damon knew, was an alliance of architects who called themselves Sala. Maybe these three were from there.

The booth opposite was occupied by a man who was the antithesis of the cool-looking architects. He wore a linen jacket heavily creased at the crook of the elbows, baggy trousers and hair the color of sewage. Damon longed to join the architects, with whom he had more in common even if he did not know them personally.

If they had bothered to look, the architects might have wondered why Damon was paying attention to the weird loner across the aisle.

"Are you Jacob Rankin?" Damon asked.

The man nodded and proffered his hand not to shake it but to direct Damon to sit across from him.

He was nursing a draft beer with beefy fingers. Even though he was not large he was imposing, exuding a kind of menacing dominance that made you keep your distance. Damon decided he was not someone you would want to, even if you could, get to know well.

"You already got a drink."

Damon nodded. "On my way in."

"Let's get down to business, then." Rankin handed him an envelope, the kind drugstores use after processing a role of film. Kodak was printed under the Snyders logo.

"What is this?" Damon asked, opening the envelope and pulling out several black and white photographs. They were grainy and the images were shot from a distance, as if the photographer was sitting in a car parked down the block. The pictures were of an unusual circular house set far back on a big lot. Behind it, off to one side, was a long building that looked like a stable and next to it a corral bordered by a fence with crisscrossed timbers. Horses grazed behind the fence.

Damon went through the selection, six in all, twice. "What am I supposed to look for?"

Rankin reached across and pointed to a figure. His nails needed trimming. "See that person?"

Damon studied the figure closely, a young woman with her hair in a ponytail, wearing jeans and a cowboy shirt. She was leaning against the fence watching a horse inside the corral. He sorted through the other photos and saw that she was in every one, sitting on the front porch, picking up the mail from an RFD mailbox, riding a horse. One photo had her greeting a man and a woman considerably older who were climbing out of a car in the driveway.

"Who is she?"

"A Fischer."

Damon looked up at Rankin in surprise. "What?"

"This is Arvid Campbell's kid. Her adopted name is Amy Jacobsson, with two S's."

"I'll be damned," Damon said, going through them one more time, staring intently. "He hired you to dig her up?"

"Yeah, three weeks ago. He was in a hurry and didn't care how much it cost." Rankin smiled. "The best client to have. Cash on delivery."

"How did he find you?"

Rankin shrugged under his baggy jacket. "Yellow pages? How would I know?"

"What's the story behind this?"

"You have to ask him but I have my own ideas."

"Like what?"

"He was all business, calling me every day asking if I got results. Pissed if I told him no. I don't think he cared about meeting her, like you would expect from a father. He just wanted to find her, prove that she exists. To me he is a man seeking revenge. Blackmail I'm thinking. I never met the guy. He left the money in a drop box. He even sent you instead of coming himself." Rankin shook his head. "Campbell wants to hold that kid over someone's head, like the Sword of Damocles."

Damon stared in surprise. "You know Greek classics."

Rankin smiled, the first time he did so. "I wanted to show off a little bit after seeing your last name." He leaned back, relaxing a bit. "A PI spends a lot of time in the public library digging up information. Once in a while I check out a good book to read."

Damon began to understand that the unkempt man sitting across from him was more interesting than he gave him credit for. So perhaps he didn't need the company of the architects after all.

"What I'd like to know," Damon said, getting back to business, "who is the mother?"

"Hey, I'm only a PI, not a wizard."

"I wonder if that's Arvid's Sword: threatening to expose her."

"Maybe so. Campbell wants you to contact the girl. He won't do it himself. All the information I have about her is inside this envelope." Rankin slid it across the table.

Damon picked it up. "Why don't you contact her? That's a detective's business, too, isn't it?"

Rankin smiled ironically. "You've read too many Raymond Chandler detective novels—Phillip Marlowe nosing into people's private lives and getting into big trouble because of it."

"You like Chandler, too? He's one of my favorite authors."

Rankin made a quirky grin. "Like I said, lots of time in the library. I've read all of his books, The Big Sleep, Farewell My Lovely, The Lady in the Lake. Crime fiction is not that different from the Greek classics, exposing human frailties, fighting to right wrongs, struggling for the answers to life's puzzles. But I'm a working stiff, not a hero. I stay away from confrontation. I turn over my findings to the client and he can go to the police or follow up himself, or file it away. It's up to him. My part of this deal is finished. I found the girl. You have everything—the legal documents proving she is a Fischer, plus the photos and their negatives. I've cleared my files."

"Is that the way you always work?"

"Especially in this case."

"Why?"

"I am a one-man business. I don't have a secretary and I don't take chances. I got child support. I won't do anything dumb enough to jeopardize my source of income. So if someone tells me to lay off I lay off. Besides," he shrugged, "the job is done and I was paid. Handsomely I might add."

THE CURSE OF THE BIG WATER

"But who told you to lay off?"

"I don't know, and I'm not going to try to find out. I got a couple of calls, the last one yesterday, an indistinct voice like someone covering the mouthpiece with a silk stocking, probably calling from a public phone booth, warning me that if I keep looking for that bitch, as he called her, I would lose my license." Rankin laughed sardonically. "Someone spying on the spy. How about that?"

"Who could take your license away?"

"Someone who knows how to fix city hall."

When Rankin said that, Sarah Rand immediately came to mind. Damon wondered if she had anything to do with this, hired someone to spy, as Rankin said, on the spy.

"The Fischer family is a rat's nest," Rankin said. "You got no dog in this hunt, so why don't you get out while you still can."

"Get out?"

"You think whoever is warning me might not do the same to you, now that you have all this stuff on the girl? Like I said, clear out while you still can. That's my advice if you want it."

7

Damon found Harris waiting for him in the Sculpture Court, walking around with his hands locked behind his back looking at the art.

"What is this?" he inquired when Damon approached.

"Mother and Child by Henry Moore. He specialized in abstracting the human figure."

Harris studied the carved granite form of rounded shapes.

"Where's the mother and where's the child?"

"You need to take into account the negative space. See the ovoid hole? That suggests the mother's womb..."

"Suggests?"

"Well, you can't know for sure. Abstract art is subject to multiple interpretations."

Harris rolled his eyes. "You can say that again."

They sat side by side on the bench next to the Horse and Rider. Harris became pensive as if holding back information.

"Bring me up to date," he said.

Damon had decided not to say anything about his meeting with Jacob Rankin until he had a chance to talk to

Arvid, and so he restricted the narrative to his private meeting with Sarah, telling Harris about her concern over the bad publicity the Fischers were facing because of Beth's death, and convincing the Minnetonka's City Attorney to postpone the coroner's report long enough to formulate a response.

Harris interrupted. "What did I tell you? She thinks she can run City Hall."

"She has her own set of rules...as well as opinions," Damon said, although he did not tell Harris she thought he looked like a vagrant.

Damon finished with Sarah's desire—more like a mandate—to have him represent the family as their public spokesman, and to do so from the Schloss, not only taking up residence there but also using CT's old office.

"More than I could hope for," Harris said, beaming. "When I asked you to be on the inside I didn't expect you to get that far."

"Not because of my efforts, I assure you."

"Who cares how it happened. The fact is, you couldn't be in a better position to keep an eye on the family. What do the others think of your moving in?"

"Not much. In fact, downright hostile."

"Good," he said. "Make someone mad enough and he will say something incriminating, so keep your ears open."

"But you can't keep assuming someone in the family killed Beth. Why don't you look elsewhere?"

"You think I've been sitting on my ass?" Harris said, irritated that his professionalism was being questioned. "I've been nosing around the Wayzata Country Club where Beth Rand was a member. Did you know your sweetheart was a scratch golfer?"

He nodded. "She was good at anything she tried."

Harris nudged Damon on the arm. "Even in bed?"

"Better," he fired back, his turn to be irritated.

"Did Beth Rand ever mention Harvey Wilson?"

Damon nodded. "She was dating him when we

met."

"Comes from old money as well. They would have been the ideal union, everyone's been telling me, but you broke them up. He wasn't too happy being replaced by a working stiff like you."

"Doesn't that make him a suspect, then?" Damon asked, looking for an opportunity to deflect attention away from the Fischers. "Like you said the other day, a jealous lover nine times out of ten."

Harris smiled. "Except for one thing."

"What's that?"

"Alibi. The night Beth Rand was killed, Wilson was balling another high society babe at a fancy BandB in St. Croix, not only getting laid but getting even, I guess."

"But that doesn't mean he's the only one out there who had reason to kill Beth."

"Process of elimination, that's way I work. And it looks more and more to me that the killing was an inside job." Harris reached into his pocket and pulled out his notebook as though he just thought of something. He leafed through it and stopped at a page, referring to a line written on it. "Does the name Jacob Rankin ring a bell?"

Damon stared, totally surprised, totally off guard, wondering how in hell he knew Rankin.

"Private Investigator, address 113 East Hennepin, Suite 207."

"That's Minneapolis," Damon said, hoping to turn the query back on Harris. "I thought you were assigned to Lake Minnetonka."

"Following up. Got a call from MPD responding to this guy brought in to the ER at Hennepin County General. They searched him for ID and came up with a notebook with your name in it. A notebook just like mine, by the way." Harris held it up and wagged it in Damon's face. "Looks like PIs and cops have at least that much in common.

"Anyway, it didn't take long to trace your name to the unit investigating Beth Rand's death. You were the one who found Rand in the water, after all—your name is writ large in the file. So the big question is, how in hell did your name also end up in a notebook belonging to a Minneapolis PI?"

Damon shrugged.

"You are a bad penny, turning up in the wrong places, first with Beth Rand and now this Rankin."

"That doesn't mean I did anything wrong."

"But death seems to follow you around."

What did Harris mean by that? "This PR guy…"

"Not PR, P*I*. What's the matter, nervous about something?"

"No, no, just wondering if he is ok. You mentioned Hennepin County General, that's all."

"He's not ok."

"Dead?"

Harris nodded. "As a doornail, on the operating table."

Damon felt the blood drain from his face. "What…" he asked, "what happened to him?"

"He was run down while walking to his car in the alley behind the building."

"When?" Damon hoped to sound only casually interested.

"Last night, around ten."

Holy shit, the same day he saw Rankin. The detective was worried about losing his license not his life. What in hell went wrong?

"So," Harris said, picking up the thread of his narrative, "why were you in this guy's notebook? Are you a client of his?"

"Me? A PR guy working for a museum?"

"Not just any PR guy and not just any museum."

Damon needed time to think. He didn't want to admit anything to an acid-tongued cop.

"I checked up on Rankin," Harris continued after Damon failed to respond. "He specializes in tracing bad apples like felons, runaways, debtors, child molesters, ass holes behind on child support. The world is full of people running from something or somebody, and Rankin made his living finding them like a bounty hunter. Not a job to be proud of. So if you are protecting him..."

"What do you want to know?" Damon asked resignedly.

"Just answer my goddamn question. How did your name get into his notebook?"

Damon knew he was no match for Harris, a professional, while Damon was a rank amateur, and so he had to be careful not to reveal too much, only that Rankin was hired by Arvid to find his missing daughter.

When he finished, Harris whistled. "You mean Rankin was looking for a missing Fischer?"

"That's what he told me."

"Fantastic! Find that girl and we'll find out who killed Beth Rand."

"Think so?"

"Can't be a coincidence. I'll put a tail on Campbell. Sooner or later he will contact her." Harris shook his head in frustration. "I wish we had more to go on. Minneapolis police searched Rankin's office and they drew a blank. It's as spare as a monk's cell. Did Rankin give you anything?" Harris asked as if in afterthought.

Damon's head was racing like an engine in full throttle. He did not want to give away the store.

"Well?"

He shrugged.

"What about photos? PIs are notorious for using long lenses and pushing 800 ASA film to the limit in order to shoot unsuspecting suspects with their pants down."

Damon slid his hands between his thighs, hoping Harris did not notice that they were shaking. God, lying was hard, against his very nature, but he had to buy time, he had to talk to Arvid first and find out what the hell is going on.

6

Harris left with a dissatisfied look on his face and the expectation that Damon would have more information when they met again.

Damon wanted then and there to drive out to the Schloss, but this was his last day of work and Troy was hosting a mini-cocktail party in his office for the staff at four o'clock to bid their collective farewell, a gathering not unlike a stage play in its theatricality. Everyone seemed to be playing a part, reciting lines they had memorized earlier.

"Wish I were in *your* shoes, living in the lap of luxury."

"Don't worry, there is no one on *earth* who could possibly replace you."

"You *are* dropping by once in awhile, aren't you? So drop by my office and say hello."

"We *will* see you at the opening of The Industrial Edge, won't we?"

Maggie had been invited to this painful farewell but, thank god, she was busy at a farewell of her own at the gallery where she was finishing her last day.

He used his final hour cleaning out his desk—the pencil holder with his astrological sign, Aquarius, on it, his seat cushion, a framed certificate of merit from the Public

Relations Council of America, among other personal items. He did not want Maggie to see them. He would not put it past her to toss them in the trash bin, he was that bitter. Moreover, he wanted her to find a barren atmosphere, devoid of any record of his presence or of any human occupation for that matter. He was not even willing to give her a leg-up and leave a note where to find things, let her struggle on her own, hoping she would stumble and cause Troy to abort her mission at the Art Center, call Sarah in desperation that he can't open The Industrial Edge without Damon, and she in turn would see the folly of her ways, isolating the museum's PR man in the Schloss, and send him back to the Art Center where he belonged.

He put the cardboard box with his stuff in the trunk of his car and got in the driver's seat, looking out the windshield but unable to focus beyond it, his mind in such a lather he left the car in park, engine idling, and sat there waiting for his head to clear.

Not only was he anxious about his job, he also knew he was in deep shit withholding information from an officer of the law. Harris asked if there were any photos and, with a nerve Damon never thought he had, he baldly lied, saying, in effect, Photos? What photos? Did he commit a felony? He didn't know the difference between a felony and a misdemeanor, but what he had done surely sounded worse than a misdemeanor. What happens if he gets caught? Prison? For how long—one year, two years? Life?

He had to stop thinking about these nightmarish scenarios. It was only making his panic worse. Think positively he told himself. You did this to protect the Fischers, clearly part of your new job description. You were doing it as a representative of the Fischer family. Surely Sarah Rand, with all of her power and influence, will support you. The thought made him feel better and it also cleared his head enough to determine a plan of action.

It was time to devote all of his efforts to the

Fischers, beginning by talking to Arvid. He put the car in gear and, with renewed determination, headed west on Highway 12, the lowering sun in his eyes. Is this what commuters who work downtown face every afternoon driving home? It seemed a big price to pay just to live on a lake—and all the bumper-to-bumper traffic, as well. He was not a lake person anyway. He didn't boat, sail or fish and if he went swimming it was in the pool at the Y.

Half an hour later he exited on County Fifteen and drove through Wayzata, following the shoreline till he reached Breckett's Point about two miles outside of town. He accessed the security gate code and followed the long drive, parking his dark blue Electra 225 behind the garage so it would remain out of sight. The old boat wasn't considered respectable. Beth refused to be seen in it despite its unique delta wing styling, angled dual headlights and the 264 Nailhead V8. The old beater never felt comfortable amongst the rich and infamous anyway, he rationalized, anthropomorphizing the forty-five hundred pounds of aging parts.

The garage was set apart from the Schloss so as not to compromise its rococo purity. There was space for at least six cars plus a service bay. The only car he recognized parked in the garage was Sarah's Lincoln. Del, the chauffeur, was more or less a retainer now, hardly ever driving Sarah anywhere anymore. He mostly delivered private messages like the one Damon got a week ago. Message-delivering was an extension of the more formal time when the rich would let their neighbors know that they were "receiving," which meant it was all right to pay a visit.

The way Sarah lived was an atavistic throwback to the days of CT. While the younger generation respected Sarah—perhaps feared was a more apt word—Damon knew there would be a collective sigh of relief when she finally died, and the old world she clung to died with her.

He had never been in the garage before and was not sure whose cars were parked there other than Sarah's

Lincoln. It occurred to him, even without any prodding from Harris, to check them out. The one that ran down Rankin must have suffered damage, like a broken headlamp or a dented grill. Just to satisfy himself that no car belonging to a Fischer was involved, all he had to do was simply check each one.

There were six overhead doors, all down. Damon came in through the service bay, a layout that would have impressed Mr. Good Wrench—tool chests on casters, an air compressor, a hoist, and shelving for anything a mechanic might need for auto maintenance, even body repair. He spotted cans of Bondo and auto paint, a sander, and a sprayer. If a Fischer car ever had a fender bender, there was no need to go to a body shop.

He was looking at the cars when the door behind him opened.

"Hey, what are you doing here?"

Damon turned. It was Del. He was not in his livery, wearing instead the pin-stripe overalls of a mechanic.

"Oh, it's you." He moved forward, a man in his fifties, sandy haired and rough-cut, with the cocky attitude men who work around cars have in the company of men who don't know a generator from an alternator.

"Karl told me you weren't moving in till Monday."

"Just dropping off some luggage," he said.

"Where are they putting you?"

"The guest bedroom."

"Yours now, huh?"

"For awhile."

"Never been beyond the kitchen, can you beat that? Twenty-three years driving Mrs. Rand and I've never been invited in. But she told me she'd remember me financially and otherwise."

Jesus, Damon thought, those were the same words she used on him. "What do you suppose she meant by that?"

Del shrugged. "Be in her will, I guess. I'll find out soon enough. She can't last much longer."

"She's tough as nails."

"What she wants you to think."

"How do you know that?"

"You work for someone as long as I have you learn things."

"Like what?"

Del looked around for imaginary eavesdroppers. "I drive her to the Medical Arts Building once a week. She sees an oncol... oncolo..."

"Oncologist?"

"That's it. She found out she has some kind of cancer, but she's not going to do anything about it. Since Beth died all the life went out of her."

"Who knows about this?"

Del shrugged.

"Why are you telling me?"

"She likes you a lot and trusts you. She told me once she wished you were her grandson. All these years being in the car alone with her, just the two of us...well she likes to talk, get things off her chest, you know? She needed to unload. She talked and I drove."

He lowered his voice. "And that's not all. I help out in the kitchen some nights and Karl tells me what he hears when he's serving. The old lady talked about changing her will. There are people in the family really worried they might get left out."

As the information sank in, staggering in its import, Damon began to understand how the rich lived in their insular, cocoon-like world. They talked freely as if servants were part of the woodwork, and if they heard anything they were expected to keep their mouths shut. Another revelation, or perhaps a flash of insight, was that Damon was now seen, at least by Del, as one of the family, not an interloper. If that's the case, Del could become a font of information, even a confidant.

He decided to test his theory. "Has there been a

fender bender lately?"

"Not the Town Car. I'm the only one who drives that one."

"Do you drive anyone else around?"

"Sure. Irene, back and forth to board meetings at the Art Center. When Edmond wants to go out, which is pretty rare, I drive him, or sometimes Miss Ellen will. I used to drive Miss Beth a lot."

Damon knew Beth disliked driving. "What about Henry?"

"He takes pride in still being able to drive. He'll never give up his driver's license without a fight. If anyone would have a fender bender he'd be the one."

Damon could not believe that Henry would run down Rankin but he would still like to check his car.

"What does he drive?"

"An Olds Cutlass. Nothing fancy."

"Who else has a car?" Damon asked.

"Dolores has a Caddie. Richard drives a C Class Mercedes Convertible.

"Arvid?"

"He has a rental. I don't know why, though, we got enough to go around." Del used his fingers to help count. "The Town Car, of course, then there's Henry's Olds, Richard's Mercedes, Dolores's Caddie, and there are two more cars, a Chevy Suburban and a four-wheel-drive Jeep."

"Eclectic."

"What does that mean?"

"Variety. What kind of car does CT drive?"

"He drives a company car which he trades every year. I don't know what the hell he has right now."

"That's ok. Do you mind if I look at the cars?'

"Sure, help yourself. I have to go shower." Del turned and walked out.

Damon turned on the overhead bank of fluorescent tubes. The place lit up like a showroom. Each car was immaculate and no doubt ran like a fine Swiss watch.

Nothing less would be allowed. He walked down the line. There was an empty space. The Mercedes was gone. The other cars were there and they all checked out. Not a nick, dent or scratch could be found.

Ok, he thought, a wild goose chase, but at least he could eliminate any Fischer car being involved. He was ready to leave when one of the garage doors hummed and began to go up. Trapped in the open, Damon ran around the big Caddie and ducked behind it. He didn't want to be caught snooping.

He glanced at the ceiling from his crouched position, wondering if the overhead lights would give him away, and then realized that they'd come on anyway when the garage door opened. So all he had to do was stay hidden.

He heard the steady purr of a high-performance engine—not the tappet noise of his V8—the authoritative sound of a C Class coming home to roost. No doubt Richard was pulling in to park. The garage door came back down automatically and settled into silence. Damon held his breath, he was only a few feet away, and caught the glimpse of well-tanned athletic legs in bright white tennis shoes go by. The exit door open and closed.

Alone again, he left his hiding place and looked at the convertible with its top down—shiny, expensive, haughty, the hood warm from engine heat, the sound of hot oil dripping into the pan, everything normal for a car just parked, everything normal except for one thing. Damon checked again to make sure. The plastic lens of the left headlight was cracked and the trim around it was pushed in as though the driver had struck something—or someone—maybe a PI named Jacob Rankin.

Arvid was having a drink on the terrace with his wife Crystal. No one else was around. Damon went into the Venetian Room to mix himself a gin and tonic from the sideboard before coming outside to join them.

The late afternoon sun was trickling through the oak leaves, caressing the flagstone, not too hot, not too cool, just right according to Goldilocks. Once again, the Fischers would have it no other way. While mixing his drink, he reflected on what he had just seen in the garage. The Mercedes had indeed been damaged, insignificant using his standards—who would bother to repair a small mar like that—but on a thirty-thousand-dollar C Class it stands out like a shaved heretic. He could have easily missed the damage had he not been looking for it. So, he thought further, is this all that happens to your car when you hit a body? He expected a broken headlight at least, a cracked grille and, if the impact were hard enough, a smashed windshield. So maybe the C Class was not involved in a hit and run. Someone might have grazed Richard's car in the Country Club parking lot. Shit happens, even to a Mercedes.

"I thought you were moving in Monday," Arvid said, the same comment Del had made. Isn't there any originality around here?

Arvid and Crystal were sitting on white wrought iron chairs next to a large round wrought iron table with a glass top. Above them a giant umbrella shaded them from the waning sun. They were nursing drinks.

"I need to talk to you," Damon said.

Arvid read the expression on Damon's face. "Whatever you have to say, you can also say to Crystal."

She frowned. "Why involve me? Your mother was a Fischer, not mine."

"You have a stake in this, too, you know," Arvid replied cryptically. Then he addressed Damon: "So what did you find out?"

"Jacob Rankin gave me the information about that woman you were looking for."

"So you got together. Good, I'll give him a bonus."

"He won't need it...maybe you haven't heard."

"Heard what?"

"Rankin is dead. Killed, hit and run."

"Jesus," Arvid muttered. "When?"

"Last night. I saw him at Whitey's on East Hennepin. He told me he got a warning to lay off or he would lose his license, and the next day he was run down." Damon took the envelope from his jacket pocket and laid it on the bench. "This is probably why he was killed."

Arvid stared at the envelope as though it was a time bomb.

Crystal reached for it. "If you don't have the nerve to look, I will." She withdrew the photos and sorted through them. "Well, at least she's pretty."

"Let me see."

While Arvid was looking at the photos, holding each one close to his face, Damon handed the business envelope to Crystal who seemed to be the one in charge.

She unfolded the sheet inside and read what Rankin had typed under his letterhead:

Amy Jacobsson, born June 8, 1939

Parents Elroy and Doris Jacobsson owner/operators
King Breed Arabians, 37415 Manor Road
Rogers, Minnesota.

"Where is Rogers?" she asked.

"North of here, not far," Damon said.

Arvid sighed. "All this time she was that close."

"Why are you trying to find her?"

"I want to accomplish at least one decent thing in my life. Coming back for Beth's funeral gave me that opportunity."

Crystal stared at her husband.

Arvid stared back. "Now that she's been found, do you think I can put the genie back in the bottle? Besides, she is a Fischer. She deserves to inherit some of Sarah's fortune. At least I can do that for her. Just like a fairy tale: she lived happily ever after."

Crystal narrowed her shoulders. "If you really want her to live happily ever after, then leave that girl alone. You will destroy her life as well as yours. Can't you see that?"

The pain and guilt in his voice was palpable. "I only want to see what she looks like, listen to the sound of her voice!" He lightened up. "I can drive by her house. Pretend I got lost, knock on her door and ask directions. She wouldn't know me from Adam."

"Listen to Crystal," Damon warned. "You might put her life in danger by contacting her. Rankin was probably killed because he was looking for her. And there might be a connection to Beth's murder. You just can't take that chance!"

Damon suddenly realized their raised voices carried in the soft summer air. He looked back at the Schloss, concerned that their emotional words might have reached the open windows.

77

8

Crystal insisted Damon take the documents and photos for safe-keeping, another responsibility foisted on him he would rather not have.

He stepped inside the Venetian room long enough to refresh his drink and headed for the library, hoping no one overheard the conversation the three just had. His mind was aflame with so many complicated thoughts his head began to ache. He sat at the table by the window where he and Sarah had their pivotal talk the other day and let his mind wander as he sipped his drink. And wander it did, all the way back to that afternoon, in this very room, where he first met Beth.

He was looking through family albums, his first assignment from Henry. When was that? My god, three months ago. Henry had left him with a stack of albums, some with delicately tooled leather covers, others plain, filled with Kodak snapshots taken with a box camera of yesteryear. The most intriguing was one whose cover of padded pink silk apparently belonged at one time in someone's boudoir. Sarah's perhaps? There was even a shoebox containing dozens of photos that were meant to be sorted and placed into albums, but never completed. Even the rich have habits not unlike the rest of us, Damon mused.

With great curiosity he began leafing through the

thick black pages. Fortunately someone with the talent of a draftsman wrote in white ink the names of those in the photos and this helped Damon a great deal. There were several of CT covering decades of his life as he went from a young man to middle age to dotage. Regardless of the moment captured on film power and strength accentuated his features, even when buried beneath the jowls, bags and walrus moustaches that made up much of his face as he grew older.

One of the photographs showed CT at his large oak desk, the same one Sarah insisted that Damon use. He turned the page quickly. Fat chance he'll ever have his photo taken sitting at it.

There was a family photo of CT and his wife Anna Spencer with their five children: Sarah, Henry, Edmond, James and Irene wearing the fashions of the time: sailor hats with ribbons and knickers for the boys, and puffy dresses with big bows for the girls, plus a collection of hounds at their feet.

Damon found a wedding picture of Sarah and Alfred Rand dated August 15, 1920. There was also a worn snapshot, probably kept in his wallet, of Rand in his officer khakis standing next to a Spad S.XIII. He flew as a volunteer in the Lafayette Escadrille during World War I, the same war that killed Sarah's brother James. Alfred survived, of course, and married into a fortune, his contribution to the family being a pedigree: he could trace his roots to Eleanor of Aquitaine while CT was but a first generation Austrian-American. Alfred Rand died during the time of World War II, of a heart attack at the age of 63.

In the satin-covered album Damon came across a series of Sarah's children, Harrison and Elizabeth, taken during their growing-up years. Thumbing through the pages it became apparent that Elizabeth blossomed early, seeming to jump fully formed from the photos.

The last page in the album was devoted to a color photo of Harrison sitting in his beloved P51 Mustang, wearing his helmet and goggles, waving at the photographer. On the opposite page was his obituary in the New York Times with the headline: Fischer Lumber Heir Dies in Air Show. He was only thirty-seven.

But Damon could not take his eyes off the photos of Elizabeth—the last one taken when she was eighteen particularly fascinated him. Her hair, set in tight finger waves, gripped her scalp like a conquistador's helmet. But it was her face he was drawn to, delicate yet strong, vain yet compassionate, firm yet gentle—contradictions he wanted to reconcile when a voice behind him said hello. He turned to see a young woman standing in the doorway.

"May I come in?" she asked and then promptly did so, no doubt used to taking matters into her own hands. When she stood in the light from the window Damon almost gasped. The woman before him was remarkably like the woman in the photograph, as though she magically stepped out of the past

She read his expression. "You must be looking at photographs of my aunt Elizabeth. Everyone keeps saying how much I look like her."

She extended her hand, strong fingers circling his. "I'm Beth Rand."

After that, she took an avid interest in his project, helping him in his research, sorting through old files and records so that, when he visited the Schloss, she had papers in neat piles with hand-written notes identifying each one. At first he was grateful for the help but as time went on he realized that Beth was more a hindrance than a help—she was in effect deciding what material was important instead of letting him be the judge. By that time their interest in each other had reached spontaneous combustion, from casual to intimate in one afternoon when the touch of a knee under the table became an extended stare which in turn became a hand around the waist that led to a kiss, then another one, longer, deeper and wetter this time, and amorous touching that hastened them to her bedroom, culminating not on her bed but on the thick oriental rug because it would have taken too much precious time to unmake the bed (covered by a revolutionary-era handmade quilt, one of CT's rare arts-and-crafts acquisitions).

An unexpected benefit of their relationship was that Beth began to open up about herself and her family, especially her close relationship to Madie, the woman-child Damon rarely saw, shielded by Mrs. Stockton when she made a rare appearance or otherwise hiding in her room down the hall from Beth's.

Madie, nee Madeline, was virtually absorbed into the deep recesses and dark corners of the Schloss. Damon even wondered if she roamed the hallways at night like a ghost in a haunted house. There were no photographs of her in the albums. It was clear that discussing her was discouraged, nor would there be any mention of her in the family history or even listed in a family tree, one of the illustrations Damon wanted to include. It was as if Madie did not exist.

"Ah, there you are!"

Damon jumped and turned from the window he was staring out of. It was Richard dressed for dinner in white trousers and a light blue aloha shirt of four-masted sailing ships.

"I saw Arvid on the terrace and he told me you were here. Staying for dinner?"

"No, I just came to unpack some things."

"Too bad. I'm really looking forward to your being around."

"Glad to hear that. I hope I don't let you down."

"Not a chance," he laughed heartily, nearly spilling his drink.

Of all those in the Schloss, Damon thought, Richard is the least opaque.

"So, what are your plans for next week?"

"First of all, have a meeting."

"I thought we did."

"That was dinner."

"What will we talk about?"

"Ground rules. After that I plan to visit the news editors of the TV channels as well as the Star and Tribune and The Pioneer Press."

"What about the Lakeshore Weekly News? Beth wrote a column for that paper. You should pay a call."

Damon had to give Richard credit for a good idea. It would not hurt to develop a relationship with the local weekly. The big city dailies and TV channels are antagonists by their very nature, no way to build a relationship with them unless it's adversarial. Damon finished his drink, making small talk with Richard, and then left. It was nearing seven-thirty, and the summer sun, made higher by daylight saving time, was still visible, though barely, through the trees. Damon backed his Buick out and made his way to Highway Twelve, very little traffic now and so he was able to cruise along at highway speed. East-west Twelve crisscrossed thoroughfares running north-south, each with signal lights: Highway 101, Plymouth Road, Ridgedale Drive, Hopkins Crossroad—if you timed it right, you could hit green all the way to the exit at Dunwoody Boulevard. He cruised under the overpass of Highway 100 doing fifty, when the last semaphore of his clear-lane challenge, Penn Avenue, pulsed yellow and then turned solid red. Several cars ahead came to a stop, their taillights bright crimson.

Damon applied his brakes, a routine action he'd done thousands of times without incident, but not this time. This time the car just kept rolling.

9

Damon pushed down on his brake pedal as hard as he could and threw the transmission into low gear. The car responded slowly but not nearly the way you expect power brakes to react. He figured he was losing brake fluid, one of the lines must have worn through. It happens in an old car like his. He put all his weight on the pedal, knowing that he had to stop the car manually, without power. Sluggishly the car slowed and came within a foot of the car in front before he was able to stop. Damon breathed a huge sigh of relief, realizing how close he came to having a serious rear-ender. At fifty mph he would have gone into the windshield given a propensity to ignore his seatbelt.

Thanking God, whoever He was, Damon carefully steered his car off Dunwoody Boulevard, following the road past the Parade Grounds to Vineland Place where the Fischer Art Center sat across Hennepin Avenue from the Cathedral Church of St. Mark.

He turned right on Hennepin and hugged the curb as closely as possible without rubbing the wheels. He crawled into Bernie and Jim's on the corner of Fremont and Hennepin, his go-to filling station three blocks from his apartment and fifteen minutes from closing.

Jim, in striped coveralls with his name stitched

over the breast pocket, shook his head when Damon told him what happened.

"Sounds like a busted line," he said, getting in the car and moving it onto the hoist. "I'll find out what the damage is, but I can't work on it until tomorrow."

Jim hydraulically lifted the car until he could walk under it, and shone his flashlight to inspect the brake drums one at a time.

"Come under here I want to show you something."

Damon crouched and joined him, amazed by the impossible-to-understand automotive underworld packed tightly—crankcase, transmission, drive train, axles, u-joints, shock absorbers, tie rods, manifold, muffler. How in the world can the human mind design all these parts and then assemble them into a functioning whole which runs without peril for thousands of miles, unless you rupture a brake line.

"See that?" Jim shone his flashlight on a piece of coiled tubing that was hanging free of its fasteners. Little drops of oil dripped from it.

"Broken?" Damon asked.

"Cut."

"What?"

Jim made a snip-snip motion with his fingers. "'Someone cut your line, probably with a shears." He shifted his beam to the other front wheel, "Here, too."

Sure enough the tubing on that side was cut cleanly as well.

"Both front wheels. What have you been up to? Looks like someone is trying to do you bodily harm."

*****

Damon walked the four blocks to his apartment on Franklin and watched TV till it was time to go to bed. He didn't want to think about anything. He slept fitfully, waking up once in a cold sweat, and lay on his back trying to remember the nightmare he was having, better than the nightmare he was having in real life.

By the time morning came he had decided to call Lieutenant Harris and tell him what happened. It was getting dangerous out there.

"May I speak to Lieutenant Harris?"

"He's not in. Give me your number and I will have him call you."

Damon's phone rang in less than five minutes.

"Where are you?" Harris asked after Damon answered.

"Home, my apartment."

"So you can talk?"

"Yes."

"Something is going on or you wouldn't call me Saturday morning before breakfast."

"Someone cut my brake lines. I almost had an accident."

Harris's voice was tense. "When?"

"Last night, driving back from the Schloss. When I put on my brakes they didn't work."

"You ok?"

"I stopped in time."

"Where is the car?"

"At Bernie and Jim's on Hennepin and Fremont."

"What is Bernie and Jim's, a diner?"

"A Pure Oil Station."

Harris took a cautious breath. "What is your car doing at a Pure Oil Station?"

"I drove it there, very carefully by the way. Jim put it on the hoist and found two brake lines cut. It was no accident,"

"I'll call Minneapolis Impound and have them send a tow truck to pick it up."

"You don't have to bother. Jim is probably working on the car as we speak."

"Working on it?"

"Sure. I have to be able to drive it. I'm moving

into the Schloss on Monday."

"Jesus H. Christ!" Harris yelled. "You know what you did? You let that mechanic of yours destroy evidence! The only fingerprints left are his!"

Damon felt his knees wobble. My god, he thought, what have I done? "It never occurred to me…"

"Never occurred to you? This could have been the break we needed—pardon the pun—but whoever cut those lines is our man. Find out who he is and we've solved the murder of your girlfriend and that PI nobody seems to care much about. By the way, what were you doing at the…what the hell do you call it?"

"The Schloss."

"Can you please tell me what that means?"

"Palace in German."

"Ok, enough with the fancy-pants crap. Who at the Schloss knows how to cut a brake line?"

"There is only one person I can think of, the chauffeur, Delmar."

Damon could hear Harris leafing through his notebook. "I've got something on him, let's see…Delmar Kominski, age forty-seven, Hennepin County Community College two years majoring in auto mechanics. Well he fits the MO but you don't need a diploma to cut a brake line. Who else might have done it?"

"Richard."

"The playboy? Why would he get his hands dirty?"

"Well, his car was damaged…"

"What the hell are you talking about?"

"I was in the garage looking at the cars, six of them…"

"Wait a minute. Hours after I told you Rankin was run down, you were in the Fischer garage checking out their cars? If I wasn't so pissed at having your own car repaired, I'd give you an E for effort, but investigating is my job, not yours."

"Ok, so I *was* checking out the Fischer cars for

front end damage."

"All right, Mr. Detective, did you find anything?"

"Richard's car, an E Class Mercedes convertible, had a small crack in the headlight lens and the trim was slightly dented."

"Well, well, well. I have to hand it to you. But you got yourself into deep trouble trying to be what Rankin was, a PI, and you know what happened to him. So cool it like I said. Stay in your apartment the rest of the weekend. I want to impound that Mercedes and have it examined by forensics but I can't get a court order till Monday. With the clout the Fischers have in City Hall it may take longer. And there is good reason to haul in that chauffeur, too." Harris sighed. "He is the one with most opportunity and knowledge to cut the lines but I can't imagine him doing this on his own. Someone must have put him up to it and I want him to tell me who it was."

Damon was concerned about the ripples, more like a tidal wave, that will rock the household.

"Maybe we should just hold off for awhile."

"Are you serious?"

"Maybe it was just a warning."

"You mean like the warning Rankin got that eventually killed him? Do you want to be next?"

10

Damon ate breakfast as if it were his last meal. How else could he describe it? He was as good as condemned, his apartment a cell on death row. Who wanted him hurt, or even killed? Richard? But how could he possibly have detected Damon hiding in the garage and checking out the damage on his car? Who else but Del even knew he was in the garage?

These and other questions nagged him like a shrewish wife. He paced the floor diagonally so he could go further without having to turn. This was awful. How can Harris expect him to stay locked in here given all the things that were spinning out of control beyond these four walls? Even his limited art collection, among them a Warhol silk screen of Marilyn, Robert Indiana's Love poster, and his favorite, a large abstract painting by a talented local artist, Jerry Rudquist—none of these inspired him as they normally would. He looked at his watch for the umpteenth time, not yet nine. He called Jim's and found out his car would be ready at ten. Harris could not possibly ground Damon for picking up his car.

He was ready to leave his apartment when his phone rang. Probably Harris calling back. What now? Damon picked up the phone and snapped a hello into the receiver.

A voice belonging a woman asked, "Is this Mr. Petroulis?"

A tentative voice, a young voice, totally unfamiliar, calling him on a Saturday morning and referring to him by his proper name. He could hardly remember the last time that happened.

"Yes," he said.

"I'm sorry to bother you but it seemed urgent." She hesitated. "I don't know where to begin."

He was going to tell her, why don't you begin at the beginning but sensed this wary caller was in no mood for jokes and so he waited for her to make her own decision, and she did: "You don't know me and it is not my habit to call a perfect stranger but this person who called me last night was, well, so desperate sounding. I don't know how else to put it. I know I'm not making much sense but this person said it was vital for me to get in touch with you right away. He did not say why but that you would explain. It was late when he called, after ten, and I wasn't going to call someone I didn't know that late and besides I had to think about it, sleep on it, and this morning, with the sun up and everything bright, not spooky, I decided to call and if you sounded weird or scary or phony or anything, all I had to do was hang up."

"You haven't heard me say anything but 'Yes.'"

She laughed lightly. "No, I guess I haven't."

Her long, rambling discourse gave him time to figure out that this voice had to belong to the girl in the photos Rankin had taken, the Horse Girl. Apparently Arvid did not take Crystal's advice. What does it matter now, Damon asked himself, the lid was blown off the whole enterprise when his brake lines were cut. He was in no mood for subtlety, yet Damon liked the sound of her voice, almost cheeky with an air of insouciance that was refreshing, and so he decided to play along. "Tell me who you are."

"No," she said firmly. "I have to find out about

you first. Tell me who *you* are."

"Fair enough. My full name is Damon Mark Petroulis. That's Greek if that matters. I'm 32 years old, my sign is Aquarius, I'm six-foot-one, weigh hundred seventy pounds, I have a BA in journalism from the University of Minnesota and I'm the Publicist at Fischer Art Center in Minneapolis. Oh, I'm also single, no serious attachments."

He thought he detected a subtle shift as though she wanted the conversation to go forward. He was completely attentive to every nuance in the way she breathed, or hesitated, or emphasized her words, even a delicate sigh that encouraged him to say:

"Is it ok now to ask who you are?"

"My name is Amy Jacobsson…"

Even though it came as no surprise, hearing the girl speak her name still caught him unprepared, causing a slight alteration in his own breathing that he was not aware of, but that she must have sensed because she, too, was attentive to every nuance coming from his side of the conversation.

"There is a connection isn't there?" she asked suspiciously. "You know who I am don't you?"

"Not personally," Damon said hurriedly. "I heard your name mentioned, that's all."

"That's *all*? You know who called me in the first place, don't you?"

Damon had to admit that he did. "Yes."

"Who is it?"

"Someone you don't know. Look, there is too much to talk about than can be covered over the telephone."

"What are you suggesting?"

"Getting together."

"I may be curious but not that curious."

"Let's meet someplace. You name it and I'll come."

She thought a bit. "I'm not taking any chances. "

Damon felt that he was losing her. "Let's meet where you'll feel safe, like the horse farm." He could have bitten his tongue.

"My god! You even know where I live?"

"I'm sorry, I said too much."

"Not near enough. If you are stalking me, I will have you arrested, right at that museum you said you work at."

Oh no, he thought to himself, I haven't even met her and she's going to have me arrested! "Please, let me explain."

There was a long pause. "I can't imagine hearing anything that will convince me to meet you where I live or anywhere else for that matter."

He could sense her ready to hang up. God, what a mess. How could Arvid do this to him? No warning, nothing, leaving it up to Damon, once again, to clean up a mess someone else made. Was there ever a worse beginning trying to build someone's trust? He couldn't blurt out that the stranger who called her was her real father, that she was heir to unfathomable riches—too laughable to be true, too preposterous to make any sense. Damon needed to have a conversation, divert the real reason for her call.

Think, think!

Then he recalled (a) the picture Rankin took of the girl on a horse and (b) lateral thinking—using an indirect approach to solve a problem.

"Have you ever heard of The Blue Horses?" he asked.

"What?" she said, taken a bit by surprise—nothing fancy but enough to keep her where she was, on the phone.

"It's a painting by Franz Marc, a German artist. It hangs in the Art Center where I work. The horses are painted blue because the artist was using that color as a visual metaphor for power. I guess you know all about horse power, right?" He laughed, lamely, of course, but he was trying.

At least she did not hang up.

"The Blue Horses happens to be one of my favorite works and it occurred to me that we can meet at the Art Center, a public place, by that painting. A certain kind of symmetry don't you think? You, a lover of Arabian Horses and I a lover of The Blue Horses. And I promise to explain everything. If you don't like what you hear, you can simply turn around and leave."

11

On his walk to the Art Center, Damon stopped by the Pure Oil Station to tell Jim that he would pick up his car on the way home, and arrived at the museum way ahead of the agreed upon time, two pm. He wandered around the busy galleries fighting off a desire to visit the administration wing and check his desk, wondering if it was still the way he left it yesterday, which seemed like an eternity ago, or that Maggie had already made a sneak raid, as silly as this idea is, and laid claim to his office with her personal possessions, whatever they might be—a potted plant, a sampler, an embroidered chair cushion. He knew he was being snide but he could not help himself, everything in his life was going haywire—he felt like a helpless pawn buffeted by people and events beyond his or anyone else's control. First he was afraid of losing his job and now he was afraid of losing his life. What kind of crazy world is this?

Stan Steppen, the chief guard, noticed Damon wandering like a lost soul. Stan was direct, if not brutally frank, never taking the time to suffer fools gladly, not even Damon. He was a practicing artist as were many of the guards working at the museum because they ate, lived and breathed art, their consuming passion.

"Hey, man," Stan said, walking over. He was dressed in light gray slacks and a dark gray jacket, white shirt and black tie, designating him the guard in charge.

"You are wearing out the terrazzo. What gives?"

"Waiting for someone."

"Female?"

"How did you know?"

"Only a female will make a man pace like that. She has to be someone special."

"I'll find out soon enough."

Stan raised an eyebrow. "Blind date?"

"Kind of."

"I heard you moved out yesterday, emptied your desk. Donna said she saw you carrying a cardboard box containing your worldly possessions."

"Only temporary."

"I hope you're right. I know Maggie is tenacious. I've exhibited at that gallery she was at. She always wanted to work here and she got her wish. To be honest with you, you might find it tough to get your old job back."

Before Damon could fire a salvo of his own—that this would never happen, not in a thousand years, if he lives that long—Stan turned his attention to the front entrance.

"Well," he said, "if that gal who just came in is your date, you are one lucky man, job or no job."

Damon turned and followed Stan's stare. Standing in front of the tall brass doors that had whisked shut behind her, tentatively looking around, was the girl in the grainy photograph, now sharply in focus. Damon hesitated before approaching, wanting a moment to study her. She was wearing a light maroon snap shirt with piping outlining the pockets, narrow blue jeans and scuffed cowboy boots. Horse Girl, all right. She wasn't so much pretty as striking, taller than average, dark brown hair that now hung loosely to her shoulders, not the ponytail in the photographs, and strong facial bones that made her look determined. As he walked toward her he saw that she did not pluck her eyebrows and wore no lipstick or makeup of any kind. The main impression he had was that she did not look like a Fischer. Around the Schloss she'd be a misfit.

She looked at him as he neared, the apprehension in her eyes changing to recognition.

"Amy?" Damon said.

"So you are Damon," she replied. "You don't look so scary."

"What did you expect?"

"I don't know. Someone older-looking maybe." Then she directed her attention to her surroundings, obviously foreign to her, a museum with abstract works of art that had no reference to the real world, and patrons were staring at the art as if they saw something she didn't.

"I've never been in here before. It's like a new world. Where are The Blue Horses?"

First things first, Damon thought, amused by her way of cutting to the chase. "In the next gallery, follow me."

They stopped in front of a painting about six feet wide and four feet high. Three roundish, dark-blue horses with black manes dominated a multi-colored landscape of an unearthly planet. A plaque next to it gave its official title as Die Grossen Blauen Pferde (The Large Blue Horses), dated 1911.

"Like it?"

She nodded.

"The painter, Franz Marc, was expressing his inner feelings rather than reproducing what he saw."

"You told me that blue meant power."

"Or masculinity."

"So you conflate the two?"

Damon could not remember hearing anyone use that verb in a long time. She was sharp, all right.

"What about red and yellow," she asked, pointing to the mountains and the sky in the background, "do those colors have special meaning, too?"

Damon nodded. "Red represents nature and yellow femininity."

She held up her hand in protest, and he saw strong

fingers that looked as if they had been rope-burned more than once.

"Have you ever broken a horse?"

"Me?" Damon laughed.

"Well, then, maybe Marc should have used blue to describe females, too."

"We are talking about a long time ago."

"No excuse."

"Ok, enough art history. At least until we get to know each other better."

"You think that might happen?" she asked, clearly dubious.

"I hope so. Let's sit down." Damon guided Amy to a bench in the center of the gallery. They were not alone, but the hushed atmosphere and the concentration of those looking at the art made it seem as if they were. As they sat down, Damon was reminded of the bench where he met with Harris—next to another horse, the Marini sculpture in the court yard. The horse metaphor was inescapable.

They sat for a moment, Damon wondering where to begin, she waiting for him to start.

"This isn't going to be easy," he said presently, "but nothing important ever is."

"I'm ready—for whatever you want to tell me, I'm ready. I just don't want to hurt anyone."

"Like...?"

"My parents."

He eyed her questioningly.

"I know why that man contacted me. It's as if I've been waiting for his call practically all my life."

Damon was beginning to think that Amy had done the hard work for him.

"This has something to do with my adoption doesn't it?"

The word adoption fell between them like something too hot to handle, as though Damon had to wait for it to cool off before he could pick it up.

"Yes," he finally said. "The man who called you is your real father."

"Real? Why do you call him real? My real father is Elroy Jacobsson."

"Well, biological, then." He looked into her eyes, wondering if this was going too far too fast.

"What is his name?"

"Arvid Campbell."

"How did he find out about me?"

Damon knew that this woman was too astute for him to prevaricate. "He hired a private detective."

"A private detective?" An aura of fear circled her eyes. The mere mention of a private detective suggested something ominous.

Damon held out his hand, hoping the gesture would calm her. "It's nothing like that. Arvid has his reasons, too complicated for me to explain here. I hope he can tell you himself. I know he wants to meet you but that is up to you, and your parents, of course." Damon hesitated, trying to read the expression on her face. "I feel this has got off on the wrong foot, I'm sorry if all this is scaring you."

"Maybe more angry than scared." She sighed. "I guess I knew down deep that sooner or later something like this would happen."

"Did your parents ever tell you that you were adopted?"

"It was not hidden. If it came up, they didn't avoid talking about it. I remember asking my mom when I was six or seven why I didn't look like her, and she used that as an opening to explain in terms that a small child could grasp."

"For what it's worth, you don't look like a Fischer, either," Damon said with no malice aforethought, in fact with no aforethought whatever, a mindless comment one might say over coffee or a glass of wine during a casual conversation, even though there was nothing casual about this one.

"Fischer?" Amy asked with renewed wariness. "I thought you said his name was Campbell."

"Oh, yes, of course, you're right," Damon replied, flustered and upset for coming off sounding insensitive. He could have kicked himself for not being attuned to her feelings. But how often does anyone have a life-changing revelation of this magnitude? He cursed Arvid under his breath for putting him in this position, this was Arvid's job not his. But then, he reflected, she had to know sooner or later, whether or not she learned it from him or someone else, so bear the burden and carry on.

"His mother's name was Fischer."

"But why does that make any difference—Campbell, Fischer, who cares? Why did you even mention the other name?" Amy stared, recognition slowly flowing over her features like an eddying pool. "Wait a minute. This muscum is named after a Fischer, some guy who made a fortune cutting down trees, is that right?"

"Yes."

"Are you saying I'm related to him?"

"CT Fischer, the founder of Fischer Art Center, is your great grandfather."

Amy stared at Damon for a moment and then forced a smile, pointing to The Blue Horses. "Is that painting mine, then? Can I take it home with me? It would look great in the stables."

She was resisting the impact of the news, not buying anything Damon was saying. How could she believe some stranger she had never set eyes on till now telling her that her great grandfather, when he was alive, was one of the ten richest men in America. And, if anything, that fortune has grown since his death.

"I know this sounds crazy to you."

Amy looked up at the ceiling. Dozens of spotlights suspended from long tracks highlighted works of art on the walls.

"So…where do I go from here?"

12

A great wave of empathy rolled over Damon as he watched this young woman struggle with the news. She sensed his concern and the barriers of suspicion and doubt began to crumble. They sat on the bench side by side without speaking, each immersed in a myriad of thoughts, absently watching those who were looking at the art, reading labels, commenting quietly about the artist's intent, looking for meaning in the lines, splashes and forms.

"What about my mother?" she asked suddenly as if she had just thought of it. "My birth mother. Who is she? Do you know?"

Damon shook his head. "No, but I intend get some answers. I'm going to call Arvid from my office." He pointed with his head. "Through that door over there." He stood. "I should bring him up to date anyway. You want to join me?"

She considered his offer. "You mean I can go in there? My first time in this museum and I can go through that door marked private?"

Damon smiled. He was really beginning to like this girl. "You might even be my boss someday," he said, only half kidding.

"I'll wait out here and look at some of this abstract art. I think I can figure out the art better than what is happening to me right now."

"Ok, I'll be right back." He left Amy and walked down the hallway so familiar to him, the one he traversed countless times, the same hallway that Henry Fischer followed as he dropped off his polished stones on his visits to the Art Center. Familiar, even hallowed, ground.

As he approached the walled-off area that was his cubicle, Damon slowed and tensed. Something was amiss but he could not identify it. Was it the air he was breathing? It seemed heavy, dense. Perhaps a change in barometric pressure, the way one senses an impending storm. Baffled, he looked into his office. Sitting at his desk was a woman pouring over a stack of files. For a split second Damon thought he was in the wrong place. This was not his office, his desk, his chair, his window. But they were, collectively, and the person in possession of them all was Maggie, his replacement, checking in early it appeared to make sure she would hit the ground running Monday morning.

Maggie looked up at him. She wore round tortoise-shell glasses that Damon thought were too large for her oval face, hiding eyes, he decided in the split second one has to make such judgments, that were direct and piercing. The two had never met face to face and so she did not know who he was and suspicion arched her eyebrows, as if protecting her space against encroachment.

"I beg your pardon, " she said coolly.

Unprepared for this, his mind on other matters clearly not connected to his PR job, Damon was flustered and he stammered, "Ahhh…" The last time he did this was in a high school chemistry class when he gave a report on distilling alcohol and a cute girl asked him what 100 proof meant. He did not know the answer, and he felt the same way now because he had not prepared himself. And how could he? How on earth could he have expected Maggie to be sitting at his desk when he walked in to use the phone, *his* phone? Two separate conflicts in his life on a collision course. Could there be anything more paradoxical than this?

"I'm Damon Petroulis,"

"So *you're* Damon. Well, what a surprise. Didn't expect to see you *this* soon."

The implication that Damon was checking up on her was not lost on him. Plus the fact that she liked to *em*phasize her words did not bode well for cordiality.

"I was in the Museum and I needed to use the phone." He could not manage to say *my* phone. "I didn't expect to see anyone here."

Maggie rolled herself back from the desk. "I'll pack up and leave. Actually this isn't officially my office till Monday."

Officially my office? What in hell did she mean by that? "Never mind," he said. "I can use Troy's phone." He said this purposely to imply that he and the Director were like two fingers intertwined—even though he had never used Troy's phone.

"That's all right, I'm gone." Maggie grabbed her handbag, a large floppy monster of soft tan leather that could have carried her life's belongings, and off she went.

Damon stared blankly at the empty chair. He did not want to sit in it and so he stood by his desk and dialed the Fischer number.

The butler, Phillip, answered after the first ring, as if he were standing by the phone in the foyer. "Fischer residence."

"Phillip this is Damon Petroulis. May I speak to Arvid, please?"

"Why, Mr. Petroulis, isn't Mr. Campbell with you?"

"No."

"He said he was driving into town to meet you."

"There must be some mistake. I haven't seen him."

"Perhaps I should have Mrs. Campbell speak with you."

Crystal came on after a moment. "Damon where

105

are you?"

"At the Art Center. What's the matter?"

"Arvid left about two hours ago."

Something fishy was going on. "Crystal, did Arvid tell you that he was going to contact Amy?"

"He knows how I feel about that," she replied.

"However you feel about it, it happened. He called her and asked her to get in touch with me, which she did. We met this afternoon at the museum. In fact she is waiting for me in the galleries."

There was a long silence. "So he contacted her after all."

"Yes, and we can't just leave it hang there. I'd like to bring Amy to the Schloss."

"I can't be responsible for this," Crystal said. "It would be unwise for you to pursue this further, Damon."

Arvid gave no warning before he opened this Pandora's box, not just open it but blast it open. And now that he had, there was no going back. Something must have happened, as if Arvid had to do it now or never and, for some reason, time had run out on him.

"Too late now, Crystal," Damon said.

"You can't bring that girl out here, not without Arvid present. Do you understand?" she said emphatically, almost fearfully.

"Ok, but sooner or later the press will get hold of the news and it will blow the lid off the Schloss. Sarah has to know about Amy before that happens. This will be an even bigger story than Beth's murder."

He returned to find Amy sitting on the bench facing The Blue Horses. When she saw him she jumped up as though greeting an old friend. They had connected—strangers initially but now two persons with a common purpose. She touched his hand with her fingers, a gesture of intimacy, at least that is what Damon wanted to believe, a brief contact charged with potential. This extremely vulnerable woman was putting her trust in him, a gesture of faith he hoped was deserved.

"Where do we go from here?" she repeated, but this time she used the plural noun, not the singular.

"To start with, talk to your parents."

She almost shuddered. "When they learn I'm related to the man who started this place," she moved her hand in a sweeping gesture, "it will come as a big shock."

"You took it in stride," Damon said, wanting to be supportive.

"Mom and Dad were already in their forties when I was adopted. I grew up with kids whose parents were twenty years younger. At PTA meetings people thought my mom and dad were my grandparents. How do you explain that? I was different without completely understanding why. I mean, being adopted is always wondering who you are. That is hard enough but now I see that finding out who you are is even harder." She reflected a moment. "So now I have a new family. Where do they live?"

"Lake Minnetonka."

Amy's eyes slowly widened as a thought took root in her head. "Wait a minute..." she began.

"What?"

"About a month ago there was a drowning in Lake Minnetonka. I saw it on the news. The reporter was doing a live remote from a place called Schloss Fischer."

Damon took his time to answer. This was not how he wanted to introduce Amy to her startling new life—a death in the family. "The woman who died was Beth Rand, your first cousin."

Amy stared at Damon in shock. "I've led a quiet life with two people I love and now, out of the blue, I find that I am related to a rich family living in something called a Schloss—and if that isn't weird enough, one of them drowned."

14

Damon woke up Monday morning with a headache. Making his head throb were Amy's words from Saturday still caroming inside his brain as well as the image of the perplexed look on her face. She wanted answers but he was not prepared to tell her that her first cousin did not drown accidentally, nor that he was having an affair with her, nor that the private detective who tracked Amy down was himself killed, nor, who knows, that Damon may also be a marked man, nor that he was a mole for the local constabulary while professing loyalty to Amy's grandmother.

All he was able to give Amy in parting was a promise that he would get back to her as soon as he heard from Arvid. He would arrange a meeting between the two. Beyond that she would have to remain in a holding pattern, like a plane waiting for a break in the storm to land safely.

After swallowing two Bayers he munched down a muffin with a cup of coffee, not at all healthful, but in his present state of mind he was not as concerned about diet as he was self-preservation.

All hell was breaking loose when he arrived at the Schloss. A white Channel 4 television panel truck with remote equipment was camped on the access road and, when Damon drove up, a female reporter stepped out from behind it and waved him over. He recognized her as Patricia Azquith, in her mid-thirties, with a tightly bound body only Pilates can sculpt, blonde hair that a breeze wouldn't dare mess with, and eyes that burrowed like a rodent after kernels, in this case kernels of information. She was wearing a pastel pink, one-piece dress that Damon realized would contrast perfectly with the row of arbor vitae she would probably use as background when she did a live report.

He rolled down his window as she approached his car. He had met her once before when trying to rouse interest in Twyla Tharpe and her dance company who were conducting a series of master classes at the Fischer. This reporter turned him down for an interview probably because she knew Twyla was a difficult person who did not suffer local reporters gladly. He had been pissed at Azquith ever since.

"What's going on?" he asked as if she were a highway patrol officer redirecting traffic after an accident.

"That's what I want to ask you."

He shrugged noncommittally.

"Come on, Damon, don't be coy. I tried to get an interview with Sarah Rand and got stonewalled. Refer all questions to our representative, Damon Petroulis. I thought you were doing the Art Center's PR so I called there and they connected me to a woman named Maggie. What gives?"

"A new assignment. But only temporary," he added defensively.

"So now you are the gate keeper for Schloss Fischer? No story unless you approve it?" She motioned behind her back and Damon saw a cameraman move into position with a Digi Super 86ll Canon on his shoulder. Damn, she was going to tape him

He held up his hand instinctively, a bad move, as if he were coming off with something to hide, what you learn not to do as an experienced PR man. He should know better

"This is my first day on the job," he said. "Tell your man to lay off and I'll get you something."

"What something?"

"Whatever brought you here in the first place."

She smiled knowingly. "You don't know do you?"

"My plate is full, pick one thing."

"I'll give you what I have and you can do the picking." Patricia referred to some notes on a folded sheet of paper. "How about the cover-up of the Beth Rand investigation surrounding her death? And driving out here we followed a Sheriff's car that was allowed through the gate, something I'd love to be able to do. What gives?" she asked again.

All Damon could do was gape. What *was* a sheriff's car doing here? Had to be Harris checking out Richard's convertible. But this soon? He needed a warrant and Harris had told Damon he could not get one till Monday at the earliest, and it was only ten. He could only repeat Azquith: What gives?

She saw the anxiety spreading across his face. "Look, Damon, I can't wait all day. I'm going on the air at noon with the lead piece, with or without a comment or update from you."

"If it bleeds it leads, is that it? Listen, I haven't had a chance to talk to anyone yet. Give me a couple of hours."

"I haven't got a couple of hours. I'll need time to prepare my material." She looked at the oversize designer watch on her slender wrist. The dial was pink with raised white numbers. No match for his Timex even though they both kept the same time. "Eleven-thirty, max."

Azquith walked away with the cameraman to the waiting truck. They had set up a small table with an umbrella and Damon could see coffee mugs sitting on the table and a paper plate of croissants, a jar of Bonne Maman blueberry preserves and cheese slices. They were prepared to wait in comfort. He wondered idly, how do you get a job like that? Much better than the one he had.

He opened the gate using the pass code and drove onto the grounds of the Schloss. As he pulled up, sure enough, there was a brown van parked in the turnaround with a Hennepin County shield on the driver's door that claimed To Protect And Serve—serve as in warrant? Damon asked himself ruefully.

Phillip responded quickly to Damon's ring at the front door. There was a look of consternation on his face. "Mrs. Sarah wants to see you right away, Mr. Damon, in the library."

He walked with heavy legs across the Great Hall, through the Venetian Room, to the library. He opened the door. Sarah was sitting in her favorite chair next to the window and standing by her side was Lieutenant Harris, dressed not in the business suit Damon was familiar seeing him in but a black uniform with silver bars on the shoulders. A wide black belt held his weapon, a revolver of impressive caliber, and a hat with a black bill was tucked under his arm.

"Thank god you are here," Sarah said and fanned herself with a lace handkerchief. She pointed to the officer. "This is Lieutenant Harris."

They pretended not to know one other and shook hands. Harris was smiling, an expression on the officer's face new to Damon.

"What is going on?" Damon asked as innocently as he knew how.

"I have a warrant," Harris said, showing Damon a folded piece of paper. "I worked overtime and got a judge to issue it first thing this morning. Mrs. Rand asked me to wait until you arrived before I served it."

"I told you about him, Damon. He's treating us like common criminals. How can this be happening?" She wailed. "He wants to search the house."

"No, ma'am, just the garage. A warrant is very specific and that's the only place I can search."

"What is in the garage? Just cars."

"There is reason to believe one of them was

involved in a hit and run."

Damon thought Sarah was going to faint. "Just a minute, Mrs. Rand, let me talk to him." Damon led Harris across the room, out of earshot. "Jesus, Lieutenant," he said under his breath, "why didn't you at least call me?"

"I didn't have time. This came together very fast. And why are you barking at me? I'm looking out for you, too. We got to find out who is using cars as weapons. Now that you're here we can check out that Mercedes."

Damon returned to Sarah and sat across from her. She needed reassuring. "There is nothing to be concerned about, Mrs. Rand. Just routine police business. They have to follow every lead and it's a process of elimination. As soon as he finds out everything is ok, he will leave. I'll go with him and make sure he does just that."

She smiled wanly. "Thank you, Damon. At least there is someone here who knows what to do."

Damon felt his nose was about to grow as he and Harris walked out of the Schloss to the garage.

"What will you do with the car?"

"Haul it in as evidence."

Then what? Damon asked himself. What do I tell Sarah? The truth for once?

They entered the work area. Del was not there. They walked into the long space where the cars were sitting. The Mercedes convertible was in its spot. Harris took out the flashlight fastened on his belt next to his holster and shined it on the front of the insolent chariot to check the damage to the fender, but all they saw was a pristine headlight the way it must have looked when the car came off the assembly line in Sindelfingen, Bavaria. Where was the crack in the lens? Where was the dent in the trim? Gone—or was never there in the first place. Damon could no longer trust his memory. Maybe he had gone mad and fallen into a time warp, hurling his confused mind into another dimension where the world was turvy-topsy rather than the other way around.

Harris was disgusted. "Goddammit, Petroulis, you

said there was damage. There is nothing wrong with this car!"

"But I swear, Lieutenant, when I saw it Friday the headlight lens was cracked and this band of chrome..." Damon rubbed it as if he could change it back to the way it was, "...the chrome was dented. I know I was not dreaming. I did not make this up."

"Like you didn't make up that business of a cut brake line? I don't know if I can trust you anymore. All I have is your word..."

"And Jim's."

"Jim?"

"My mechanic."

"Great. An open and shut case—you and that gas station attendant. You have made my job impossible!" Harris grabbed the warrant out of Damon's hand, tore it into small pieces and threw them on the concrete floor. "Let someone else clean up the mess."

When Damon returned to the library, he did not have to lie to Sarah. The car had no damage and Harris had left, exactly as he promised. As he reported this to her, she gave a long sigh of relief. He wished he could sigh, too, but he had nothing to be relieved about. Someone had repaired the car over the weekend to hide the fact it had been in an accident. Did Richard take it to a garage over the weekend? Or did Del fix it? He certainly had the tools.

"I never want to see that man again," Sarah said.

"Who?" Damon asked, his mind on other things.

"That Lieutenant. Don't ever let him come into this house again."

"Yes ma'am," Damon replied, knowing he had no power or authority to keep the lieutenant at bay, not with two murders to solve.

Sarah stared out the window. "I'm tired," she said. She did indeed appear to be spent. The wattles on her face sagged even more than usual and pulled the flesh around her eyes downward, giving her a hangdog appearance.

"I'm going up to my apartment."

"I need to talk to you about a reporter out on the main road. She's planning to do a story."

"I know. There was a call from the interphone by the gate. What is her name, Azquith?"

"That's the one. She is going to do a live remote this noon and I have to prepare a statement. We have less than an hour."

"You handle it, Damon."

She did indeed look tired, almost defeated, so unlike the Sarah Rand he had seen up until this day. He recalled what Del had told him in confidence: She was dying of cancer.

"We should have a family meeting."

"Talk to Henry."

"What about Richard and CT?"

"Talk to Henry," she repeated, and struggled to her feet as though a chain were dragging her down.

"May I help you?"

"Give me your arm."

He walked with her slowly to the secret panel that opened to her private elevator. He pushed the button for her and the stainless steel door slid open.

"Do you want me to come up with you?"

"I'll be fine." She stepped in and turned around. "I am counting on you, Damon," she said as the door began to close, "to take care of things."

15

Damon found Phillip having a cup of tea at the kitchen table, a rectangle of heavy oak where the help took their meals. Phillip was alone, an old man more comfortable in his past, a throwback to the butler of Old England, proper to a fault, dressed in a black coat without a wrinkle, stiff collar and slim tie, discrete and faultless.

He looked up.

"Mrs. Rand went up to her apartment. She was tired."

"A very trying morning, Mr. Petroulis."

The afternoon isn't going to be any easier, Damon thought.

"May I bring you tea?"

"No thanks. Mrs. Rand wants me to see Henry."

"He is in his apartment. Shall I see if he is available?"

Damon nodded.

Phillip talked into the intercom, a wall-mounted affair with a button that Phillip pressed to make his connection.

A tinny voice came out of the speaker, "Yes?"

"Mr. Petroulis would like to see you, sir."

"Send him up."

Damon was surprised that he was being invited to Henry's lair, his first visit to the recluse's inner sanctum, having met him, up till now, either in the library or in CT's old office.

"Have you been to his apartment, sir?"

Damon shook his head.

"Take the elevator, not Mrs. Rand's, but rather the service elevator across from the main staircase. Mr. Henry occupies the entire third floor."

The elevator lifted Damon slightly faster than bread dough rising, and came to a sluggish stop at three. Damon exited into an expanse as large as a basketball court with room for bleachers. The space was supported by center beams running the length of the Schloss. The floor was not separated into rooms as Damon had expected, but was one large space separated by function: sitting room, bedroom, kitchen, and a laboratory the likes of which Damon had never before seen. And everything was messy. Clearly the cleaning staff was not allowed up here.

Henry was standing before a long workbench under a bank of windows that looked out on the lake, a commanding view stretching into Brown's Bay. In the winter, when the leaves of the giant old oaks are gone, Damon was sure Henry could see Wayzata. If the windows were clean, that is.

He was wearing an apron of heavy material, what appeared to be leather, and his shirtsleeves were rolled up to the elbow. He was grinding a stone on a large wheel. Surrounding him was an array of cutting tools, tumbling machines, metal trays, and wood drawers with labels of exotic sounding names:

> Turquoise
> Agate
> Malachite
> Jasper
> Dolomite
> Obsidian
> Petrified Wood
> Rhodonite

Sodalite
Lapis Lazuli
Apatite
Epidore

Damon stood by, waiting for Henry to invite him in but, because of the noise of the grinding wheel and his total concentration on what he was doing, he did not notice Damon had already entered his private domain. Probably the entire Schloss would have to collapse before he took notice.

Finally Damon said in a loud voice, "Thank you for letting me see what polishing a stone looks like!"

Henry turned and smiled. He truly was in his element. He flicked the toggle switch of the big electric motor mounted behind the grinder. A drive belt connecting the motor pulley to the grinder slowly lost speed and finally stopped—the subsequent silence had a presence all its own, like the negative space in an abstract sculpture, a companion to the noise it had just replaced.

Henry held up the stone he was polishing, the size of a half-dollar. The light green was deeply veined with darker streaks of green, which seemed to flow like slow-moving lava.

"This is malachite, a carbonite mineral found in the Southwest where copper is mined. I started out with a flat piece and I'm rounding it using a 100 diamond-grit wheel. You have to be careful, though, because it will rub your skin off. That's why stone polishers have what are called zombie fingers." He held up his hands, palms outward, to show his fingertips. Where you usually see delicate whirls and ridges there was only smoothness.

"See? No prints."

For the first time Damon became aware of what the hands of a stone polisher look like—hardened, strong and featureless. He hadn't noticed this before because Henry always put his hands in his jacket pockets or curled his fingers into his palms, even when they met to talk about the Fischer family history—a self-conscious affectation he used in public but here, in the safe haven of his studio, Henry was himself, unburdened by the Fischer mantle, even expressing pride in the physical toll stone polishing took on his hands.

It was clear that Henry was proud of his craft and enjoyed talking about it, that part of his life in which he felt most comfortable and in control. The outside world he generally shunned was the opposite of this. He was his true self up here, in this aerie of sorts, above the evils that crawled and slithered across the floors beneath him. Yet, was he able to escape them altogether?

Damon had a sudden, unnerving image of these tough callous fingers wrapped around a pretty woman's neck, or cutting through a brake lining or, if required, repairing a small dent in a fender.

He dismissed these crazy notions as the meanderings of an overzealous imagination. He had to take better control of himself.

"Sarah asked me to talk to you about preparing a statement for the press. A TV news crew is parked outside on the main road."

Henry went to the kitchen sink and washed his hands, drying them with a paper towel from a roll suspended under the cabinet, and led Damon to the open space that was his living room: a black leather sofa worn almost gray, an odd assortment of easy chairs, floor lamps, a chest of drawers, a very large oval braided rug and, except for a television sitting on a table, that was it. Henry could afford the most lavish life style, yet he chose to live like a man on a pension.

He went to the chest and pulled open the top drawer. Damon watched as he rummaged through an untidy assortment of files. He reached down deep and came up with a small bundle of envelopes held together by two crisscrossed red rubber bands.

He walked over to the sofa and sank into the leather with a small grunt. Damon surmised that, for

Henry, standing at his work bench was preferable to sitting on a sofa—the image alone disturbing enough: an old man watching television rather than an old man at his workbench, vital in strength and purpose and a mind alive with creative effort.

Come to think of it, not too bad.

He looked at Damon. "I fear your original job description to help me write a family history has changed."

"Indeed it has, Mr. Fischer. I hope I am up to it."

"I don't know if anyone is," he said cryptically and handed the envelopes to Damon.

"What are these?"

"Letters written a long time ago, letters I believed would never be brought in the open, but I fear we no longer have that luxury. Sarah and I feel you cannot represent the family without understanding what we are up against. That is why we are entrusting you with this information. But you must hold it in the strictest confidence."

Damon looked at the envelopes uncertainly, the caveats from Henry so forbidding that he wondered if he should even touch them.

"Go ahead, read the letters."

"If you say so." He undid the rubber bands and sorted through the envelopes, four in all, addressed in a woman's handwriting to Henry Fischer, but there was no return address. They were postmarked in the summer of 1937.

Damon opened the top envelope and unfolded the letter, handwritten in a woman's neat script. It read:

July 10

Dear Uncle Henry,

I was hoping you would come today but I guess you have more important things to do. I'd walk out of here but they keep a close eye on me. Even if I tried, how would I get home? They locked my clothes away and I don't have any money, even bus fare. At least I'm not restricted to my room. I can wander around like the other inmates (I call us that because what else are we?) but there is someone always keeping an eye on me. I never thought it would come to this. Please visit.

E

Damon guessed that E stood for Elizabeth, Beth's aunt. He opened the remaining envelopes one at a time and read:

July 18

Dear Uncle Henry,
That awful doctor is like a warden. He gave me some medicine in a small paper cup. It made me throw up. I think he is trying to induce a spontaneous abortion, but I've been able to fool him. Now I take a pill but I hold in my mouth till he leaves and then spit it out in the toilet.
This place is evil. Can't you do something to get me out of here?

E

July 26

Dear Uncle Henry,
Everyone in this godawful place looks at me as if I were a criminal, even the other women who are here for the same reason as I am. So I made a bad mistake, who are they to judge? I know you forgive me but it's not you I have to convince, it's Granny. Please help me—I'm

running out of time.

E

August 3

Dear Uncle Henry,

I don't know what you said, but it worked. I'm getting out of here tomorrow. That doctor still keeps telling me I will regret my decision, even while I'm packing. He just won't give up! Can't wait to see my new digs. Anything will be better than this prison. Thanks for everything!

E

August 4

Dear Uncle Henry,

This new place is nice, sort of far away, but I guess it's better not to be too close to home so people don't get nosy. Wouldn't want anything bad to happen to the family! Speaking of family, I thought Delmar was picking me up but I got a ride in a rented limo. Can't take any chances that someone might find out about me, right? Well, beggars can't be choosers. Doesn't matter. I'm going to have my baby after all!

E

That was the last letter. Damon set them on the sofa cushion between him and Henry, who was looking down at his hands, probably wanting to get back to work.

"Did you ever visit her?"

Henry shook his head. "I regret that I did not."

"But you did convince Sarah to move her to another place where she could have her baby."

"I had a moral obligation. I am apposed to abortion." Henry looked up, the expression on his face a mixture of guilt and regret. "Nevertheless, I should not have interfered. The biggest mistake of my life."

Damon waited a moment before asking the inevitable question. "Why do you call it a mistake?"

"Ask me who the baby's father was and you will know why."

"All right," Damon said, puzzled as to why Henry was finding it so hard to tell him. "Who was he?"

"Arvid Campbell."

Henry stared down at his shoes, scuffed and stained. He rose and walked over to his workbench, turned on the electric motor and began polishing.

Damon could not be sure but he thought he heard him say, "God help us all."

16

CT's office was heavily redolent with memories of the old man—Damon could almost smell the cigars he probably smoked, feel the power he must have exuded, hear the deep growl of authority that must have been his voice. And mixed in with this ineffable past was the present expectation that Damon be like him, replicate the old man's authority in order to save the family from imminent doom.

He opened CT's roll-top desk, the inside neat as a pin, even the cubbyholes had been dusted. He placed his notepad on the desk surface, which showed signs of wear along the edge, as though CT's forearms had rubbed away the gloss.

What would CT have done at a time like this, Damon asked himself. Would he have dodged, dissembled, delayed? No, CT would have faced his problems head-on, not giving a damn about public pressure or censure. He was his own man, self-made, and he didn't owe anyone anything.

Well and good if you were CT, but Damon wasn't. He was not the master of his fate but rather the victim of it—and so, he told himself, forget thinking you are a latter day CT just because you are sitting at his desk, and be the man you are, out of your depth, struggling against all odds—as in odd family—and proceed from there, not from advantage but, if one can mix a metaphor, a disadvantage. What he needed was a strategy, a plan of attack, and he was far from having anything even approaching that. He had bits and pieces of a large tapestry but he was not able to see it as a whole.

Damon began making bullet points on his pad, whatever came to mind, what the Surrealists called automatic writing—prodding the unconscious until a buried thought bubbles to the surface, exposing it so that the conscious can examine it, roll it around in the head to see if anything makes sense:

> Letters to Henry from E (Elizabeth) who is in abortion clinic against her will
> Henry, anti-abortion, helps her have her baby
> Sarah is against the birth to preserve family honor but agrees through pressure from Henry who regrets his decision
> Elizabeth has the baby but gives it up for adoption (deal with Sarah?)
> The baby is Amy
> Henry says Arvid is the baby's father
> Elizabeth is the baby's mother
> Arvid and Elizabeth are Amy's parents
> Arvid and Elizabeth are first cousins

Damon stared at the last line as though it were a live hand grenade he had to run away from in order to keep from getting blown up. Had he touched upon something so shocking, so abhorrent, so calamitous that a proud family would go to any length to suppress such a terrible secret, even murder?

There was no time to reflect on the impact of such a possibility. He had only a few minutes to deliver a statement to Azquith. But what can he say that would satisfy her insatiable need for news while hiding from her what amounted to the news story of the year, earning her a

Peabody or even a Regional Emmy?

He flipped over the offending page of notes and started on a new sheet, writing down what in the PR trade is known as boilerplate, scanned it several times till he had it memorized, and walked outside to meet his fate.

Azquith was watching him from the main gate as he walked down the private drive toward her. The sun was nearly vertical. High noon was approaching, reminding him of Gary Cooper in the movie of the same name checking his six-gun to make sure it was loaded. He wished his was.

"Well," she said, apparently surprised that he really showed up, "you kept your word."

"I wouldn't be long in this business if I didn't."

"What have you got?"

He began reciting his prepared talk about how the police were diligently investigating Beth's death, the family was bearing up as well as it could, an announcement will be made in a few days...

Azquith stared as though in shock. "Is that it, is that all you've got?"

"For now..."

"What were you doing all morning in the Schloss, playing tiddlywinks? The Sheriff's car left about an hour ago, burning rubber. What was that all about?"

Damon shrugged.

"Don't bullshit me. Investigative reporting is not a hobby. I followed Lieutenant Harris and interviewed him outside the Sheriff's Office. Want to see it?" She led him to the truck. A door in back opened into a dark interior with two television monitors providing the only light. A technician was sitting at a control board in front of one of the monitors.

"Tom, bring up the Harris interview."

The screen was a blur of fast-moving images and garbled sounds and, suddenly, there was a close-up of Harris glaring into the camera. A handheld mike was parked in front of his face, the fingers holding it belonging to Azquith off-camera.

"Tell me what happened this morning at the Fischer Mansion, aka Schloss Fischer, on Lake Minnetonka," came her disembodied voice. "I understand you were there with a warrant. Does it have anything to do with the untimely death of Beth Rand?"

There was no doubt Harris was fighting mad and was willing to take it out on the Fischers and, by extension Damon as well, even if he risked a reprimand from his superior.

"One of the Fischer automobiles was suspected of being in an accident..."

Azquith interrupted, "What kind of accident?"

"Hit and run."

"Hit and Run?" Azquith repeated, and paused to allow the words to sink in. "Are you implying someone in the Fischer family was involved in a crime?"

"In Minnesota a hit and run is a misdemeanor."

"Unless, of course, it results in injury or death. Then it's a felony, right?"

"You know your law."

"Just part of my job. So tell me, was there an injury or death?"

Harris either squinted at the sunlight or winced, maybe both, Damon could not be sure.

"Sorry I can't tell you that."

The camera followed the microphone as it moved from Harris to Azquith, who stared into the camera lens with deep impact. "I can only assume that the Sheriff's Office would not serve a warrant on one of Minnesota's most prominent families unless a crime was involved."

Damon watched as the screen went dark. He had to admire her reporting skill if not her underhandedness. They stepped outside and stood in the shade of the truck.

"Do you want to add anything?" she asked.

"Looks like you got your story."

She gave him her sitting-in-the-catbird-seat smile.

"While you were in the Schloss making up crappy excuses I was doing my homework. Accident reports are easy to access and there aren't that many involving a hit and run. In the past two weeks I found only one that involved more than a damaged vehicle, and that was a private detective killed in the alley behind his office on East Hennepin. Does that ring a bell?"

Damon was bushwhacked and it was clear that Azquith could see the distress in his eyes. "Patti, you can't go on the air with pure speculation."

"My interview with Harris is not speculation. Rich people don't go running down detectives unless there is something to hide."

"Ok, I can tell you that Harris checked the family cars and found absolutely no damage to any of them. Maybe that's why he stormed out of here because he was expecting to find evidence."

"But he had to have probable cause to get a warrant issued in the first place. Was that detective working for the family? Does it have something to do with Beth Rand's murder?"

"Wait a minute—what are you talking about?"

"Hey, don't go all naive with me, Damon. The talk of the town, whether truth or rumor, is that Beth Rand was murdered, she did not drown accidentally. So it makes sense for the family to hire a private eye to help them nail the killer. And if they did, let's assume the detective found something incriminating, maybe pointing to a member of the family, and he got iced for his efforts."

Damon had to give her credit for a vivid imagination, but her method was like throwing mud at a fence to see how much stuck. "You've been watching too many Dragnet shows on TV."

"And you're a blank screen, Damon. You know what happens to your name when I leave the O out of it, don't you? You get *Damn*—exactly how I want to express my frustration with you."

"You are clever, I'll give you that."

"I don't want clever, I want content."

Damon sighed inwardly. He had plenty of content all right, and that was the paradox he was facing. He was a PR man first and foremost, and getting a feature on television was what he was paid to do. 'I don't care what you say about me as long as you spell my name right' was his eleventh commandment, but in this case he was not trying to build an audience, he was trying to prevent an audience from building.

He needed to buy time. "This is my first day on the job..."

"Oh, yeah, I forgot about that, you left the Fischer Art Center for bigger fish, if you don't mind my play on words."

"I do mind." Jesus, she was annoying.

A flash of an idea sparked in her eyes. "I got it!" she said. "We'll do a human-interest, live, right here in front of the gate. I'll save my interview with Lieutenant Harris for tonight. It's on tape anyway. I'll ask you what it's like behind the scenes, describe the inside of the mansion, what it's like to work for the Fischers, that kind of stuff."

*****

They waited under the umbrella for twelve o'clock to arrive—along with Tom, the cameraman, a twenty-something whose stringy blond hair hung to his shoulders—and went over what amounted to a mini-dress rehearsal: look into the camera (except when answering Patti), smile (do not frown) stand erect, (do not slouch), don't be nervous (ha!).

Damon was wearing jeans and a short-sleeved shirt, too casual for a television interview, even one at noon whose viewers consisted mainly of shut-ins and mothers with babies. He was more appropriately dressed for stocking grocery shelves than representing the Fischers on television. He hoped no one in the Schloss was watching Channel 4.

He was far from composed when the cameraman began counting down with his fingers—three, two, one—and pointed at Patti who suddenly assumed her professional persona: confident, authoritative, in charge.

"This is Patti Azquith broadcasting live from fabled Lake Minnetonka, at the gated entry to the home of one of Minnesota's most famous yet least known families, the descendants of CT Fischer, lumber baron and founder of Fischer Art Center. With me today is Damon Petroulis, erstwhile Director of Public Relations for that museum, who recently ended his career there to become the spokesperson for the Fischer family. Behind me, leading up this heavily wooded road, is the Fischer mansion, too far away and too hidden to see from here. The family calls it a Schloss..." Patti suddenly pointed the mike at Damon as though it were a dagger. '"What does that mean, Damon?"

Damon was already put off by her referring to him as "erstwhile director," and was ready to pounce on that unfair description, but now he suddenly had to respond to what amounted to a patronizing question.

"Ahh," he said, struggling to collect himself, "it's German for Palace." He decided to expand on his answer and let her know he was not simply decoration. "CT Fischer was proud of his Austrian heritage and built his residence in the rococo style, which was the architectural fashion of the eighteenth century, just as the International Style is the architectural fashion of the twentieth..."

Patti forced a disingenuous laugh and pulled the mike away. She did not know what the hell he was talking about and she was not going to lose control of her story. "Damon's first television interview in his new job and he's giving me a lecture on architecture," she said into the camera, scolding him for his impertinence.

Thus began what can only be described as the interview from hell.

"Tell me about this so-called Schloss," she continued. "I've sailed by it on Lake Minnetonka but you can't see much with all those trees. It has to be pretty imposing. Describe it to us, Damon—paint some word-pictures for our viewers. That's what you did when you worked at the museum isn't it, paint word pictures?" Patti was virtually wallowing in her cleverness.

He was ready to wring her neck. "If you ever took the time to visit the Art Center, Patti, maybe you wouldn't need word pictures."

"Touché, Damon, but right now I'm hoping for a simulated tour of Schloss Fischer. How many rooms? What's the décor like?"

As much as he wanted to escape this third degree, he could not walk away. To do so would be like a sentry leaving his post. He took a deep breath to calm himself and replied in measured tones: "I never counted them all but my guess is twenty rooms…"

"Twenty? Must be an army living there."

"No uniforms, Patti, just a private family that happens to go back several generations. In the last century the rich built grand palaces to express their wealth. Look at James J. Hill's home on Summit Avenue in St. Paul. Same thing."

"But they must rattle around in all that space. Public records show only Sarah Rand and her brother, Henry Fischer, live there."

"There are other family members and a staff to serve them." He hoped the camera, staring at him like a Cyclops, was not exposing his pent-up frustration, especially since it was recording every word and every expression on his face.

"So who else shares this grandeur with Sarah and Henry?"

Resentment was now piling on top of his other negative emotions. Here was this twit who thought of herself as some sort of Grand Inquisitor referring to members of an elite society, persons she had never met and never will meet, by their first names as though they were old friends. "Mrs. Rand and Mr. Fischer," he said, emphasizing their titles, "do not live like hermits. They share the Schloss with several other family members."

"Like who?"

"*Whom*," he corrected, savoring a millisecond of satisfaction

"Forget the grammar lesson, Damon. Stay focused, if you can, and try to answer my question. Who else lives in the Schloss?"

And so he answered, helter-skelter, rattling off the names of those who clearly preferred to remain anonymous. He realized, as he responded like a wide-open spigot, that Patti was cleverer than he, baiting him, heating him up into saying more than he intended.

"Wait a second, let me get them straight. Richard Rand—he is…" Pattie held the mike under Damon's nose waiting for him to fill in the blanks.

This was not the image Damon wanted the public to see in his first day working for the Fischers. In the PR business, the first image is the one that lasts. No, he had to appear confident as though he intended all along to talk about the residents of the Schloss—normal people, not a mysterious family hiding behind its wealth.

"Richard is Sarah Rand's grandson. He is a twin of Beth Rand…"

Patti interrupted and looked into the camera. "For those of you who may not recall, around a month ago Beth Rand drowned in Lake Minnetonka and it is possible she met with foul play. To learn more about this, see my interview with Lieutenant Harris of the Hennepin County Sheriff's Department tonight on the Six O'clock News." Patti smiled like a flower in full bloom and turned her attention back to Damon.

"How old is Richard?"

"Twenty-nine."

"Is he married?"

"No."

"An eligible bachelor, rich beyond all our dreams, and he still lives at home with Grandma?" She asked in mock surprise. "You'd think he could afford a Schloss of his own."

Damon tried to smile but his jaw was too tight. "He and Beth, being single, elected to live with Mrs. Rand. Their mother, Dolores, also lives with them. She's a widow. Her husband Harrison died in an air show accident a few years ago."

Patti nodded. "Yes, I remember hearing about that. Are there any other children, if I may use that word, besides Richard?"

"A brother, CT-Two."

"That's odd calling him Two instead of Junior."

"Technically he is not a junior, he is CT's grandson and so he's CT the second."

"But why CT-Two?"

"A kind of nickname."

"Because he bears CT's name, does he run the family business?"

"Fischer interests are far and wide, not only forests but also paper mills, transportation."

"And CT-Two is the head honcho over all that?"

"There are division managers who take care of day-to-day operations."

"So CT-Two is kind of a figurehead?"

"Well, I wouldn't say that," Damon said feeling the ground shifting under him.

"I've heard that a family business rarely survives past the second generation."

Just then the cameraman raised a hand and began twirling his finger in the air.

"Looks like my time is drawing down. Thanks for giving me the opportunity to talk to you, Damon Petroulis, and giving us some insight into the Fischer family." Then she looked full into the camera. "This is Patti Azquith broadcasting live from Fischer Mansion, oops, Schloss Fischer, on Brecketts Point in Lake Minnetonka. Now back to the studio and the rest of today's Noontime News."

The light on the camera went off.

"Is this over?" Damon asked, his collar damp.

"Yep." Patti handed the mike to the cameraman who began to wind up the long cord that connected his camera to the power source in the van. "Thanks for your help, Damon. This has been an eye opener, so far, anyway. There's more to find out though, so why not chat for awhile."

"I thought we were done."

"The live broadcast anyway. But I am still curious, wondering if there is a successor generation for the Fischers. You don't think CT-Two is up to the job?"

"I didn't say that."

"But you meant it. I could see it in your eyes."

Now that Patti was not on camera, the pressure over, she was relaxed. She seemed even downright nice. Television is a tough business, all right, you get everybody angry and then you have to make up to them.

"I will say this: Beth was heir apparent."

"And she's dead, so don't you think there will be a power vacuum when Sarah dies?"

"Very likely."

"How about Beth's twin, Richard?"

Damon thought of Richard's designer tennis shoes and well-tanned legs. "Not Richard."

"What about Irene Campbell? Anyone in her family capable of taking over?"

Damon hesitated a moment. "Well, her son, Arvid, but he moved away a long time ago. He returned for Beth's funeral." Damon felt he had to one-up Patti on pithiness. "He reminds me of a mystery guest on 'I've Got a Secret.'"

Patti perked up. "Why do you say that?"

"Hard to figure out. A misfit. You know, every family has one—siblings who don't get along, that sort of thing."

"Campbell," Patti said thoughtfully. "Wasn't there

a curator at the Art Center in the 1940s named Campbell?"

"That's right. Irene was divorced, and when she married Daryl Campbell, Arvid took his name."

"I learned about Campbell from the Tribune's morgue."

The morgue was the daily newspaper's archive, containing every issue and every column of every paper, much of it on microfiche.

"I should interview *you* for the family history." Damon meant that as a joke.

"You want me to do your homework for you, is that it?"

"No," Damon replied defensively, "my history is based on family records, not newspaper files."

"Well, that could explain the difference between public relations and the Fourth Estate."

Damon forced a smile. "It doesn't explain anything, Patti, except your argumentativeness."

"It's my nature, Damon, sorry. But I do my homework before starting on a story. At least give me credit for that."

"I do...."

"You're not sore at me?"

"No, of course not."

She made as if to follow the cameraman who was standing behind Damon. "Oh, before I go, I want clear up one thing."

"What's that?"

"The funeral."

"Beth's funeral? That was private."

"Yeah, there were so many cop cars you would have thought the president was there, but we covered it from a distance. Our cameraman shot some footage from across the road that we never used. I looked at it this morning and when the family came out of the church there was a heavy-set woman, plain looking, with another woman at her side, like a companion. They were holding hands."

"No one special," he said offhandedly, not wanting to make too much of it.

"Maybe the Fischers have someone hidden in the attic, someone they don't want to talk about or let the public see."

Damon laughed. "Like Bertha Mason?"

"Who?"

"Mr. Rochester's wife in Jane Eyre."

"Oh, ok, but she still begs a lot of questions, doesn't she? The Art Center's PR man is assigned to write a family history. While he is digging around he discovers a crazy woman like Mr. Rochester's wife, someone the Fischers want to keep under wraps. In the middle of it all CT's great granddaughter dies under very suspicious circumstances, which Lieutenant Harris is investigating, not to mention the mysterious hit and run of a Private Eye. This is not the stuff of a novel, this is the stuff of real life."

"Don't say anything about her will you? Things are hard enough for Madie without turning her into a spectacle."

"Her name is Madie?"

Damon looked skyward in frustration. How could he be so careless?

"What is wrong with her?"

"Nothing is wrong with her!" His angry retort only gave credence that something indeed *was* wrong with her.

Patti snapped her fingers. "I have an idea—I'll call her the Poor Little Rich Girl."

Damon felt prickles on the back of his neck. He turned and realized that the cameraman, standing a few feet back, had his camera on his shoulder, and the light on it was glowing.

"Are you recording this?"

Patti beamed like a saint on a stained glass window. "Only for verification."

"We were speaking off the record!"

"I never said that." Patti looked at her cameraman. "Did I, Tom?"

Tom shook his head. "Nope."

"What are you going to do with it?" Damon shouted, helpless rage shaking his torso.

"Madie, Poor Little Rich Girl, will be the wrap-up of my piece on the Fischers. I can use footage of her at the funeral, the poster child of The Family Without a Future—what a great tag line. But I have to move fast if I want to get it on before twelve-thirty." Patti headed for the truck, filled with energy and burbling excitement.

"Thanks, Damon!" she shouted over her shoulder. "Be sure to watch Channel 4!"

17

Damon trotted up the drive to the Schloss, anxious to get to a TV set to see how much havoc Patti had created. What a way to start your first day protecting the Fischers from nosy reporters. He had failed miserably, and the prospect of facing an angry Sarah only worsened his frame of mind. He understood now how unprepared he was to have taken on this assignment. Publicizing modern art is far more predictable than keeping private the foibles of an old-line family.

Where the hell do I go from here? he asked himself as he came through the front door of the Schloss and headed for the White Room where the television was located. He saw no one, and felt at least thankful for that. He turned on the set and sat in one of the overstuffed chairs waiting for the tube to heat up. It was twenty past twelve, maybe too late for Patti to have put her story together. He sat through what seemed interminable commercials for gastro-intestinal remedies and the weather report before the anchor, Bill Carlson, came back on. Bill was a pleasant personality with whom Damon had good rapport—he was not at all like Pushy Patti.

Bill stared into the camera with the gravity of an undertaker. "We have a follow-up report from Patti

Azquith on assignment at Schloss Fischer in Lake Minnetonka. Patti, you are on."

The scene shifted to Patti standing where she had initially interviewed Damon. "Thanks, Bill. As you recall in my opening segment I interviewed Damon Petroulis, former PR man for the Fischer Art Museum, now working for the Fischers in their efforts to turn around a tarnished public image caused by the untimely death of Beth Rand. She was being groomed by her grandmother, Sarah Rand, to take over the family's far-reaching business holdings once Mrs. Rand died. I asked Damon who else in the family could replace Beth and, let me preface this by saying this is a Channel 4 exclusive, he told me there is not one Fischer descendant, not a single one, with the acumen and the smarts to take over. After further inquiries, this reporter discovered yet another family member who has up till now remained in total obscurity, someone who can only be described as the symbol of a once great Minnetonka dynasty that is now in decline—The Family Without a Future.

"This heretofore unknown Fischer descendant is known only as Madie. Despite a talented gene pool, she somehow missed the swim and grew up a recluse in the bowels of the grand mansion that is her home, a Poor Little Rich Girl. Madie is seen here in this video clip of the funeral of Beth Rand at the Episcopal Church by the Lake two months ago."

The screen showed footage of Beth's funeral as the family came out of the church to ride to the cemetery. Madie was seen shuffling next to Mrs. Stockton, head down, her body a mass of puffiness without definition.

"There you have it, Bill," Patti said, winding up, "the latest on the Fischers. In the meantime I will keep working on this story to update our viewers. Until then this is Patti Azquith reporting from fabled Lake Minnetonka, home of the un-fabled Fischer family."

Damon turned off the television and bent over, his head in his hands, expecting the door to burst open and an angry Sarah, Henry, Richard—*somebody*—to come in and finish him off, he was that badly wounded. The longer he waited the worse it got. Doesn't anyone around here watch the noontime news? He lowered his hands and looked up. Maybe no one had seen it, after all. Who but shut-ins have the time to waste watching television in the middle of the day?

Perhaps he had got away with it, and the comforting thought brought to his mind a New Yorker short story titled "Dyson on the Box" about an Oxford professor who was interviewed on local television—the box as the Brits call it—and his performance was terrible, so terrible in fact he was embarrassed to return to the campus, expecting students and faculty alike to snicker as he walked by. But, he discovered to his amazement and relief, that no one had seen the interview and some actually apologized to him for missing it. Maybe Damon lucked out like Professor Dyson—saved by turned-off TVs.

Slowly, rational thinking began to replace his sense of impending doom, but he knew even this was short-lived. Television editors monitor each other's newscasts and sooner or later he would get inquiries from the other Twin Cities TV stations. And so would Margaret Martin, gossip columnist at the Tribune, who had her nose in everything. All Damon had, really, was borrowed time, not more than twenty-four hours, before he would have to face the consequences of his errors. The only recourse was a family conclave where he would brief everyone and take the fallout. Hearing it second-hand from Damon was better than hearing it live from Patti. At least he had time to prepare for the onslaught. And, if Sarah fires him, so what? Worse things can happen. He has employable skills—move away, start over, others have done that, why not he?

He rose from the chair, walked upstairs to CT's office and sat at the roll-top desk, staring at the phone. Preemption in the PR business is better than reaction and so he girded his loins, metaphorically speaking, and spent the rest of the afternoon calling the media, not to put out fires because he realized after his second call that, even though he thought his world was coming apart, the rest of the world did not. No one brought up Patti's report, either because they considered it gossip or because they didn't think it was newsworthy enough to follow up. After the second call he found his rhythm, introducing himself as the new spokesman for the Fischer family and to direct inquiries to him rather than the Fischer headquarters in Wayzata or anyone else in the family. By and large the afternoon went pretty well and by five o'clock he was looking forward to cocktails on the terrace, ready to take on all comers.

He went to his bedroom to freshen up, the same room he shared with Beth, the room where he saw her alive for the last time. It was eerily transcendental—even in daylight with the afternoon sun streaming in, he felt as though he was trespassing. He shrugged it off, showered, changed into dinner attire and walked down the grand staircase, through the Great Hall to the terrace where Phillip had set up the bar.

He made a gin and tonic and sat, sipping and looking out at the expanse of lawn to the lakeshore. If you've got it, he thought, flaunt it, and the Fischers had no problem doing that. Half an hour and a second gin and tonic later, he was still alone. Where the hell was everyone? Six thirty came, dinner hour, and Damon went inside to the Venetian Room. He found himself alone there, too. He helped himself to the buffet—breast of chicken, baked portabella mushrooms, green salad, rolls and butter and a Burgenland Pinot Noir from an Austrian estate. He hoped he had not sold his soul for the good life, but right now he wasn't going to think about it. What he did think about, though, was how Amy was doing. He wanted to call her, she had given him her number, but he had no reason to. As far as he knew Arvid had not turned up. At least he hadn't seen him or anyone else for that matter, and so he was relieved to have dinner by himself after a day fraught with hazard and uncertainty.

He sat down in the middle of the long table, looking both to the right and to the left at empty chairs. Still, dinner alone had all the gravity of a last meal. It was unsettling, as though he was being boycotted, and wondered if the family had seen Patti Azquith's slamming report after all. Could their absence mean they were shunning him, treating him like a leper?

Damon tried to shake off his unease, making an effort to convince himself this was the result of an overactive imagination, and returned to CT's office where he reviewed family records till it was time to call it a day, and what a day it was.

*****

Sleep came grudgingly. The large bed he once shared with Beth was more like a vacant lot, and in the dark the period furniture evoked a gothic past of secret rooms, gloomy passageways and creaky staircases. He made noises each time he turned—thumping the pillow with his fist, grunting loudly, sliding his legs back and forth on the bed sheet to remind himself and the unknowable out there that he was a corporeal presence, not a phantom.

When he finally did fall asleep he dreamed, recreating in Surreal imagery the night Beth disappeared and his desperate search only to find her in the water by the boathouse, limp as a figure in a Salvador Dali painting—real but unreal, there but not there, conscious but subconscious.

He was jarred awake uncannily at about the same time he awoke the night Beth died. He sat up and looked around, his eyes darting from gloomy object to gloomy object—the chest, the chairs, the vanity, the ancestor paintings from CT's collection, the door to the hallway, heavy and forbidding, like the portal to a crypt. He sat up cursing himself for letting his mind wander into the nether side of sanity. This is ridiculous, Petroulis, his inner voice scolded, and he slammed his body back down on the mattress, closed his eyes, and lay there but he could not relax—stiff enough to fool an embalmer.

A half hour passed and he knew there was no more sleep this night, so he got up and walked to the window looking into the predawn gloom at the expanse of lawn and the lakeshore in the distance. An eerie sense of déjà vu came over him and, as if in a trance, he dressed and walked into the hallway in his bare feet, as he had done when he was looking for Beth. Retracing his movements, he stopped at Madie's bedroom and peeked in as if expecting to see Beth sharing Madie's bed as she had done before. Once more he could barely make out the heavy lump that identified her, surrounded, almost buried, by her vast collection of stuffed animals. They were everywhere—on the floor, on her bed, lined up along the wall, displayed on shelves. He carefully shut the door to this magnificent obsession and her gargled snoring. He walked down the wide staircase, through the Great Hall to the terrace and then outside, the dewy grass tickling his bare feet. He came to the lake and, as before, the Chris-Craft was tied to the dock, rising and falling to the gentle swells. Opposite, on the other side of the dock, was the boathouse, a silhouette in the slowly lightening sky.

He approached and went inside, switched on the overhead light and looked again at the marine paraphernalia—oars, life buoys, cans of gas, folded canvas, rope neatly coiled on hooks, fish poles. He walked to the edge of the sloping concrete floor and waded in a few inches letting the water lap around his ankles. He stood there contemplating life, death and everything in between, and then, drawn as if by some inexorable force, he worked his way in the shallow water, and climbed onto the dock. He looked down into the gray liquid where he had found Beth submerged and stared as if hypnotized. He did not know how long he stood there, transfixed, frozen by the memory of jumping in the lake and hauling out Beth's unresponsive body. He felt tears running down his cheeks, a rare display of emotion. Was he crying for her, for himself, for his inability to save her, for the mess he now found himself in...

His concentration was unexpectedly broken by the prickly sense that he was no longer alone, that someone was approaching him from behind. He began to turn, not from caution but from curiosity, wondering who else had got up early for a walk down to the boathouse, but before he had a chance to turn fully and see who was there, a rope was suddenly flung over his head and tightened around his throat. In a millisecond he went from a man contemplating life to a man fighting for it. He gripped the rope desperately as it began to crush his Adam's apple and then worked his fingers backward to those holding the rope, and he clawed at them, trying feverishly to loosen the death grip. Of all the wild thoughts coursing through him, he was able to determine that these were not normal fingers, but rather fingers hardened from years of labor, not just any labor but the labor of polishing stones. But *why?* Why was Henry trying to kill him?

Damon's scratches were met by a cry of pain and the rope went limp, enough for Damon to fill feverish lungs sucked dry of air. He lurched forward and fell into the water, making an untidy splash like the one he heard the night Beth died. He slowly sank into a torpor where nothing mattered—life, death, or anything in between.

The cool water felt so good against his burning throat, he just wanted to lie there on the bottom of the lake and let nature take its course. Dying is easy, living is hard, his slowly disconnecting synapses were signaling him. If he was this close to death why not simply take the last step, quiet the thumping heart, close down the last neuron and end the short, happy life of Damon Petroulis, to paraphrase the title of Hemingway's great short story. *Why not simply die?* Another *why* question, except for the

145

negating adverb. He was ready to call it a day—call it a life, actually—when that word *why* intruded itself back into his waning consciousness and alerted him in a way nothing else could. He had to find the answer to that inflammatory question, *why?* Like a fish that had been out of the water and then dropped back in, a reverse metaphor if you will, he sprang to life, his hands pushed on the sandy bottom and he shot to the surface. He broke it in a sluice of lake water mixed with sputum from his mouth, and he collapsed over the dock, his legs still in the water, slack-jawed—his chest heaving, his pulse racing—but his eyes, in contrast, were heavy-lidded and stared unblinking at the wood planks running the length of the dock.

PART II

18

"Sir, *sir!* Mr. Damon! Wake up!"

Damon felt his shoulder being shaken. He turned his head the other way and found himself staring at a pair of white Reeboks inches from his nose. He moved his eyes upward, expanding his line of vision to include two bare ankles and the bottom of a pair of sweatpants.

"Why?" he asked, the word etched, it seemed, for all time in his brain cells.

"Sir?"

"Why do you want me to wake up?" He realized now the voice belonged to Phillip.

"Why, indeed, sir. You look the worse for wear."

Damon pulled himself up and out of the water, turning so he was sitting on the edge of the dock with his legs dangling in the lake. "What time is it?"

"Five thirty."

"What are you doing up so early?"

"I walk along the lake every morning, sir. It's part of my daily exercise regimen. You had an accident, Mr. Damon. Your neck is bruised."

Damon touched his throat with gentle fingers, reminding him of his near-death experience which, now in the dawn of a new day, seemed like a bad dream.

"It was dark. I fell off the dock and hit the edge."

A lame explanation, but all he could come up with. He was still in a state of incomprehension, that employment by the Fischers had come to this. First someone tried to kill him by cutting his brake lines and now someone tried to strangle him. Was there a conspiracy to eliminate Damon before he found something so incriminating that the Fischers would go to any length to hide it? And even before this, was Beth killed for the same reason? She was his lover after all. Perhaps there was fear she was confiding in him.

Phillip sat on the deck cross-legged. "Mr. Damon, if this were not the same spot where Miss Beth died, I could buy your story."

"Ok, someone threw a rope over my neck. We fought here on the dock and I was able to free myself but I lost my balance and fell into the water."

Phillip shook his head. "Terrible things are happening. More than anyone can imagine. Mr. Damon, for your own good and for the good of the family may I give you some advice? I am speaking out of turn but you must leave Schloss Fischer. Please…before anything else happens."

"You mean next time I might not be so lucky?" Damon asked.

"I cannot say. But you have stirred up a hornet's nest. Not you personally, Mr. Damon, but your presence in the Schloss has created, how shall I put it, a dangerous imbalance which is unleashing forces beyond your control, beyond anyone's control…" Deep creases fissured his forehead as he spoke.

Damon looked out at the lake, slowly turning blue as the sun asserted its presence for another day. "Phillip, how long have you worked for the Fischers?"

"Thirty-five years."

"That makes you part of the family, doesn't it?"

"How so, sir?"

"Well, in your position you must overhear conversations. I'm sure the family says things, even revealing private matters in your presence. It occurs to me that you are the one who knows the family history better than anyone. I should interview you."

"You are giving me too much credit."

"I don't think so. Thirty-five years covers a lot of ground. You were here before CT died and I can't believe you are not privy to family secrets and, like a loyal servant, you keep quiet. You wouldn't have told me to leave the Schloss unless you knew what is going on behind the public facade the Fischers are so desperate to preserve."

Phillip squirmed under his sweatpants. Even dressed casually he had the demeanor of a man still in his starched collar and black waistcoat.

"What would you say if I told you it was Henry who tried to kill me?"

Phillip shrank as if being prodded with a live wire. "Not possible, sir, not Mr. Henry."

"Who, then?" Damon said, trying to back Phillip into a corner. "The hands around my neck were not the hands of someone who sees a manicurist. I visited Henry in his studio. He showed me his fingerprints that are worn smooth from polishing stones. You could tell they had the power of vices. I know, I felt them."

"Perhaps a stranger attacked you."

"Perhaps? Phillip who are you protecting?"

"It is not for me to say."

"Well, it is for me. I scratched those hands deep enough to draw blood. All we have to do is look at Henry's hands and that will be my proof. If he tried to kill me then he had to be the one who also killed Beth, and we have solved the crime. Won't Lieutenant Harris like to hear that?"

"Mr. Damon, if you proceed with this line of reasoning you will be disappointed."

Damon pulled himself to his feet. It was harder going than he imagined. He teetered a bit and Philip rose with him and held him by the arm.

"We are going to Henry's studio and find out right now."

"Mr. Damon, you need to go back to bed and get some rest."

"No," he replied stubbornly. "I have to find out now. And you are going with me."

"And then, what, Mr. Damon?"

"I will call the Lieutenant and tell him we have Beth's killer. And then I can go back to the Art Center because my work here will be done. I've had it with the Fischers, Phillip, I've done the dirty work, now let someone else do the cleaning up."

"If you insist." Phillip spoke as though he were dealing with a recalcitrant child and deciding to let him have his way. He helped Damon walk across the yard to the rear entrance. It was slow going as Damon's head began to throb.

They stopped by the lawn furniture on the terrace and Damon sat down. "Just give me a few minutes." He breathed deeply and rubbed the right side of his forehead. "My head is killing me."

"Will you let me call the doctor, Mr. Phillip?"

"Only after we've seen Henry. That's the deal."

"Very well, sir."

After a few minutes Damon got to his feet. "Ok, let's go."

They went inside to the elevator and took its slow ride to the top floor. The door slid open and they entered Henry's domain, shadowy and forbidding. They heard subdued snoring and the shifting of a body as they walked across the floor of Henry's makeshift bedroom.

Henry suddenly raised himself on his elbows. "Who's there?" he demanded.

"The man you tried to kill." Damon could feel Phillip shaking with fear next to him.

Henry swung his bare feet to the floor. He was wearing an extra large t-shirt that hung on him like drapery. He folded his hands in his lap as though he was hiding them.

"What are you talking about?"

"You know," Damon demanded. "Stop playing dumb with me."

"Phillip, explain this will you? It appears Damon is either drunk or gone mad."

"Stand up and show me your hands!"

Henry stared in disbelief. Phillip nodded as though signaling Henry to play along. "All right if you insist. But you better have a good reason for interrupting me in this inexplicable manner." He stood and his extra long shirt covered his bare thighs. He opened his hands and held them out. He turned them palms up and then palms down. Damon stared.

Henry's hands were as Damon last saw them, gnarled, fingertips smooth, skin coarse but there were no scratches on either of them.

19

His eyelids no longer able to shutter the sunlight streaming through the windows, Damon looked from his bed at the offending brightness, and then checked the clock on the nightstand. Damn, he slept the whole morning away—it was twelve noon.

After leaving Henry's apartment utterly mortified, Damon returned to his room to lie down just for a few minutes but instead he fell asleep and sleep he did, till noon—paraphrasing the title of a Max Schulman best seller a few years ago. Schulman went to the University of Minnesota as Damon had, attended classes in Murphy Hall as Damon had, got a degree in journalism as Damon had. But the comparison ended there. Schulman went on to become a famous novelist and screenwriter while Damon was neck deep (pun intended as he felt the bruise on his throat), a victim of attempted murder—twice in three days!

He could not tell if his neck was red from the rope or red from the unremitting embarrassment he absorbed after demanding that Henry show his hands, convinced that this scion of old money, son of CT Fischer, tried to choke him to death. The *why* swirling in his head was still there, but it had to be redirected away from Henry and toward someone else, someone with motive and strength to end his life. So now it was not only *why*, it was *who* as well. Too much to absorb, too much for his muddled brain to make sense of this confused mess. There was only one person he could turn to: Lieutenant Harris.

Damon was dismayed as he recalled the shock on Henry's face as well as the disappointment that followed after Damon realized his awful mistake. There was no going back, no way to mend the broken bond between them. Henry had trusted Damon implicitly and Damon betrayed that trust by accusing Henry of trying to kill him. He now was worse than damaged goods, there were no goods left to damage or even to rehabilitate. Damon was finished at Schloss Fischer. He will pack his overnight bag and get out of here. But where can he go? Home, of course, to his apartment but what about his job at the Art Center? That was where home really was, where he looked forward to going every morning. He was probably finished there, too. No doubt Maggie had sunk her talons into the PR department, turning it into her own and changing its character forever. No, there was nothing in front of him but bleakness and failure. He was through, finished, kaput.

He went into the bathroom and stared at his reflection in the mirror. He was gaunt, his body white except for the redness around his neck. His pain now was more mental than physical. He had survived the attack, in terms of still having a beating heart and a functioning brain but the intangible part of him, his morale, his spirit, his gumption, his drive, his self-image, were all gravely injured.

He turned away and got in the shower, the hot water helping assuage the cold assessment he had made of himself.   He shaved after toweling off, careful of the whiskers around his Adam's apple. Then he dressed, wearing a shirt with a collar that hid the bruise and left his room, in his frustrated state totally forgetting to pack his bag and bring with him the clothing he stored in the closet. He navigated the hallway, staircase and Great Hall without being seen. He made it to his car behind the garage and drove down the long lane to the security gate, using the code he was provided to open it. In his rearview mirror he watched the heavy gate swing shut. It was as if he were closing the book after reading the final chapter. Everything behind him was fiction, ahead lay reality. He turned onto County Road 19 to Wayzata and pulled into the parking lot of Hart's Café, its deep overhang held up by square columns clad in sandstone. He found a spot in the shade of an Aspen tree and sat for a while staring out at Lake Minnetonka, the bane of his existence. He worked to turn his negative thoughts around by trying everything including Dale Carnegie's five-step sales rule for success: Attention, Interest, Conviction, Desire, Close. Well, he got attention all right and interest, too, but he lacked conviction and desire, without which there was no close, meaning there was no sale. Damon realized he could not let himself go on like this, down the road to failure.

He got out of his car more resolutely than when he climbed into it back at the Schloss and walked into the now quiet Cafe, idle between lunch and dinner. He sat in a rear booth, facing front and leaned against the red leatherette cushion.

A thin-faced waitress wearing a lace apron over her black uniform brought the set-up: paper mat, silverware wrapped in a napkin and ice water.

"Eggs over easy, toast and crisp bacon and coffee, lots of coffee."

She opened the menu for him and pointed to a line near the top: Breakfast served 6:00 a.m. to 11:30 a.m.

"Oh."

"How about meatloaf?" she asked

Damon knew from experience working in his father's café that meatloaf was ground-up leftovers.

"No thanks." He said and studied the menu.

Her boniness seemed to get more brittle as she waited for him to make up his mind.

"Ok, BLT." At least he'd get bacon.

"White or whole wheat?"

He hesitated a second too long.

"Whole wheat," she answered for him and noted it

on her pad. "Say," she added looking down his shirt collar, "that's some bruise."

While waiting for his order Damon went to the phone booth on the opposite wall and called Harris's office. The Lieutenant came on the line quickly, as though Damon was his number one customer and Harris was competing for the Sales Person of the Month Award.

"You survived the weekend?" Harris asked.

"Barely."

"What does that mean?" Harris asked, concerned.

"I'm at Hart's. Do you have time to come over?"

"I'm practically there."

When Harris walked in Damon expected to see him wearing his rumpled suit but he was once again in uniform.

The officer sat across from him and placed his hat, with a black bill and a leather sweatband with tiny air holes, on the table.

"You are not in mufti," Damon said.

"The only other time you saw me in uniform was when I came to see Sarah Rand. I thought that would impress her but I was wrong."

"Why this time?"

"Inspection," he said by way of explanation. "Once a month we dress up for parade."

"Just like the military," Damon said.

The waitress came through the swinging door from the kitchen with Damon's BLT and a mug of steaming coffee. The toasted sandwich was cut into four triangles. Toothpicks with decorated tops held them together.

She lit up when she saw Harris. "Lieutenant," she said warmly, "you never come in this time of day."

"Have to see my friend here," he said, nodding at Damon.

The waitress's demeanor immediately changed. Damon was no longer a stranger, he was a friend, now that

Harris vouched for him. "You didn't ask for cream," she said to Damon as though he was a guest in her house, "but I brought it anyway."

"Thanks."

"Coffee for you, right, Lieutenant?" As she walked away she swung her scrawny hips the way Lauren Bacall swung hers in To Have and Have Not. The results were mixed.

Harris pushed himself into the corner of the booth and stared at Damon. "You sounded really anxious over the phone," he said. "Are you all right?"

"No." He pulled his collar away from his neck.

"Jesus, what happened?"

"Someone tried to strangle me." He went on to describe in detail his unreal morning, including Phillip finding him collapsed on the dock and Damon's subsequent confrontation with Henry.

Harris shook his head. "I told you to be careful."

"Careful?" Damon stormed back. "I drive home like any human being and my brakes fail. I walk down to the lake for a stroll and someone tries to strangle me. What the hell am I supposed to do? Quit living?"

"You almost did. Clearly, you have scared someone enough to want to silence you. Anything happen over the weekend to change the dynamics?"

"Arvid was supposed to meet me Saturday but he never showed up."

"Why didn't you tell me about this?"

"I just did."

"Look, Damon, you are supposed to report everything to me, whether you think it's important or not—and in a timely fashion. Anything else you've been holding out on me?"

"Well," Damon said, "I met Arvid's daughter who was given up for adoption at the museum Saturday. The one Rankin found. She…"

"You *what*?" Harris shouted loud enough for his voice to be heard throughout the restaurant. Fortunately the place was empty except for them, and the only turned head belonged to the waitress who was really startled.

"I was going to tell you but..."

"Who else knows about this?"

"Arvid."

Harris sighed in frustration. "Damn it, why the hell are you keeping vital information from me?"

"I didn't want to drag Amy into this. She's a nice kid."

"Her name is Amy? Amy what?"

"Jacobsson. Her adoptive parents own a horse farm in Rogers. They breed Arabians."

Harris smiled ruefully. "So you took matters into your own hands to meet up with this woman who may very well be the reason behind what's going on, unless you haven't given it much thought."

'What do you mean?"

"Can you imagine how threatened the Fischers have to be to discover another heir to the family fortune?"

"No one else knows about her."

"You don't know who Arvid might have talked to. How about his wife? Maybe she spread the word, even if he didn't. Do you think that girl is safe any more than you are? We have to get to her before the killer does. Where does she live?"

"In Rogers. I have the address."

"We're going out there—right now."

"Wait a minute, Lieutenant. She just learned that she's adopted. We don't even know if she talked to her parents yet. This could be a real shocker."

"Too bad."

"I'm not going to be part of this," Damon said, thinking about Amy, an innocent person he had befriended, who trusted him, and now he was asked to betray her confidence. "Find someone else to be your inside man. I quit."

"Quit?"

"I moved out of the Schloss. I'm heading back to

my apartment. That's why I wanted to see you, to tell you to find another patsy."

"You can't quit now. We're getting close, I can feel it."

"So can I," Damon said rubbing his neck.

Harris leaned forward and put his hand on Damon's arm. This was the first time Harris showed his avuncular side. "This adopted kid is our first real lead. And we have to make sure she is safe."

"How do you propose to do that?"

"Put her under police protection until we find our killer."

"Police protection?"

"She should move out of her house. We'll put her in an apartment where we can keep an eye on her."

Damon was appalled. "You can't do that!"

"Why not?"

"She just found out she is adopted. Her world has been turned upside down and now you want her to move out of her house?"

Harris shrugged dramatically. "You want her to be another victim?"

Damon put down his sandwich. It no longer tasted good. In fact, it tasted awful.

Harris was losing patience. "I don't have time to waste worrying about hurt feelings. This kid's life is in danger and she has to be warned. Finish your sandwich, we're driving out to Rogers."

"There has to be another way."

"If you have a better idea tell me now or get your ass in gear."

Damon looked up at Harris. "Let me handle it."

"You handle it?" Harris chortled. "This is police business not a PR campaign."

"Hear me out, Lieutenant. She is in a very fragile state. She only learned her real background on Saturday when we met at the Art Center. I don't know if she's even told her parents. Can you imagine the turmoil in her mind?

161

And now you want her to leave home and hole up in a strange apartment?"

"And you hear me out, Damon. You also are in danger. The next attempt on your life could be the last. And if you are seen together with that girl, you both are sitting ducks. No, I can't let you do that. I would be failing my duty as a cop. Both of you need protection."

"How are you going to protect me?"

"That will be tougher because I still need you in the Schloss. But you don't have to worry. I will make sure the police keep an eye on you."

"How can you do that? Who's going to let a cop into the Schloss?"

"I'll have a surveillance team watch the place."

"You think you can park a squad car on the road and not be seen?"

"We'll use a boat, the lake is full of them."

"A boat?"

"Lake Minnetonka has two hundred miles of shoreline. You don't think Hennepin County has a boat?"

"Yeah, but a boat fitted with surveillance equipment?"

Harris nodded. "It cruises the channels and bays like anyone else enjoying a Sunday afternoon outing."

"But how will you know if I need help?"

"You'll carry a wire. We can be ashore in a matter of minutes."

Damon groaned. "This is completely out of hand."

"Look at the bright side. This might be over in a few days."

"So I'm still a piece of bait for you. Is that it?"

"That's the whole point. If you bow out now, we'll lose access to the Schloss. Don't fail me, Damon. You didn't tell anyone you were leaving did you?"

"No, but the way Henry looked at me I didn't have to. I'm just as good as canned."

"Don't jump to conclusions. As I see him he prefers playing the role of a recluse and he won't tell anyone."

"What about Phillip?"

"Butlers are discreet or they wouldn't be butlers. From the way you tell it, you have an ally in him. Just go about your business as though nothing happened."

Damon shook his head. "I was so convinced Henry Fischer tried to kill me. I never really paid any attention to his hands until I visited his studio and saw him polishing stones. They are those of a blacksmith, strong and rough, like the kind I felt around my neck. I was convinced there were scratches on his hands, but when he showed them to me…nothing."

"When you fight for your life everything gets exaggerated. You were caught by surprise, the rope around your neck was tight against your throat, you were choking. So there is no guarantee you actually succeeded leaving any marks. You may have thought so."

"I did not imagine that yowl of pain."

"The only way to know for sure is to go back to the Schloss. If you are right, someone in that place has hands that are scratched and you are the only one who can find out for sure."

"What about my bruise. How do I explain that?"

"Keep wearing a shirt with a collar. I didn't notice the redness until you pointed it out."

"What about Amy?"

"Amy?"

"The adopted girl."

"Like I said she has to be warned. I'll leave right now. Give me her address."

Damon shook his head. "I can't let you see her alone."

"So what do you propose?"

"I'll talk to her, explain everything. She deserves that, Lieutenant."

"Not without me."

"We can't go together in a squad car."

"You go in your car and I'll follow behind. I can't

163

let you out of my sight."

"This sounds like something out of 'The Big Sleep.'"

Harris smiled. "We already covered film noir. This is the real thing. No more going off on your own. Got that?"

164

20

Damon got it all right but he didn't especially like it. He understood rationally what Harris said was true, he should not go off on his own, but emotionally he was resentful being told what to do. Nevertheless he listened without protest as the officer outlined how to handle the visit to the horse farm.

"I'll park out of the way while you go to the house and see the girl. How you say it is up to you, but she has to be told about the risk she is facing. Explain that she will be better off under police protection. We have a safe house, an apartment in Wayzata where she can stay until we untangle this mess. Then she can return home. I can't force her to do this so it's up to you to convince her and her parents that this is the right course. If she agrees bring her to me."

"And if she doesn't?"

"Then we'll put a surveillance team on her and follow her wherever she goes." Harris studied Damon's face for signs of a fault line. "Think you can handle it?"

Damon nodded that he could, but he was still far from convinced this was the right course, scaring the hell out of the girl. There had to be a better plan but for now this was the only way for him to see Amy again. Standing next to Harris's squad car, the two unfolded a road map across the roof, baked hot by the sun, and checked the location of the farm where Amy lived with her mother and father.

Damon climbed into his car and took off for Rogers, a town he had never before visited. In his rear view mirror he watched Harris fall in line behind him, a few cars back. For a while, like a silly indulgence, he considered speeding up and trying to lose him but it didn't matter. Damon wasn't being tailed, they both were going to the same place. The whole thing felt like something out of a Keystone Kops two-reeler. Maybe he was trying to hide his nervousness. Harris was asking him to do the impossible.

He turned onto 101 and headed north. The countryside never appealed to him and here he was, driving past farms and hamlets and grain elevators not by choice but by fiat. Once he got out of this mess he swore to himself he never again would venture any farther west than St. Louis Park, the first ring suburb where he grew up and went to high school.

He exited 101 to Highway 55 and drove past the Medina Ballroom, home of polka music and schottische dancing, a sprawling clapboard building painted red. Three miles later he turned onto a gravel road that seemed determined to shake his car apart, leaving behind clouds of dust enveloping Harris's trailing squad car like a re-enactment of Pompeii, giving Damon a moment of perverted pleasure. He found Manor Road and turned left, following a split-rail fence painted white to a wood sign that read: Home of King Breed Arabians, Elroy and Doris Jacobsson Proprietors. There was an asphalt drive leading to a single-story house, nearly circular in shape. A nearby stable and a pole barn completed a bucolic picture framed by an expanse of pasture, a scene pastoral, idyllic, serene—the antithesis of Damon's inner sanctum. This is where Amy lived, where Rankin took his stealth photographs. Damon drove past the house a hundred yards or so and parked under a tree, the engine idling. Behind him on the gravel road, his police car glazed in gray dust, Harris slowed down, probably puzzled as to why Damon parked so far from the house. But Damon needed time to reassess his situation, his assignment, even his purpose in life. He sat for a while pondering these inexplicables and, finding nothing but hollowness, he backed up and turned into the driveway of King Breed Arabians, resigned to his fate. Harris was no longer to be seen, hiding somewhere on that gravel road. With the Lieutenant no longer in his line of vision he was no longer in Damon's train of thought. He turned his attention to the house in front of him

The twelve-sided structure, a style new to Damon even exposed as he was to contemporary design, made it seem almost round, though segmented into a dozen flat walls. The low-rising roof was peaked with a large rounded skylight of clear plastic. Damon was impressed. The Jacobsson's had a keen sense of architecture. As he approached the front door set inside a narrow porch to protect visitors from the elements—for him, though, the elements were not natural like rain or snow but rather emotional like fear and trembling—the door unexpectedly opened and a man appeared behind the screen, a man in his sixties, tall and angular, bald with a wedge of hair circling his head. He wore denim pants and shirt, wrinkled and worn, unprepossessing, the uniform of the working man.

"Mr. Jacobsson?" Damon asked

"I was watching you drive by, sit under that elm for a time, and then back up like you weren't sure of the address, so I figured you did not come here to look at horses."

Jacobsson's directness made Damon wonder if Amy told her parents of their meeting. He climbed the steps to the porch slowly, each step tentative. "No," he replied. "I came to see Amy."

Jacobsson eyed Damon as he might evaluate a

horse. "I thought you might wait awhile before showing up."

"Then you know who I am."

"If I were a gambler, which I am not, I would bet you are Damon Petroulis."

"You should have been a gambler, because you are right."

Although a stranger, Damon was nevertheless known to Amy's parents, a circumstance as contradictory as his ambivalence. "So you were expecting me."

"If not you, then one of the Fischers." He sighed. "Now that it's out in the open, there is no reason to keep the secret any longer. I knew sooner or later it would have to come out."

Jacobsson opened the screen to usher Damon inside. Looking around, he realized the interior was divided into two sections—a perimeter for, he presumed, bedrooms and bathrooms, and a central area, open like the nave of a church, with a kitchen, dining space and parlor. Double doors led out to a rear balcony.

The walls were unadorned except for a display of photos of Arabian horses and blue ribbons hanging under them. 'Tis a Gift to be Simple, Damon thought, the Shaker song playing in his head.

Jacobsson led Damon to a brown leather sofa on the far wall, sharing the space with its mate, a brown leather armchair.

"Sit down," he directed. "Amy is in the stables with her mother. We have a new foal, born yesterday. Before you go see her, I think you and I should have a little talk."

"That's fine." Damon hesitated for a moment. "What did she tell you about me?"

"Between the tears and the accusations you mean?" Jacobsson said, smiling but his smile was far from friendly. "I think you can appreciate the atmosphere around here after she came back from her meeting with you on Saturday."

"Sorry I put her through this."

"You're just the messenger."

"How is she doing?"

"Is that why you came to see her?"

"I just want to make sure she is not hurt any further," Damon replied.

"She always knew she was adopted, she just didn't know she was a descendant of CT Fischer. Like most adopted children she was happy to remain ignorant of her true origins. Some kids go looking for their natural parents but Amy believed as we do that Doris and I are her real parents, and she was satisfied to be who she was, Amy Jacobsson. And then she got that phone call from Arvid Campbell…"

"You know him?"

"Not personally, only as Amy's natural father. It wasn't till she talked to you, when she came home and spilled everything like a burst dam, that I learned he was the one who called.

"She was very agitated, and I did not want to pry, but deep down I knew it was about her adoption. I guess I knew sooner or later the call, or something like it, would forever change things for us. We were doing fine, living out our dream."

Jacobsson leaned into the corner of the sofa and crossed his legs. "I started this horse ranch on a shoestring, only a teacher's salary, which in those days was not much. Sometimes you make deals, you can call it a compact with the devil, in order to realize your dream and my dream was to be a successful horse breeder. If it weren't for the Fischers I wouldn't have what I have today." Jacobsson uncrossed his legs and used them to prop his elbows. "You might say I sold my soul."

Damon was beginning to wonder if this is the way the Fischer clan worked—suck you into their vortex until you are so deep down there is only one way to deal with it: sell your soul, which apparently was happening to Damon as well. And now he wondered if he could ever extricate himself.

"You made a financial deal with the Fischers?"

He nodded. "Therein lies a story if you care to hear it."

"I would very much."

"As I said I was a school teacher, a damn good one. I taught Biology at Northrop Collegiate, right around the corner from the Fischer Art Center, and the school had a lot of financial support from the family, especially Irene Campbell, who is still involved in the museum." Jacobsson looked up from his lap and into Damon's eyes. "You know her, of course."

Damon nodded assent.

"Anyway, one of my students was Irene's niece Elizabeth Rand …"

Damon interrupted. "Elizabeth?"

"Amy said you are working on a family history, so you know the whole clan right back to CT."

"I've done a lot of research, but I don't know much about Elizabeth—she remains largely a mystery. What was she like? Please tell me about her."

Jacobsson became reflective. "To begin with she was beautiful, too beautiful for her own good, and rich, too rich also for her own good. Either way, a bad combination. She loved attention but if some kid played up to her, she immediately suspected he was interested in her because of her wealth. You have to remember that CT was one of the richest men in the country. You are talking about one big fortune. So Elizabeth had this dichotomy, a split personality, Poor Little Rich Girl you might say."

In his mind Damon did say, recalling Patti Azquith's pejorative use of the phrase.

"And then this beautiful kid who had everything anyone could want dropped out of school. One day she was in class and the next day she was not. She had perfect attendance. One of her traits was being organized. She always had her homework handed in on time, and she was never late to class. Punctuality was a virtue to her. And one day she was absent. Ok, I thought, she must be sick, which was unusual for her. And then she was gone the next day and the one after that. A week passed. I thought she was seriously ill or had an accident. I inquired in the office but no one had any information. I gave her an incomplete for the quarter grade, hoping she'd return for the next quarter. Then the school year ended and I forgot about her, being busy in my summer job working for a horse breeder in Rogers and wishing I could have my own place just like his when I got a call from Sarah Rand."

"Elizabeth's mother."

Jacobsson's eyes widened with the memory. "That was an amazing moment, getting a call from the Fischer doyenne. She asked me to drive out to Schloss Fischer and meet her in the library. She didn't tell me what for but I knew it must have to do with Elizabeth because she was my only contact with the family. But why me? I was only a biology teacher, not the school principal." Jacobsson stopped to reflect a moment. "I tell you I never saw a place like that palace. It was as if I was put in a time machine and sent back to the eighteenth century. A butler showed me in. It was so quiet I thought I was in a mausoleum. You whispered instead of talking out loud.

"I was ushered into this library. There was beautiful carved wood everywhere, moldings and bookcases with curved glass doors. The ceiling was covered with paintings set in fancy plaster frames, and the parquet floors…"

"I know it well. I've had meetings in that room with Mrs. Rand."

"Then you know what I'm talking about."

Damon nodded.

"I could tell even before she started speaking that she was a force to be reckoned with. I was curious of course why she summoned me, like having an audience with a queen. But I just sat down across from her as if I was the stable boy who came to tell her that her stallion had been shod. She was not a woman of small talk, getting right to the point and it shocked me."

"What did she say?"

"She knew everything about me, how much money I made, how much was in my savings, how much I could expect to get after retirement. It was like a lecture, like she was admonishing me for not doing better in life."

"How did she know so much about you?"

"Private detective."

Damon's antennae went on full alert. "Private detective? Know anything about him?"

"I asked her who he was. If people are blunt, you have to be blunt right back. I told her I was offended that she had me investigated as if I were a common criminal. She became defensive, which is the way people are who can't admit they did anything wrong. I pressed on, wanting to know who it was and finally I got a name out of her."

"What was it?"

"Rankin. I can't remember the first name. That was nearly thirty years ago."

Damon stared as though he'd seen a ghost. In a way he had, Rankin as a young PI.

"What's the matter?"

"Oh, nothing," he said, catching himself. "Time sure flies, doesn't it?"

So Rankin was no stranger to the family—working both sides of the street, first for Sarah, and then Arvid who had to know of Rankin's earlier involvement. This was not a coincidence. Was that why Rankin was killed? Damon quickly refocused his thoughts. He could not let Jacobsson become guarded. There was more to learn, maybe another shocker.

"So Sarah was interested in how much you made?" he asked, expressing the right amount of interest.

"Not only that, she knew my love of horses and my dream of breeding Arabians."

Damon was beginning to connect the two: the salary of a teacher and the tastes of the landed gentry. "She offered you a deal?"

Jacobsson nodded. "I was wondering what in hell she had in mind. She told me what a great teacher I was and how much Elizabeth liked me. I was her favorite pedagogue is the way she put it. I was really flattered. Teachers eat that stuff up. Long ago I read a novel by Somerset Maugham—about a school teacher, don't ask me the title as I can't remember it, but what I do remember is him saying that teaching is worth the effort even if you have only one student who wants to learn. Elizabeth was like that for me, until she got into trouble that is."

"Trouble?"

"Mrs. Rand told me Elizabeth was pregnant. That's why she was pulled out of school, sent away from prying eyes and nosy gossips, especially the press. Oh how Mrs. Rand hated the press. And then she hit me with the bombshell: would Doris and I adopt the child, sworn to secrecy, of course. We had none of our own and so we agreed, a decision that completely turned our lives around. I not only realized my dream, retiring early to start the business, which by the way, is doing very well, but we also had the good fortune to have this wonderful girl to raise. No matter what anyone says," Jacobsson added defensively, "Amy is our daughter and always will be. She understands that, too. But since Arvid came back and messed things up our world has turned upside down. I don't know where we go from here." Tears began to well up in his eyes and spill over. Jacobsson swept at them as he would a horse fly, apparently embarrassed to show emotion. "She is our entire life," the breeder said, "now they want her back."

"You will be ok," Damon said. "You said so yourself, no matter what happens she will always be your daughter."

"But why did Arvid contact Amy? I know Mrs. Rand kicked him out. But why did he come back and contact her? If Mrs. Rand swore me to secrecy, then he was supposed to keep the secret, too."

Unless, Damon suspected, Sarah herself decided

to break that promise after Beth died.

"I want to talk to him."

"I do, too," Damon replied. "But I haven't seen him since Friday."

Jacobsson snorted derisively. "He probably ran away like he did after Amy was born, and left another mess of his own creation."

He was right about a mess, Damon thought. "Mr. Jacobsson, I want to share something with you, something you need to know." Damon hesitated. The conclusion he had reached in the library, using the Surrealists' method of automatic writing, was on the tip of his tongue but he still found it difficult to tell him why Amy was given up for adoption.

"What's the matter?" Jacobsson wanted to know.

"Amy's birth parents, Arvid Campbell and Elizabeth Rand, were related."

"They can't be. They don't have the same name."

"Arvid's mother, Irene Fischer, married a second time to a man named Daryl Campbell. Arvid took his name. Arvid and Elizabeth were first cousins."

Jacobsson leaned back, his face slack, his eyes dilating. "Oh my god…"

21

Strangers only a half hour ago, the two men were now bound by the common knowledge of an act neither wished to express openly, yet they could feel it crawling on them like vermin.

Damon had never before given much thought to this Biblical taboo except for familiarity with Greek custom in earlier generations, before his parents emigrated to America. It was not uncommon in small isolated villages for kin to marry and have children, given the limitations of travel and minimum exposure to unrelated people. But this was something done from an uninformed culture, assuming that intermarriage strengthened the bloodline, not weaken it. However, in modern society, committing such an act exposed a character flaw so awful it would stain family honor, but would it be motive enough to commit murder?

But now the problem was how to break the news to Amy—that she was not a love child but the bastard child of a mean order. This was at the forefront of the unspoken thoughts between Damon and Jacobsson.

"The good thing is that Amy is wonderfully normal," Damon began. "She is healthy, strong, gifted, beautiful…" As Damon described her in such glowing terms he felt the anticipation of seeing her again, talking to her, getting to know her, taking her out on a date. "I'm sure she can handle whatever life throws at her."

"I taught biology and know a little about genetics. What if she carries a recessive gene that won't become evident until she has children of her own, or her grandchildren?"

"At least she will be able to make an informed decision."

He watched Amy's adoptive father struggle with the news—a man full of fear and anguish, being tested in a way he could never have anticipated.

Presently, Damon asked, "May I see her?"

Jacobsson's eyes moistened. "I suppose you came to give her the bad news."

"That's your responsibility."

Jacobsson led Damon out the back door to a spacious fenced-in back yard. "Do you like horses?" he asked, relieved to change the subject.

Damon never gave them a second thought unless he saw them in a Shriners parade.

"They are beautiful animals," he said hoping not to reveal his ambivalence. He looked around at the impressive spread before him.

"We have seventeen acres of meadow, a 35-stall barn, and an indoor arena." Jacobsson pointed to a wood building connected by a covered walkway whose roof was a good twelve feet high, presumably to accommodate horse and rider. "That is where we train. We also have an outdoor ring and nine paddocks."

They walked down a lane of compressed dirt with stalls on either side, fitted with Dutch doors framed in white wood. The smell was what hit Damon first, a kind of tart sweetness hard to describe—a mixture of manure and horseflesh. Arabians stretched their necks out of the upper half of the stall doors. Majestic heads of varied hues— gray, chestnut, black—with intelligent bright eyes, alert ears, and snorting noses pointing in Damon's direction, the animals curious about the stranger walking by them.

Jacobsson was in his element. "Look at them, the large eyes, prominent dish, small muzzle, finely tipped ears—all the marks of great breeding. "

"They have different colors."

"Not different, unusual. Arabians were once thought impure because of their coloring, and now they are sought after. We began by breeding a Raffidles mare to an Azraff-Sirecho cross-stallion. Their foal produced many other great foals, and we have won a number of prestigious awards."

Damon was impressed even though he was not at all familiar with horse talk, as he was inclined to call it.

Jacobsson stopped in his tracks. He sighed heavily. "This is Amy's life. What will happen to her now? I can't imagine anyone in the Fischer family accepting her. What about Sarah? What will she think when the grandchild she gave away turns up? How are you going to handle that?"

Damon fully understood the man's concern. "I don't know," he admitted.

"If you don't know, then why are you here?"

"I am concerned about Amy's safety."

"Safety?" Jacobsson said, staring anxiously. "Jesus, what now?" He opened the bottom half of a Dutch door and stepped into an empty stall. "Come in here, we have to talk some more."

Damon joined him and the smell was even more redolent inside the narrow confines. Standing in the home of one of King Breed's majestic Arabians, he felt somehow privileged.

"Mr. Jacobsson," Damon said, "it's not as bad as you think. This is a precautionary measure." Damon explained as calmly as he could, trying not to add to Jacobsson's anxiety, the reason for his visit, and the fact that a police officer was waiting in a squad car down the road to place Amy in protective custody.

"That is the same officer investigating Beth's drowning. He is convinced that Beth did not die accidentally but was murdered." Damon decided this was not the time to tell Amy's father that there were also two attempts on his own life. Jacobsson had enough hard-to-swallow items on his plate. "So this officer, his name is Harris by the way, is concerned about Amy, as he should be. There is no way to know if she is in danger but he can't take any chances."

"What does protective custody mean?"

"She will stay in a safe house for the time being. No one but the police will know where she is."

"Doris and I won't know where she is either?"

Damon shook his head. "The police are trusting no one until this is solved. Not even me."

"But I don't want her hidden away. She would be a prisoner. That's not Amy. Look around. Do you think anyone who has lived here her whole life can be cooped up in some secret place?"

"If she refuses to leave, Lieutenant Harris told me they will put a 24-hour surveillance team on your property and follow Amy wherever she goes."

"You mean police cars will be parked up and down my street and following us around? Think what that will do to my business. This is insane."

"I know, but there is another way, an idea that's been going through my mind ever since I drove out here."

"What's that?"

"She'd be safe in my apartment."

"Your apartment? Where?"

"Minneapolis, on Franklin not far from the Art Center."

Jacobsson eyed Damon suspiciously. "And where will you be, on the sofa in the living room?"

"I'm not staying in my apartment. I'm at the Schloss. Amy will be ok there. No one but you, your wife and I will know where she is."

"What about that cop?"

"He won't know."

"You are not going to tell him?

"Nope."

"You are either crazy or clever, I haven't decided which."

"Neither have I."

"So what is your plan? How are you going to get Amy out of here without that cop seeing you?"

Damon shrugged, realizing he had not thought this through all the way. "I will have her hide in the back seat. He will assume I left alone."

"I have a better idea"

Damon felt relieved. Jacobsson was now beginning to act like a co-conspirator. He needed Amy's father on his side.

"What is it?"

"We have a back road we use for the horse trailer. It comes out behind the property. Use that."

"And leave Harris waiting in his squad car? He could be there for hours." The thought amused Damon. This was a wild idea but he was determined to follow through. "Is it ok if I talk to Amy about this?"

Jacobsson shrugged. "I have no other choice do I?"

"The choice really is hers but you also have to be a part of it. We need to trust one another."

"Speaking of trust what will you be up to while Amy is hiding in your apartment?"

"I will return to the Schloss and keep digging. Sooner or later the person behind all of this will slip up. And Amy has yet to meet her new family. When that happens..."

"The shit hits the fan?"

Damon smiled. "Something like that."

Jacobsson opened the stable door. "Ok, let's go talk to her. She's in the end stall with Doris, checking on a new foal, a beauty. We still need a name for him. Follow me."

Damon walked behind Jacobsson down the long center aisle to the end of the barn, dodging an Arabian that extended its neck for a closer inspection of the stranger. An occasional snort and slam of a hoof on the wood floor let him know that these animals were not to be taken casually.

"Be careful," Jacobsson warned, "sometimes they nip at you."

Damon heard sounds of neighing and clomping emanating from the last stall on the right. He peered in and saw Amy and her mother with a shiny-black baby horse, what Jacobsson called a foal. It was remarkably coordinated for being only a few hours old, standing on spindly legs, getting accustomed to its new world, eyes wide and expressive, nostrils expanded. Damon was duly impressed, realizing how long it takes a human infant even to roll over or sit up.

Amy and her mother stood next to the newborn, clearly filled with admiration and pride, both wearing the uniform of a horse breeder; bib overalls, loose fitting shirt with long sleeves and rubber boots. Their hair was tied up in buns.

"Amy," her father said from outside the stall, "You have company."

Amy looked past her dad at Damon. If she was surprised she did not show it. "Hello. I didn't expect to see you again so soon."

"I came to see what a real horse looks like."

"Honey," Jacobsson said to his wife, "this is Damon Petroulis."

Mrs. Jacobsson glanced up briefly and went back to tending the foal. Damon could sense that she was having a problem separating the messenger from the message.

As for Amy, she looked different from the time he saw her at the Museum and also, paradoxically, the same. The difference, Damon realized, was the venue. Here Amy was in her milieu, the context of her life, comfortable and in charge. At the Art Center she was out of her element, a little awkward like the foal that was trying out its legs. Either way Damon was pleased, both with the memory of her from Saturday and with the real person in front of him now, tall, self-possessed, pretty, even prettier than he remembered, a truly desirable woman. He had to check himself thinking like this, but he could not ignore how much she affected him.

Doris was much shorter than Amy and it was obvious they bore no physical relationship. And why should they. Amy was adopted, after all, but yet one could not escape their close relationship, the strong mother-daughter bond between them.

Next to them was a bucket. Damon looked down at it.

"Mild Iodine solution," Jacobsson said, "to clean the umbilical stump and prevent infection. He's a healthy looking animal isn't he?"

"Yes, but where is the mother?"

"In the paddock. The foal has already nursed and in a few minutes we'll let her newborn out to join her. But we still don't have a name. Got any ideas?" Jacobsson asked jokingly.

"Well," Damon said, "Amy admired the great painting of The Large Blue Horses at the Fischer. Why not name him Blue Horse?"

They all made faces.

"Look at his coloring, there is almost a blueness in the shiny black. Don't you see it?"

"Maybe so…"

"How about Blau Reider, then—Blue Rider auf Deutsche?"

"An Arabian with a German name?" Jacobsson said doubtfully, but then he understood the significance of the name—providing a bridge perhaps across Amy's new, uncharted road.

Jacobsson glanced at his family for consensus. "Ok, Blau Reider it is. I'll have a sign made for his stall. I was thinking of selling him but now he will stay with us."

Amy was beaming.

"Doris, let's you and I go to the house and let these two young people have some time together. We have things to talk about, too." Jacobsson took her hand as they walked down the center aisle and disappeared through the stable door at the opposite end. Damon could sense the enormous emotional weight he was carrying that he would soon share with his wife.

In the stable, there was a moment of silence broken only by the short breaths of the foal and its nervous energy. Being alone with Amy and her new foal was a spiritual moment for Damon—sharing her company and that of a newborn creature was a unique experience, and he marveled at the wonder of it all. Was it the unfamiliar— the foreign bucolic atmosphere, the miracle of birth, the attention of a remarkable woman? No doubt all of the above.

Finally Amy broke the silence. "Let's take Blau Reider to see his mother. Time for a snack."

She opened the half door and the foal, as if on cue, followed her. They walked out into a small pasture enclosed by a white-painted fence, a paddock as Amy called it, where a giant Arabian was nibbling on grass. She was majestic, sleek, indifferent to the presence of the humans, even to her own offspring who ran over and leaned under his mother's hindquarters and grabbed a nipple which he hungrily suckled on. It was an extraordinary scene.

"Something new for you isn't it?" Amy said, sensing his wonder.

"Awesome."

"Everyday stuff for me."

"Like modern art is for me."

"We each have our passions."

Damon nodded.

"What brings you here?"

He shrugged, not willing yet to commit himself to

the hard cold reason for his visit, wishing this transformative moment would go on endlessly. "To see you."

"Well, here I am."

They both laughed, trying to disarm one another. "Blau and his mother need time alone. Want to walk around so I can show you the rest of the place?"

"I'm your guest."

Amy led him down a wide path to the big training arena and they went inside. The broad circular expanse was free of columns, the open span supported by J-joists that ran out from the center like spokes on a wheel to the wall. It allowed for riding freely in any direction. The floor was dirt and pockmarked from hooves.

"What is that little hill in the center? It looks like a pitcher's mound."

"For young riders to help them mount their horses."

"You think of everything."

They walked to an enclosure with a small fence and inside were bales of hay. "Want to sit here?" she offered. "My favorite place. We don't have any riders till three so we can be alone here for awhile."

The smell of fresh hay was powerful as well as addictive and he seemed not able to get enough of the aroma as he breathed it in. "I think I could get to like to this place of yours."

"Ever ridden a horse?"

"No."

"Would you like to take riding lessons?"

For Damon her offer was heaven sent. "I'd love to."

"When do you want to start?"

"Well…" he said and hesitated.

"Well what?"

"After things settle down. That's what I want to talk to you about."

She became attentive, having patiently waited for

him to explain why indeed he came to see her. "So there is something going on, something I need to know about?"

"Yes" and he went on to explain as he did to her father that Lieutenant Harris was in his squad car ready to take charge of her fate, at least for the foreseeable future.

"Are you going to tell me that the Fischers think I'm a threat, enough of a threat to want to harm me?" Amy finally asked the salient question. Was she after all the ultimate target?

Damon admired her directness even if it put him in a delicate position. "We don't know but it has to be a factor. That's why Lieutenant Harris wants to protect you."

"They don't even know me."

"I can only speculate that Arvid talked. He has a big mouth."

"I don't think I could ever call him father."

"Your father is Elroy Jacobsson." Damon believed that with all his heart.

"But what should I call him, Arvid or Mr. Campbell? I can't call him father."

Damon never considered the many intangibles adopted kids must face when or if they meet their biological parents. "Maybe someone has written a how-to book."

Amy smiled. "Maybe the bigger question is what will he call me?"

"We'll just have to wait and see."

Amy pushed loose straw around with the toe of her boot. "So you want me to move into your apartment?"

"Only for a short time."

"And Dad agrees?"

"He wants to know where you are. If you go into protective custody no one will know except the police."

"Will I be safe?"

"I wouldn't suggest it if I did not think so. "

"How long will I have to stay there?"

"I have a feeling, a gut instinct if you will, that

things are coming to a head. I will talk to Sarah and arrange a family meeting, get everyone together and bring you out to the Schloss to meet them."

Amy almost shuddered. "It's scary."

"You have to do this sooner or later, claim your rightful place in the family. And don't worry, you won't be alone. I will be there with you."

The firmness of his commitment calmed her. "You don't have to do this, you know—getting so involved. It's my problem not yours."

"I was ready to quit but Lieutenant Harris talked me out of it," Damon said. "I realize now I can't do that. There is no one you can trust but me. I'm not a Fischer and I can walk away if I want to while they are locked inside their narrow world, as if they were in a prison. You know, Amy, you have the same advantage as I do, you can thumb your nose at them. You possess a power they fear, and that may be the reason why you are a threat."

Damon stood—time to change the subject. "Better get ready. Pack some clothes for a few days and I'll drive you into town. Your dad said there is a back road out of here so we don't alert Lieutenant Harris sitting on the road in his squad car."

"I don't think he will be a happy camper when he finds out we snuck out on him."

"More like a hornet."

'You think this is wise?"

"I want to get to the bottom of this on my own. If I get it wrong the police can take over." These words were far more prescient than he realized when he uttered them.

22

Damon waited in the big arena, walking the perimeter and looking out over the chest-high wall at the spread that was the home of King Breed Arabians. It was an impressive layout made possible by the bribery of Sarah Rand and the selling out of Elroy Jacobsson in order to realize a dream. But now that dream was becoming a nightmare whose ending was still in doubt—a nightmare of indistinct images moving furtively in a bleak landscape of dung piles under a dulling sky.

He jarred himself back to the scene before him— idyllic, serene, gallant horses grazing on green fields, white fences of broad Xs, elm leaves moving in the breeze, the sky blue, the sun intense. Life was supposed to be like this—full of rich promise and benevolence; not dark, brooding and stripped of meaning.

He sighed and checked his watch. Amy should be ready by now. He walked the perimeter again, and a third time before she came back lugging a backpack over one shoulder, the strap on the other side hanging free. Nearly an hour had elapsed. What had taken her so long? When he saw the sag in her torso, the slog in her walk, the look on her face—he knew why. Jacobsson must have told her about the unnatural relationship between her natural parents. As difficult as it was to learn this from her parents, it was far better for her to peer into this chasm now rather than fall headlong into it, innocent and unprepared. But no matter when she learns of it, now or later, how will she deal with this knowledge?

Damon had become, through no desire of his own, responsible for this young woman. And it hit him that he could not feel sorry for her, or for himself by extension, but rather be her rock, her support, her strength vicariously applied. He had to be strong for her, had to secure a future for her, had to save the Fischer reputation for her, not for Sarah or Henry, not even for Beth's memory. Damon had to do it for Amy.

She was angry. Angry at him, her parents, the Fischers, the world. "Why didn't you tell me?" she stormed as she approached him. She flung her backpack on the dirt and raised dust.

"It was up to your mother and father."

"Mother and father? Brother and sister?" Tears suddenly formed in her eyes.

"Not brother and sister, cousins."

"You think that makes me feel any better? Why didn't you say anything Saturday? Or weren't you man enough?"

"I didn't know then. Even if I did, how could I blurt out something like that when we had never met before?" He was trying to reason with her unreasonableness.

"Even the hint of it stinks. I feel like I fell into a manure pile and couldn't get out." Amy sat on a hay bale and put her hands to her chin, staring down. "Well," she said working hard to pull herself together, "we have to get out of here. Riders are showing up in a few minutes. This was my class but Dad will take over." She sighed deeply and stood, grabbing her backpack and dragging it along the ground. "Ready?"

"Wait for me here. I will bring the car around; then show me how to get out to the highway." Damon left

188

her and walked to his car parked behind the house. He stayed close to the wall to make sure Harris had not moved from his surveillance position and spot him. One damned thing after another, he thought, as he got behind the wheel and turned over the engine. When will it be over?

He pulled up to the wide entry of the barn where Amy was waiting and she climbed in. The road they were on was a narrow lane with a pair of gravel ruts that led behind the barn and between two pastures, again separated by X-framed fencing. They drove in silence, broken only by Amy giving him directions to Highway 52. Going this way took them through Rogers, a town punctuated by a vertical white water tower and the typical collection of a small town: hardware store, grocery store, feed store, farm implement dealer and, at the edge of town, a used car lot. The main street led him to the intersection with the highway and he turned left, merging into the line of steady traffic heading for the Twin Cities.

As Damon speeded up Amy began to unwind, the changing scenery giving her something else to look at, diverting her attention away from the horse farm to an urban setting. Maybe taking her away from familiar territory will be good for her, from the bitterness she left behind, hoping it would not trail after her like a panting hunting dog.

It was nearly six when he pulled into his apartment building on Franklin Avenue and parked in his assigned slot. He had long ago become desensitized to the smell of a parking garage but this time dripped oil and dank concrete assailed his nostrils like putrid offal.

They took the elevator in silence to the second floor and walked down the hall to his door. Inside she exhaled as though she had been holding her breath. "So this is what a bachelor pad looks like."

"It's home."

She looked into the kitchenette, the bath and finally the bedroom where she dropped her backpack on the floor. A black and white print by Cy Twombly hung over the dresser.

Amy studied it. "What are all those spots supposed to be for? Do they have special meaning or is it just pattern?"

"He's a minimalist, less is more. "

"I have to get used to it."

"'Want me to move it? I have a signed Robert Indiana titled Hexagon Eight. It's more literal."

She shook her head. "I'm not sure what literal means any more."

"I have an idea. How about a drink? Something to soothe the nerves and then I'll go shopping. The Wedge Co-op is right around the corner."

"Can I go with you?"

"Wish you could but you better stay inside. I'll make dinner and then drive back to the Schloss to spend the night."

She looked around in dismay. "I'll be alone."

"I'll come back tomorrow."

"Then what? Is there a plan?"

What plan he asked himself, when there are so many unknowns? "What I want to do is bring you out to the Schloss. Do you think you are up to it?"

Amy shrugged. "Why put it off any longer? I have to meet my father sooner or later."

"And the rest of the family."

"I wonder who will be more scared, them or me?"

"My hunch is them. You represent the unknown. All that has happened since Beth died is because of you."

"Including what happened to Beth?"

Damon nodded.

"Then I will be the one who is more scared."

"Maybe not. Having spent a lot of time with the Fischers in the past three months I learned one thing: family honor and reputation are everything. This is all Sarah talks about. And then to discover that…" Damon stopped talking. The word stuck in his throat.

"That's all right Damon, just say it. Incest, isn't

that the word you want to use? Well, I'm the one who is suffering most. Shouldn't the Fischers be more concerned about me?"

"They are probably afraid you will expose them for what they are: secretive and duplicitous. You are living proof of what they have been hiding for a generation."

"How do you think they will react?"

Blow the lid off the place, he was thinking, but said aloud, "Once they meet you they will realize what a wonderful person you are."

"I hope you are right," Amy said almost wistfully.

Damon studied her, taking in her poise, her beauty, the implicit strength of her slender body, and decided that if anyone could handle the truth, she could. He said so.

She smiled, "You've been a rock, Damon, and if it weren't for you I don't think I could manage any of it."

Feeling a whole lot better, Damon went to the kitchen to make drinks. "Do you prefer Scotch or bourbon?"

"I have no favorite," Amy called from the living room.

"Oh by the way," he said as he prepared Scotch on the rocks, "if the phone rings don't answer it." And as he said this, the phone indeed did ring as though the hand of a fickle fate deemed it so, the persistent sound was uncanny and unsettling. He picked up the phone on the third ring.

The voice on the other end was exasperated, impatient, angry. "Goddammit, Damon, where the hell did you go? I waited and waited and finally went up to that farmhouse and looked around. No car. How the hell did you get away without my seeing you? I'm ready to wring your Goddamned neck!"

Who is it? Amy mouthed.

Damon covered the mouthpiece. "The cop."

"Petroulis, are you there? Say something!"

"I'm here."

"Where is the broad?"

If Harris could see her, he would not use that word.

"You copped out, if I may use a bad pun because that is how I feel, and you are number one on my shit list."

"Calm down."

"*Calm down?* I'll bet a month's salary, which is probably not as much as you make, that she is with you. I can charge you with kidnapping, a federal offense. You can go to Leavenworth for twenty years. I want to talk to her."

"She's not here," Damon said, and realized right then how easy it is to dissemble, especially if you think you have the cause on your side. But his confidence was beginning to unravel. God, what have I gotten myself into?

"I'm not taking your word for it. If that girl is there I will arrest you for kidnapping."

"You wouldn't do that."

"Try me. Kidnapping is a serious charge, even worse because she is a woman. The county attorney is a personal friend of mine, and I might be able to convince him that you violated the Mann act, better known as the White Slavery Traffic Act. How do I know you aren't transporting a woman against her will for the purpose of prostitution?"

"Jesus, Harris, you can't be serious."

"After you left me cooling my heels in my squad car for an hour and a half you think I'm not? I called the precinct station on Lyndale and they are sending over a couple of beat cops who have fun with drunks and disorderlies, so you better have your hands ready to cuff or you'll end up with a battered head." Harris hung up. The monologue was over.

Damon rubbed his forehead beaded with sweat. Amy stood next to him, her cheeks flushed with anxiety.

"My god, Damon, what is wrong?"

"We have to get out of here."

"Why?"

"Too much to explain now. Grab your backpack.

Let's go."

Amy ran to the bedroom and joined Damon at the front door. "What about the drinks you just made"

"Let the cops have them."

"What cops?"

"From the precinct station right around the corner—they are coming to arrest me," he said breathlessly and grabbed Amy's hand. "We'll take the stairs, faster that way, and I don't want to run into them in the elevator."

The pair took the steps two at a time down to the parking area, their clunking heels reverberating off the metal treads. Damon pushed the heavy security door open and ran to his car with Amy right behind. He backed out, burning rubber after he threw the gears into forward, and turned left uphill on Franklin cutting off a driver who gave him the finger. He barely reached the crest when, in his rearview mirror, he saw blinking red lights and then the sound of a police siren. The squad car turned into his apartment alley.

That was close, he thought, and then wondered what the cops will do when no one answers—break down his door? He wished now he had left it open. Too late for that. He hoped LeMay, the building super, shows up having heard the sirens and unlocks the door with his master key. If not, Damon wondered, will my homeowners insurance pay for the damage?

"Where are we going?" Amy asked, next to him on the front seat, speaking for the first time since they ran from the apartment.

Her comment startled him because he had no plan beyond running from the police. My god, running from the police, how weird is that—the PR Director of a respected art institution is a wanted man. He imagined himself on a poster, grim-faced with a day's growth of beard and a reward of $10,000 dead or alive.

Damon waited impatiently for the light to change at Blaisdell Avenue and continued east till he reached

Third Avenue when a thought came to him. He followed
Third Avenue, passing parked cars whose owners lived in
1930s vintage apartment buildings of red brick facades
with window ledges and lintels trimmed in Mankato
limestone.

He pulled into the driveway of a motel kiddy-
corner from the Minneapolis Institute of Arts.

Amy peered out the window. "What is this?"

"The Fair Oaks Motel."

"A motel?" she asked guardedly.

"And a restaurant. I know this place." He needed
to reassure her. "This is where we house visiting artists.
David Hockney stayed here when the Fischer organized an
exhibition of London pop art before anyone ever heard of
him."

"I've heard of him."

"Our show helped jump-start his career. When I
picked him up at the motel, he asked if he could drive my
car. I said sure, what could possibly go wrong. He pulled
out and went into the left lane, forgetting he was not back
in London, and we nearly collided with a car coming
toward us. It was a close call." Damon laughed at the
memory.

"You lead an interesting life, much more than
mine." She reflected a moment. "Would Franz Marc have
stayed here?"

"Had there been a retrospective of the Blau Reider
painters and the motel was here, he probably would have."

"Only asking."

"It wouldn't have mattered anyway. He died in the
Battle of Verdun in 1916."

Amy seemed genuinely saddened. "Who knows
what else he would have painted."

The thought of someone dying before his time had
an uncomfortable parallel to their own perilous existence.
They fell into a somber mood, which for an instant had
been lifted by the humorous story of Hockney's left-
handed driving.

He parked in front of the office. "Wait in the car. I'll get two singles."

Behind the desk the night clerk, a young man letting his blond hair grow long, was drawing on a sketchpad with an art pencil of soft lead, making thick abstract lines. Damon recognized him from previous visits—an art student at the Minneapolis College of Art located behind the Art Institute.

"What are you working on?" he asked.

"Automatic writing, like Jackson Pollock when he was at the Art Students League."

"He did ok. Hope you do, too."

"There is only one Pollock." He closed the pad and slid it under the counter. "So what brings you in, another opening, another show?" he asked.

"Personal this time. Got two singles?"

The young man shook his head. "Pretty busy. Got a double in back. No view of the park, so I'll give you the Clergyman's rate."

Damon looked through the window at Amy sitting in the car staring back with the weight of the world on her shoulders.

The man behind the desk followed Damon's gaze. "Oh, you are not alone."

"So much for the Clergyman's rate?" Damon asked smiling.

"I'll give it to you anyway. You bring us a lot of business."

"Thanks," Damon said and signed the register. As he returned to the car, he wondered how to break the news that he and Amy will have to share a motel room. He climbed in, but did not start the engine.

"I remember an old film from the thirties with Clark Gable and Claudette Colbert—'It Happened One Night.'"

Amy stared at him curiously. "What made you think of that?"

"Hear me out. Colbert plays a rich runaway and

Gable is a reporter secretly trying to get her story, and they have to share a motel room after their car breaks down."

"Oh, oh," Amy said, starting to get the point.

"Gable stretched a clothesline and hung a blanket between the two beds."

"Are you saying this is what you will do?"

"Either that or sleep on a bench in the park."

She smiled but it was a wan smile, unable to conceal the hurt she was suffering. "I'd rather know that you are on the other side of a blanket."

Damon started the engine. "Let's park the car and have a bite to eat. You must be hungry."

"Famished."

The restaurant faced the corner of Third and Stevens Avenues and provided, through the large windows, a clear view of the Minneapolis Institute of Arts, a classic example of neo-Roman architecture, with a grand entrance of columns supporting an unadorned pediment.

The restaurant, too, had a classic style but much more recent, an atavistic throwback to Art Deco—chrome and Formica. The nearly empty dining room had a hushed atmosphere which suited the newcomers as they sank into a leatherette booth opposite one another.

Plastic covers meant to keep the menus clean were smeared with fingerprints. They ordered grilled cheese sandwiches and iced tea. They sat quietly sipping from straws and staring, not at each other but out the window, at the lone waitress, the order window behind which the chef, if he can be called that, was making their sandwiches.

Finally Amy broke the silence. "What did that police officer have to say?"

And so Damon told her that Harris was going to arrest him, but he decided not to bring up kidnapping or the Mann act. Things were bad enough without hauling Harris's histrionic threats into the conversation. "That's why we left in such a hurry. Harris was sending over police officers from the Bryant Station to arrest me. Remember those lights and the siren behind us?"

Amy nodded. "Are you sure this is worth the risk, trying to help me I mean, maybe even losing your job and ruining your career?"

He had to think about that even though the answer was obvious. "Yes, it is worth the risk."

"But why?"

"For one thing, the police have to follow procedures and I don't. I have access to the Schloss. Sarah hates Harris and doesn't want him around and I have the advantage of being on the inside. Besides, if Harris has his way I'll be in jail and you'll be in protective custody. Neither one of us wants that."

"No, of course not," she said. "But what are you going to do?"

Damon shrugged. "I wish I had a plan. Maybe I should say there is no way to plan. Just get in the way, and see what happens. With you in the picture things have to boil over."

"And that means we go to the Schloss?"

He nodded. "I'm not going to tell anyone we're coming, just surprise them. Show up at the door and Phillip will let us in."

"Phillip?"

"The butler."

Amy stared in wonder. "Is this my new world? A butler answering the door?"

23

They finished their dinner by sharing an apple pie alamode because it was advertised as homemade and it turned out to be surprisingly good. Their forks touched at one point and for Damon it was more like a small bolt of lightning. As far as he could tell Amy did not share his reaction.

He moved the car to the front of their unit, number 18. The only luggage was Amy's backpack; they left too hurriedly for Damon to bring anything. He unlocked the door and they went in, tentatively, as though they were burglars casing the joint to see if anyone was home before stealing anything.

They turned on every light, a reflection of their nervousness, and sat at opposite ends of the sofa watching television without talking until the ten o'clock news came on. It came as no surprise that the lead story was about the Fischers. Patti Azquith was standing next to the anchor desk wearing a one-piece dress of bright red, her script in her hand staring at the camera full on.

"What is the latest on the Fischer case, Patti?" the anchor, Dave Moore, asked. "I know you spent much of yesterday at the—what do you call it—Schloss?"

"That's right, Dave, the German word for Palace."

Patti replied and showed an expression Damon could only describe as a smirk.

"And you have more news to report?"

Patti stared intently into the camera as though she were talking directly to Damon. "I can now confirm that the private detective who was run down in the alley behind his office was Jacob Rankin. What I cannot confirm is that a car belonging to one of the Fischers might be implicated in the hit and run that killed that detective. I spoke to the officer in charge of the investigation, Lieutenant Harris of the Hennepin County Sheriff's Department, but he will not confirm or deny a connection. If there is, this will be the second death tied to a famous family living in a famous palace on the lake the Dakotah Indians call The Big Water. But is the lake big enough to maintain its image of serenity and beauty because of a crime wave engulfing one of the towering families of Minnetonka, if not all of Minnesota?"

Patti paused for effect, letting the import of her comment sink in, and then she continued:

"I also asked the Lieutenant for an update on Damon Petroulis, the Fischer Art Museum's erstwhile publicity director, whom I interviewed in front of Schloss Fischer on Lake Minnetonka and has not been seen since. Harris told me that Petroulis is missing, the Lieutenant calling him a fugitive from justice. Last seen earlier this evening fleeing his apartment on Franklin and Lyndale, Petroulis was in the company of a young woman, a woman of mystery you might say, because Harris would not reveal her identity except to say she was in her late twenties and might be a hostage. Harris warned that if anyone sees Petroulis, approach him with caution. He is a white male of thirty-two, six foot one, dark hair, of Mediterranean cast, and well-built. We are doing our best to identify that woman, and we were able at least to learn from the Lieutenant that she lives on a horse farm near Rogers. By the morning news we should have a clearer picture of her, not only who she is but why she is with Petroulis and whether or not he has put her life in danger."

As Azquith was delivering her report, Amy inched her way across the sofa until she was next to Damon, their hips touching. She pressed herself against his shoulder. "I can't believe this is happening."

Damon tried to reassure her. "Azquith is only fishing."

"Fishing for me, and she'll find out who I am. My name will be all over the news by morning, mom and dad's name, too. What have I done? Why did I agree to do this?" Amy began to cry.

Damon watched her sniffle for a moment and then, as if it were the natural thing to do, put his arm around her. She responded not by pulling away but by laying her head on his shoulder.

"I put you up to it," he said, his lips close to her hair. It smelled of fresh shampoo.

"This is not your fault," she said, her words floating into the room. "I was the one who came to see you. All you did was tell the truth about who I really am, and it opened up a strange new world, one I find hard to accept. I yearn to go back to the way it was but that is impossible." She tensed and lifted her head, turning to look at him straight on, her eyes unblinking, burrowing into his. "I still have this terrible self-doubt. Do you think I am up to it?"

"Of course you are," he replied, a bit too casually, not understanding that Amy was close to an emotional breakdown. "Why shouldn't you?"

"What do you mean, why shouldn't I?" she repeated testily.

"You just asked me if I felt you were up to it and I said of course you are, because I know you are a strong person."

"Don't talk to me like that unless you mean it."

Damon sighed heavily. "I do mean it, Amy. How often do I have to tell you that you have more going for you than most women your age."

Amy glared. "Now you are patronizing me like

some kid whose dog is lost."

"I am not patronizing you!" he snapped back. "Give yourself some credit."

"Oh really?" Amy stood, her arms akimbo, and faced Damon, still sitting on the sofa. "First you say I'm strong and then you say I should give myself some credit as though I am not strong. Which is it?"

He stood and faced her. "I wouldn't be going to all this trouble if I did not think you are the most interesting woman I have ever met."

That stopped her but only long enough to re-arm. "Are you serious? A person like you, sophisticated, intelligent, too handsome for your own good, telling me I'm the most interesting woman you ever met? Give me a break. I can't imagine you having any trouble attracting plenty of so-called interesting women."

"For god's sake, Amy, why are you talking like this?"

She extended her arms in a sweeping motion. "This can't be the first time you've been alone in a motel room with a woman. I'll bet you've had lots of conquests, maybe dozens."

The conversation was out of hand, all emotion now, the floodgates of propriety had been breached and everything was caught in a flood of raw feeling,

"Well, maybe not dozens..." he said, smiling broadly, the wildly exaggerated number striking him as pretty damned funny. But the look on her face told him that this was not funny to her and she was fighting back, hyperbole her weapon.

"Oh really? If not dozens, how many? Twenty? Thirty?" When he did not reply she said, "Are you ready to add one more?"

He stared at her, knowing where she was going with that one.

"Oh," she said when he did not respond. "I guess a non-answer means I'm not that interesting after all."

"You *are* interesting, Amy!" he blurted, feeling

like a spinning top, winding down, ready to tip over. "I never said you weren't. You're beautiful, sexy!"

Tears welled in her eyes. "Then why don't you have the curiosity to ask me?"

"Ask you what?"

"How many boyfriends I've had?"

This was the last question he ever expected to hear from her. He had to stand back mentally and stop acting like a child caught up in a silly argument. This one was far from silly. It was fraught with meaning, unexpressed intentions, even fear as these two vulnerable persons, thrown together in a place where neither one wanted to be, trying to find out just how far into unfamiliar territory each was willing to travel.

The tears building in Amy's eyes spilled down her cheeks. She brushed them away with both hands, trying to regain control.

"Oh my god," she said through her fingers. "I said things I've never said to anyone, not even to myself. What is happening to me?"

Damon exhaled, working to calm his jangled nerves. "You are under a lot of pressure. And it's my fault, too, I should be more sensitive to your feelings."

She nodded thanks and finished wiping the tears with the butts of her hands. "Still, I overreacted. Forgive me."

"No need to. Actually," he ventured, "it was rather refreshing."

She smiled, the standoff over.

They both looked around as if checking the room for the first time—the worn carpeting, the cheap landscape print on the wall, the tired wallpaper, the drooping curtains drawn over windows that needed cleaning (perhaps a metaphor for their own states of mind)—but they were really recomposing themselves, facing the reality they were in but at the same time seeing that they had changed significantly. Their relationship had shifted to another plane even though neither realized it clearly nor fully understood it.

"What did you pay for this place?" she asked.

"I got the clergyman's rate."

She eyed him curiously.

"A discount, not because I am a man of the cloth but because I bring them business from visiting artists."

"Like David Hockney."

"Exactly."

"Why wouldn't you put someone like Hockney at the Radisson? It's fancier."

"But lacking character. Artists like funky not fancy."

She mused on that for a while. "Now that I am a Fischer I will have to learn more about the art world."

Mentioning Fischer changed the atmosphere, a reminder of what lay before them; tomorrow would be the most demanding in either of their lives.

As if he needed no further reminder, Damon looked at his watch. "Getting late."

"I guess we better turn in." Amy picked up her backpack. "Mind if I use the bathroom first?"

While Amy was in the bathroom, Damon took the opportunity to go outside to his car for a length of nylon rope he kept in the trunk. It was convenient for tying down the lid when he had an oversize load, like the time he bought a new microwave for his apartment. He looked for a secure place to tie the rope, and tested a curtain rod over the double windows. It held and he wound the other end around the frame of a landscape print hanging above the headboard. As cheap as they were, motel prints were clamped solidly to the wall in case anyone tried to purloin one. In the closet he found a spare blanket on the top shelf and slung it over the rope, copying the makeshift separation between the twin beds he'd seen Clark Gable create in 'It Happened One Night.' Feeling a bit smug Damon sat in the only easy chair to await Amy's reaction when she came out of the bathroom. He wasn't disappointed.

"You did it!" she exclaimed, wearing a robe tied tightly at her waist making it seem more slender than it really was.

"Just like the movie."

"You are very resourceful." She laughed, clearly delighted that he would go to all this effort for her, not only to make her feel more at ease but also respecting her privacy. "Which side do you want to sleep on?" she asked.

"Since I'm left-handed, why don't I take the left one?"

His decision had the added benefit of facing the bathroom where he could undress. Then it hit him—he ran out of his apartment with no time to pack a bag.

"Damn! I don't have anything to sleep in," he said out loud, not meaning this for Amy as much as venting his frustration. "I have clothes at the Schloss but they don't do me any good here, and I can't sneak back to my apartment. I'm sure Harris has someone watching it."

Now safely behind the curtain, Amy replied, "Speaking of Harris wouldn't he be surprised to see us sharing a motel room."

"I doubt this is what he meant by protective custody."

They laughed, whatever awkwardness they initially felt about their arrangement was now past.

"Can I use some of your toothpaste?" he asked, heading for the bathroom.

"Ok but I don't know you well enough to use my toothbrush."

"A finger will do."

Damon stripped down to his underwear, shut the lights and slid under the sheets, his mind on the girl three feet away, separated only by a hanging blanket. The stuff movies are made of, he thought. He tried with all his might to fall asleep, counterproductive to say the least, until he recalled a method of relaxing one part of your body at a time, starting with the fingers, then the hands, wrists, arms, and so on until you succumb to the inevitable. He finally fell asleep, however fitfully.

"Damon?"

"Huh? What?" He stirred and looked at his watch, pressing the light button to see the dial better. Half-past one.

"Are you awake?"

He turned on his side facing the blanket. "Anything the matter?"

"No, just thinking about things."

"What things."

"What will happen tomorrow, and after that?"

He stared at the blanket, his eyes adjusted to the semi-dark, noticing for the first time the Navajo motif— earth tones with what amounted to stick figures of persons and animals, not that different from images on Mimbres Indian pottery from the American Southwest he saw at the University of Minnesota's Art Gallery on the top floor of Northrop Auditorium.

"I wish I had an answer for you."

"I wasn't really expecting any, I just want to talk. I was wondering what will happen to me and you, too, when the dust settles. I mean will we still see each other?"

"I suppose so, but things will be different. In a way you will be my boss."

"Boss?"

"Even though the Fischers don't have any say in day-to-day operations they still endow the museum, and the Board is full of Fischers, including Sarah who is chair emerita. It would not surprise me if once you are settled in, you will be named to the Board and then we will see each other at board meetings."

"Only at board meetings?"

"Don't forget I'm just the PR guy."

"Are you saying there will be a class distinction

between you and me?"

"I don't see us ever sharing a motel room after tonight." He meant this as a joke but there was an element of sober truth in what he said. When the dust settles, to use Amy's phrase, their relationship will be most certainly more formal. She will have money and position while he will have only position, that of a PR man.

Damon heard her shift as though she was turning toward him and leaning on her elbow. He imagined what that must look like.

"Why didn't you answer my question?" she asked.

"I did."

"No, not that one, the earlier one."

Damon was having trouble figuring out what Amy meant. "Earlier one?"

"When I was really mad at you, I said, why don't you ask me how many boyfriends I've had."

Damon was suddenly alert, his brain as sharply attuned as it had ever been, wondering what Amy was driving at—was she ready to start their fight all over again or was she actually going to confide in him?

"I took that as a rhetorical question," he said, "the kind you ask for effect when you don't expect a reply."

"You can still answer, rhetorical or not."

"Now?"

"You just said that this will be the last time we will ever share a motel room together, so you better ask me now because it will never happen in a boardroom."

"Ok, how many boyfriends have you had?"

Even though he could not see her he knew she had to be smiling. "None of your business."

24

Morning came suddenly it seemed, it was dark and then it was light, the sun announcing itself not slowly but in a rush, poking through the upraised branches of the gnarled old oak trees for which the motel was named and through the windows of unit 18, awakening Damon with a start. He looked around, disoriented for a moment, and then noticed the hanging blanket, its Navajo design much more vibrant in the full sun.

The door to the bathroom was closed. Amy must be in there. He drew the hanging blanket back enough to peek at her bed. It was neatly made, no trace of her presence. Disappointed that he at least did not see a pillow with the indentation of her head, he redrew the blanket and lay back.

"Amy," he called at the closed door, "you in there?"

"Yes, are you decent?"

"All covered."

She opened the door wearing fresh clothes she must have stored in her backpack—tailored cowboy jeans and a light blue blouse with a long collar.

"How do I look?"

"Great."

"I thought I'd better dress up for the Fischers.

Speaking of dress," she said, "what did you wear to bed last night?"

"I was in my altogether."

She walked past him. "In that case I'll wait for you in the restaurant."

Damon joined her in fifteen minutes, having showered but feeling less than kempt with a day's growth of stubble on his chin and day-old clothes on his back. He slid into the booth across from her feeling self-conscious, a handsome, well-dressed woman with a man who looked as if he had slept in his clothes—not too far from the truth.

The restaurant was busy with the sense of urgency that breakfast diners have in a motel, ready to hit the road, not so different from what Amy and Damon were feeling.

"What's the drill?" she asked after they ordered.

"We can't use my car. I'm sure the license number and description are on every police blotter in the Twin Cities. I'll call Jim at the station on Hennepin. He keeps a couple of loaners for regular customers and maybe he'll let me use one of them."

"What are you going to do with yours?"

"I'll park it over there, on Twenty Second Street where those mansions are."

Amy looked in the direction he was pointing—a row of stately 19th century homes of brick facades and slate roofs.

"The car will sit there for a couple of days before it is tagged, and then towed to the impound lot where it will sit for another couple of days before anyone at the police department is the wiser. By that time..." his words trailed off.

Amy waited expectantly. "By that time what?"

"I will have a big parking ticket."

Jim was waiting at the entrance in a loaner, a Chevy Impala with high miles, but also with good tires and a tuned engine.

"I need a ride back to the station," Jim said.

"Ok, but you drive," Damon said.

After introductions, he and Amy climbed into the back seat.

"You need it for long?" Jim asked over his shoulder, driving on Twenty-Second toward Hennepin.

"A couple of days."

"Since your car isn't in for service I have to charge you."

"Not a problem."

"But you'll get a discount."

"Why?"

"You brought me a new customer."

"I did?" Damon asked, wondering who Jim was talking about.

"Yeah, that gal who replaced you at the Fischer, Maggie..."

"Maggie Bovin?" Damon asked, not wanting to believe him.

"She drives a nice car, an Audi. Nicer than yours," he said jokingly but Damon was not amused.

"That doesn't surprise me."

"She spoke highly of you. Said she had big shoes to fill." Jim waited for a reaction and when he didn't get any he said, "Say, when are you going back to the Art Center?"

"By the end of the week," Damon said, with all the confidence he could muster.

After dropping Jim off at the station, Damon had Amy drive. "I'm sure the cops will be watching the entrance to the Schloss. They don't know the car and they don't know you. I'll hide in the back seat."

"Will there be any police inside the grounds?"

"They can't do that without permission and Sarah hates the cops. Once we get inside we will be ok."

They drove the rest of the way in silence except for Damon giving directions, west on 12, take the Wayzata exit and follow 15 through Navarre, where directions became more detailed as they neared Breckett's Point and the entrance to Schloss Fischer.

Damon ducked down on the floor between the front and back seats. "See anything?" he asked, his voice disembodied like a ventriloquist's.

"Nothing."

"No squad car?"

"Unless it's parked in the woods."

He gave her the code to open the main gate and silently it swung open.

"Follow the lane till you get to the garage, a long building with apartments above it. Beyond that is the turnaround to the Schloss. Drive right up to the front entrance like you owned the place."

"You sure?"

"You are a Fischer now. You have to behave like one. Besides if we look unsure of ourselves, we might cast suspicion. Anything out of the ordinary may be seen as a sign of danger and someone may very well call the police."

Amy did as told and parked under the arched portico, designed more for shiny motorcars than a well-used loaner.

"Leave the keys."

They approached the large paneled door, Amy a tentative step behind, and it opened before Damon had a chance to push the bell button.

Phillip, in starched white and pressed black, stared at him.

"Mr. Damon! I was wondering whose car that was. Thank heaven you are all right. Mrs. Sarah has been beside herself ever since Lieutenant Harris called to tell her that the police are looking for you. I think he used the word dragnet. This has been a very stressful time, none of us has slept in two days."

In his agitated state, he did not focus on Amy until he closed the door behind him. "I beg your pardon for ignoring you."

Amy didn't mind, she was looking in wonder at her surroundings. There was much to behold for someone raised on a horse farm—a granite floor expanding to the grand staircase and, straight ahead, the Great Hall leading to the terrace decorated with fake Doric capitals surmounting salmon-colored pilasters and lighted recesses of carved marble putti.

"Phillip, this is Amy Jacobsson."

Phillip lost the color in his cheeks for a moment but quickly recovered. "Mrs. Sarah wanted to be informed the moment you arrived. She will meet you in the library."

Just like always, Damon thought.

"May I escort you to the White Room while Mr. Damon visits Mrs. Rand?" Phillip said to Amy, bowing formally.

Damon took Amy's arm. "She is coming with me."

Phillip stood his ground. "I'm sure Mrs. Sarah wishes to see you alone."

Damon wondered if Sarah was already a step ahead of him, sensing that his absence had to do with finding Amy, and she was afraid he might bring her to the Schloss. Well, he would find out soon enough.

"I think she will want to meet Amy."

"Mrs. Sarah is...well, to be honest, we are all concerned for her health."

Amy hung back. "Maybe you should go alone."

"No," Damon said to her without taking his eyes off the butler. "Phillip you are going to have to stop protecting Mrs. Rand."

Phillip stared as if shell-shocked. "Mr. Damon, how can you say that?"

"Because it is true. You know who Amy is, don't you?"

The butler cast a downward glance, wanting to look at her but still unable to admit that the past had become the present.

"I know *of* her, Mr. Damon, I do not know her."

"The time has come, don't you think, to *know* her?"

Phillip finally looked at Amy, who in turn looked back at Phillip, a stand-off, if you will, the moment two duelists eye each other before firing their weapons. Privately Damon admired Amy for not withering. She was learning fast.

"Amy must meet Sarah and the rest of the family. I've gone though hell and I'm not going to..." Damon stopped, realizing he was letting his pent-up emotions get the better of him. "Sorry, I don't mean to take it out on you, Phillip, but the Fischers have got to meet Amy, starting with Sarah."

"Very well, sir, I will inform her, but that doesn't mean she will see the young lady. I will do my best to transmit the urgency of your message. Please wait in the Venetian room." Phillip walked off, not purposefully—the trademark of his profession—but reluctantly, slow-stepping as if he were avoiding cracks in a sidewalk.

Damon used the time waiting for Phillip's return to give Amy a primer on the excesses of rococo architecture, hoping it might take her mind off what could easily be another excess: the impending meeting with her grandmother, the woman responsible for her adoption. Although Amy smiled appreciatively, she was clearly preoccupied.

"Do you think Mrs. Rand will like me?"

"Grandmother," Damon corrected, "and she will."

"How should I greet her? Just say hello? Give her a hug?" Amy thought about that for a moment. "Probably not."

"Just be yourself."

"I'm not sure who that is any more."

Phillip returned with an impassive expression on his face. If there was emotion hidden beneath he did not reveal it. "Mrs. Sarah will see you now."

"Both of us?"

Phillip nodded. "She asked that I not escort you."

"That's all right. I know the way."

"I hope you do, sir." With that enigmatic statement Phillip left them.

"Ready?" Damon asked Amy.

She nodded assent with a deep sigh and together they walked to the library. Sarah was sitting in her customary chair, looking out the window, dressed in a flowered caftan that was her *faire habiller du jour.* She did not turn to look at them until Damon addressed her. "Mrs. Rand?"

She shifted her body to face them but did so with effort. Even in the few days since Damon last saw her she seemed to have failed.

"Sit close to me, Amy, so that I can see you better. My eyes aren't as good as they used to be." When that time was she did not say.

Amy sat as directed, her back erect, her hands in her lap, her feet crossed at the ankles, as she might for a job interview.

"I never expected this moment to come, but now that it has I feel a great weight lifted from my shoulders."

Amy remained silent

"Won't you say something, my dear, so I can hear the sound of your voice."

Calling Amy "my dear" was music to Damon's ears.

"I'm sorry, Mrs. Rand."

"Don't be sorry, and don't call me Mrs. Rand. Beth called me Granny. You may if you wish."

To Sarah a wish was not a wish at all but a directive made to appear as though a personal choice could be made, especially if it flattered her. Was Sarah, by virtue of having Amy call her Granny, admitting her to the family's inner circle? So far, Damon thought, things are going reasonably well, better than expected, not perfect but then this is not a perfect world.

"You are my new granddaughter. I lost one but gained another."

"Wasn't I always your granddaughter?" Amy asked.

Sarah smiled, appreciating Amy's directness. "Yes, that is true. As I look at you now, I see an attractive, self-possessed young woman and it makes me wonder if it was the environment you grew up in or your heritage that made you the person you are. I like to think it is the latter, that it is Fischer blood in your veins." Sarah stopped for a moment of reflection. "For nearly three decades I have not had to think about your birth. But now, it has to be acknowledged, even though I did not want it so."

"I did not want it either," Amy replied, "But now we both have to live with the fact that I am a Fischer. You may not like it, Mrs. …Granny, but here I am."

"My dear, this is not about you personally. You are a capable woman and for that I am pleased, but we all would have been better off if you had not learned who you are."

"There is more to it than that, isn't there?"

"What are you driving at?"

"I know the whole story," Amy continued, "how you bribed my father to raise me to protect your family from scandal."

"Who told you?" Sarah asked.

"Father."

"He was sworn to secrecy." Sarah looked disapprovingly at Damon. "Are you a party to this?"

"I was the go-between, Mrs. Rand. Amy and I met at the Art Center on Saturday."

Sarah smiled for the first time. "So your first encounter was at the museum my father founded. Rather like fate, don't you think?"

"Yes, I suppose so."

"*Suppose* so? Is that how you feel about your heritage?"

"Other than being shocked you mean?"

"Don't you feel privileged?"

"Why should I?" Amy fired back. "I will always carry the stigma of my birth, that my parents were related. How can I feel privileged about that, just because they were both Fischers?"

"It would serve you well, my dear, not to bring that up."

"Am I an embarrassment to you? Because I am the product of...of incest?" The word spilled out like an overfilled glass that itself fell to the floor and shattered. It was so startling Damon almost drew back. But sooner or later it had to be said. That took guts, Amy, Damon thought, that took guts.

Sarah's eyes widened, the grayness in them turning dark. This may have been the first time the word was uttered in the Schloss. "You have overstepped the bounds of propriety, Amy."

"You just don't want to face the truth! For you it's a scar on that family history Damon is working on. I have to live with the knowledge every day of my life. I grew up the daughter of a horse breeder. I never wanted anything different from that! And now I will forever carry the stigma of being not only illegitimate but also..." she searched for an appropriate word "...stained!"

"Please, Amy," Damon interjected. "Don't talk like that."

"Why shouldn't I?" Amy replied out of anger and frustration that somehow Sarah deserved more sympathy than she did.

Sarah struck a conciliatory tone. "Amy, you must understand that what happened long ago left a stain—yes you may call it that, but the stain is not you, my dear. There is no reason to think you are not normal in every way."

Amy was fighting back tears. "I just want to lead a normal life."

"In that case," Sarah replied, "go back to your

horses and forget about us. There is no reason you need to be a part of this family. A mistake that was made years ago does not need to dictate your life now. I admit my involvement in hiding you from my world, and for that I ask your forgiveness. We have been pillars of the community, leaders in culture and the arts. I have spent my life building that reputation and I cannot let it be destroyed by a mistake made a long time ago."

Sarah allowed time for the gravity of her statement to sink in, and then she said, "You can rest assured that I will make it up to you."

Those words sounded all too familiar to Damon. Was Sarah trying to buy off her granddaughter the same way she bought off Jacobsson?

"Make it up to me?" Amy asked.

"Financially of course. You will never have to worry about living comfortably."

"Money in exchange for silence, is that it?"

"My dear," Sarah said, shifting uncomfortably in her chair, "there is no need to put it in such blunt terms. Look at how I helped your father."

"Buying me off doesn't make me feel secure," Amy said, "it makes me feel *in*secure."

Damon's heart sank. The interview that had begun with so much promise was now turning into what amounted to a family feud.

"To assume somehow that you have to bribe me in order to keep my silence indicates that you really don't think I have all those fine attributes you just gave me. It was a mistake to think I could come here and be welcomed. Maybe Damon thought so or hoped so, but I can see now it was a waste of time. I will be just as happy to be rid of you as you are to be rid of me!"

Silence fell in the library, as heavy as a body hanging from the gallows. Sarah's shoulders sagged, her head bowed, she seemed not to be breathing and for a moment Damon was concerned that she was having a stroke.

"Are you all right?" he asked her.

She looked up, her face drawn. "When I was young I would have fought back, but I am too old now." Then she looked at Amy, an expression not of condemnation but of admiration. "You are strong-willed, you speak your mind, you have the courage of your convictions. You remind me..." she hesitated... "you remind me of myself."

The heaviness in the air cleared as though a fresh breeze came through the window. However self-directed, Sarah paid Amy not only a compliment, but sent her a signal of a truce as well. The result was a moment of quiet introspection for Amy and Damon, who both wondered if the old lady really meant it or was using blandishment temporarily to disarm her rival—what other word better fits the relationship between the two—in order to attack at a later time when Sarah got her strength back.

"You don't believe me?" she asked, reading the doubt in their eyes. "Yes, Amy, you do remind me of myself, talking adamantly to my father, who thought I was a spoiled brat. I remember many times, here in this very room with my father sitting where I am sitting—he trying to hem me in and I trying to break clear. We had a war of wills, my father and I. But it wasn't until after his death that I was able to assert myself in the family. He was preparing me although I did not know it at the time, to toughen me up in the only way he knew how—he was, after all, a nineteenth century self-made man. I can see myself reflected in his fierce pride, that nothing must ever hurt or compromise the Fischer name. His moral attitudes carried over from his century to mine, whether right or wrong that is the way I am, a product of my father's generation."

Sarah stopped to catch her breath. What she was saying was, after all, breathtaking.

"And now I have met you near the end of my own life. We have not had a chance to get to know one another very well but in the time I have left, I want to make up for that as well as I can. I only hope you are willing to let me do it. That is all I can ask of myself or of you." Sarah stared at Amy for several seconds. "I no longer see you as a threat. Now I see you as a woman with a promising future, and with strength of character that clearly reminds me of Beth. I lost one granddaughter but gained another, and I would be grateful to have one last chance to come to terms with my regrets and make peace with myself. I deserve that opportunity, don't I?" Sarah smiled. "Wouldn't it be a fascinating development if, when I die, you, my dear, carry on for me, becoming the new Sarah?"

Damon recalled reading in a literature class in college Somerset Maugham's memoir, 'Summing Up', giving a name to what most people do as they age, recalling their ups and downs, their successes and failures—in effect reviewing one's life close to the end of it. This is what Sarah was doing, summing up.

Maybe this was hiding inside her all along and Amy's presence gave it voice. However it worked, Damon was grateful that for all the risks and setbacks of his own life—too early for him to sum up but still part of the record—he made the right decision to bring Amy to the Schloss. He looked at her, trying to read her reaction as she sat across from Sarah, but she seemed mesmerized, and what was going through her mind Damon could only guess. He realized that Sarah was in effect giving Amy the keys to the Schloss.

"I was faced with a sense of leaving behind unfinished business and, with it, despair, but now I see that I may have time to make things right again. How many people get a second chance like mine?"

Amy stood and, completely surprising Damon, bent over Sarah and embraced her. The old woman shied back at first, decades of propriety honing her instincts, but then she extended her wizened arms in return, her paper-thin skin hanging from her bones like dewlap. Tears fell from their eyes. And it wasn't long before Damon joined the chorus of weepers. How could he not? All his prayers had been answered. At least for the moment he thought so.

"Well," Sarah said, wiping her eyes and composing herself. "What would CT think of me now?"

"He would be proud, I'm sure," Damon said.

"Proud of an emotional free-fall?" Sarah said doubtfully, but Damon understood that Sarah was using hyperbole. One last mental portrait of the crusty, hardheaded businessman, CT Fischer, was being laid to rest. A new generation was taking over.

"And now, my dear, I have a party to plan," her lined face brightening and seeming to shed years from her age. "I will call a gathering of the clan to dinner so you can meet everyone. How does that sound?"

"This is all so sudden," Amy said doubtfully. "Couldn't we wait till another day?"

"I told you I have no time to waste."

"All right, but I didn't bring anything dressy to wear."

Sarah cast an appraising eye. "I'll bet you are close to Beth's size. We haven't touched her room since she died and her closet is full of possibilities. You will be a special guest of the Schloss tonight, cocktails and dinner and then you will spend the night in Beth's room. How does that appeal to you?"

Amy looked at Damon for verification. None of this was in the playbook when they left the motel, and to be honest Damon did not have a plan beyond seeing Sarah. As a last resort they could turn themselves in to Lieutenant Harris. But having Amy stay in the Schloss—when it comes to protective custody what better place than right here? He smiled approvingly.

Sarah said, "Damon, you already have your room. So everything is working out, isn't it?" She gathered the folds of her caftan across her lap. "I have things to do," she said. "You two enjoy the rest of the day. Since this is your first visit to the Schloss I think it would be ideal for Damon to show you around. You know the territory by now, Damon. After all, you are writing a family history.

Start out in CT's office. I like the symbolism of that, and then show Amy the rooms that CT designed after the rococo style of Schloss Leopoldskron in Salzburg. My father was very proud of his Austrian heritage. Remember that, my dear: you have Austrian blood in your veins." Sarah stopped talking long enough to savor the thought.

"And when you finish the tour, take the Chris-Craft out for a ride. CT named it *Das Boot*, a name with a ring of authority, what CT liked, what made him a strong leader but," Sarah added with a soft sigh, "not a very patient father. I can hear the engine from my apartment with the windows open. The last time was when you and Beth took the boat out, so I will sit by my window and listen for it."

"Did you ever take it out Mrs. Rand?"

"A woman driving *Das Boot*? No, I rode in it."

"How about now?"

She smiled patiently. "My days on the lake are over, Damon. But I do like to hear the sound of that engine. It brings back fond memories."

"Ok, I'll take her out as soon as we do the tour of the Schloss."

As Sarah began to pull herself to her feet, Amy got her under one arm and helped her up.

"Let me show you the secret door that takes me to my apartment." Using her cane, Sarah walked slowly across the parquet floor to the fake bookcase. She pushed on the frame and the hidden spring released the bookcase door, opening it.

Amy peeked in, duly impressed.

"There once was a circular staircase but I replaced it with an elevator after I got too old to climb stairs. A family secret I now share with you." Sarah smiled benevolently. "After you come back from your boat ride, ask Phillip to call me and I will take you to Beth's room. No one has been in there since…since she passed away. Anyhow, Beth left behind quite a wardrobe."

"Will you help me pick something out?" Amy

asked.

Sarah stepped into the tiny elevator and turned to face them. As the door began to close, she said, "I will be delighted."

25

Amy and Damon climbed aboard the Chris-Craft, their weight bobbing the boat, and they cast off letting it float away from the dock before starting the engine. Damon pushed the starter button and the inboard Chrysler V8 came to life. He gave the engine full throttle as they left the dock to make sure Sarah heard them leave. He really liked the Chris-Craft, not because he was a boater, but because he admired it as a work of art worthy of being in a maritime museum. It was a commuter boat owned by an independent transit company to take passengers from the end of the streetcar line in Excelsior to Wayzata. CT bought the boat when the company went broke and he converted it into a cabin cruiser with a salon, two berths, a galley and a toilet. Made of deep-red mahogany and teak, the boat was 38 feet long, and sported two decks, each with its own windscreen. The upper deck had a canvas cover to protect the bridge where the helm was located. Damon liked standing behind the wheel, enjoying a commanding view of the lake.

Amy sat next to him on the bench. "I have never been on Lake Minnetonka before, only driven past it."

"You don't have a sense of its size till you get on it," Damon said, steering *Das Boot* into the middle of Brown's Bay. There was the usual traffic of a summer's day, sleek cabin cruisers, pontoon boats, an occasional speedboat pulling a skier. He followed the channel markings he had learned from Beth. She knew the lake as she knew the palm of her hand, and Damon kept the Chris-Craft at low rpms because he did not.

"So what do you think of the Schloss now that you've seen the inside?"

"Can I speak frankly?"

"To me? Of course."

"Stuffy."

"I agree with you. It feels and smells like a mausoleum."

"I could never live in it."

"I'm living there, but only temporarily." He looked across the water, back at the receding image of the Schloss roof. "I suppose one can get used to anything."

"Tell me about Beth," Amy said. "Maybe that's why I'm reacting the way I am. Sarah comparing me to her makes me uncomfortable. You and Beth were very close weren't you? Were you lovers?"

"That is a pretty direct question."

"I'm direct. That's what Sarah likes about me, remember?"

"I guess I was waiting for the right time."

"What's wrong with right now? We're alone in the middle of a huge lake."

"Are we having an argument?" Damon asked. "Seems as if we are."

"We don't know each other well enough to have an argument."

"But well enough to talk about our private lives?"

Amy looked across the bay. The heavily wooded shoreline occasionally allowed a glimpse of a large, well-manicured lawn and an impressive house behind it. "Whatever happens to me now, Damon, inexorably involves you. Without you I wouldn't be here and I can't imagine my new life without you in it somewhere, somehow."

"I already told you, we'll see each other at board meetings."

"Don't make me laugh. I didn't buy that the first time you said it and I don't buy it now."

"So you think you and I will have a special relationship?"

"Like you had with Beth?"

The question embarrassed him. Was he a prude, after all, unwilling to talk about his private life especially with someone who was stirring him in ways no other woman ever had? He admitted to himself that, yes, he wished to be with Amy the way he was with Beth, but how do you say so in a way that does not sound self-serving, like a pickup line? And he had to admit to himself that there was so much more than a sexual attraction in his feelings for Amy. "My relationship with Beth has nothing to do with you, Amy."

"Oh yes it does," she said, so firmly it startled him. "Can't you see that? When I was Amy Jacobsson, you could say that your relationship with Beth had nothing do with me. But I'm not a Jacobsson anymore. That woman no longer exists. The person you see now is expected to be the new Beth, according to Sarah, and meet a family who may not like me. That makes me feel really scared. I can't face them alone." She looked at him questioningly. "I need you, Damon. You at least know these people."

They rode on in silence, the rumble of the engine beneath their feet providing the only accompaniment to their thoughts. Amy knew he had been intimate with Beth. He didn't need to admit that. But Amy also knew he was attracted to her, and she needed to hear him say something reassuring, that what he felt for her was unique and not a copy of a former relationship.

Damon could see Amy's consternation. He understood that, along with all the other factors she had to confront, the shadowy figure of Beth was held up for her to emulate.

Beth was dead, for Christ's sake!

He decided their conversation needed what his boss, Troy, would call a decent interval, a change of pace, a diversion, not changing the subject so much as letting it simmer on the stove while waiting for the rest of the meal to be ready.

"Last night, in the motel," he said, "When I asked you how many boyfriends you had, you told me it was none of my business."

She nodded.

"Well, maybe now it is my business."

"So you want me to answer the question? Ok, then, ask me again."

"How many boyfriends have you had?"

"One."

"One?"

"In high school. His name was Tommy Nelson."

"Tommy?" The name did not have the gravity of a full-blown love affair. More like a teenage crush, acne and all.

"So how did you meet?"

"We sat across from each other in biology class and when we had to dissect a frog, the teacher paired us off, two students to a frog."

Damon burst out laughing.

"Why is that funny?"

"A cut up frog does not sound very romantic."

"That is how we got to know each other. He was so shy in fact that I had to ask him for a date."

"Really?"

"To the Sadie Hawkins Day dance. I think he wondered why I would ask him. I was a head taller."

And probably ahead of the girls in beauty, Damon thought. "Why did you ask him?'

"I guess I felt sorry for him. He was really smart, but very shy."

"Did he say yes?"

"He did, and he gave me my first corsage."

"Very gallant." He put the emphasis on the second syllable. "I'll bet there were a lot of guys jealous of Tommy."

Amy did not respond and Damon wondered if he had been too presumptuous.

Finally, she said, "Thinking back, I was shy too. Maybe that's why I dated him, because he was not a threat."

"I don't want to be a threat either, Amy. You believe me don't you?"

She nodded. "Yes, I do."

Nothing more needed to be said, right now anyway, and they relaxed in each other's company, having portaged potential rapids in their relationship. Damon steered the boat into the wide body of water known as Lower Lake with more room to maneuver and he opened the throttle. *Das Boot* picked up speed impressively. Amy stood to let the wind blow through her hair. She was smiling and so was he.

They were so absorbed in their shared moment, in the implicit connection they had made, that they were not aware of a boat with a long antenna and large searchlights coming up their port beam, overtaking them at a steady clip. Only when Amy turned and saw the approaching boat did she react.

"Look, Damon, that boat is coming toward us."

He looked over his shoulder. Printed in large capital letters on a chocolate brown stripe that ran along the hull was the word SHERIFF and in smaller letters Hennepin County. A voice amplified by a bullhorn commanded him to "Cut your engine!"

"Damn," Damon said, wondering why he was being hailed. He wasn't speeding, hell, there were boats flying by him leaving huge wakes. Was this a random check for alcohol? Or had the license expired? No one had taken the boat out in months so maybe that was it. Well, no big deal. Whatever the reason, he throttled back and let the water drag *Das Boot* to a stop.

He turned to check the patrol boat more carefully. A man in a business suit was standing next to the driver, holding onto the windshield to maintain balance. He had a fedora on his head to ward off the sun and it cast a shadow obscuring his face, but there was something about his posture, stern and unforgiving, that rang a warning bell in Damon's head. Staring hard, he finally realized with a sinking feeling that it was Lieutenant Harris, wearing a self-satisfied expression of victory.

"Well, well, well," he said in a mocking tone as the two boats bumped gunwales. "I finally caught up with Bonnie and Clyde."

The driver of the boat, a muscular officer in an orange life vest, reached out with his free hand and held *Das Boot* close enough for Harris to climb aboard.

"Want me to hang around, Lieutenant?" he asked.

"Keep patrolling, Ned, but stay in sight. Never been aboard a Chris-Craft before and I'd like to enjoy it for a while."

The officer pushed away and throttled off, leaving a white-water wake behind him.

The Lieutenant settled himself on the bench seat next to Amy. He checked her over as he would a prize steer. "So this is the damsel in distress."

Amy frowned. "I am not in distress."

"You may not be but your boyfriend sure is."

Damon turned up engine revs slightly to make headway. "How did you find us?"

"Petroulis, you would not even make a lousy armchair detective. Remember I told you we have 24-hour surveillance on that pile of stone you call the Schloss? This morning a strange car was spotted parked in the portico. Didn't look as if it belonged there and the deputy on duty called me. I checked the license and it turns out that the car belongs to a guy named Jim Watson of Bernie and Jim's, a filling station near your digs, right Petroulis? And you also have your car serviced there, even had the brakes repaired after the lines were cut, as I recall.

Anyway, I joined the surveillance team. Eventually we see you walking out on the dock with this young lady and take the Chris-Craft out for a spin. You left a trail a kindergartner could follow."

He turned his attention to Amy and extended his hand for her to shake. "May I introduce myself as the man left stranded in front of your house yesterday afternoon for nearly two hours?"

"How do you do?" she said politely but her eyes expressed concern. She had finally met the officer who was in hot pursuit.

"Better than I was yesterday," Harris replied and then looked at Damon "MPD missed you leaving your apartment by a minute. Where the hell did you go?"

"A motel."

"A motel?" Harris grinned. "Well, you had to hide out someplace, I guess, but I never thought about canvassing motels. I thought you had better scruples."

"What are you talking about?"

"Do I paint a picture like you see at the Art Institute? Shacking up in a motel? Bet her dad won't be happy to hear about that."

"Nothing happened."

"Sure, like Adam didn't touch Eve."

Damon fumed. How could he tell a hardboiled man like Harris about the blanket between them, the inherent innocence of recreating a scene from a movie Harris no doubt knew since he, too, was a fan of 1930s films. Damon glanced at Amy for silent affirmation but all he saw were her cheeks turning crimson from embarrassment.

Harris also read her distress and backed off. "Never mind. What motel was it?"

"The Fair Oaks, across from the Art Institute."

"We'll question the night clerk."

"Don't you believe me?"

"It's not my business to believe, it's my business to verify." He sighed in frustration. "I'm taking you in."

"Where?"

"A holding cell to await arraignment." Harris turned to Amy. "As for you, young lady, I'm taking you back home to have a talk with your mother and father to convince you that you should be under protective custody. I can't force you to do it but maybe your parents can talk some sense into you."

Damon stared through the windscreen at the water, wanting to hit the throttle and turn the boat hard to starboard, flip Harris into the water and let him swim to the patrol boat some hundred yards away.

But while he reflected, Amy acted. She stood up and hovered over Harris, who seemed taken aback. "Do you know who you are taking to?"

He stared in surprise at Amy's abrupt display of power and authority.

"I am a Fischer. Does that mean anything to you? If you arrest Damon, don't you have to arrest me as well—aiding and abetting a fugitive—because I was a willing participant? If you try, I have a feeling the whole damned Fischer establishment will come down on your head. What is Damon being charged with anyway? You implied that he was taking advantage of me, but that is ridiculous. The only thing you can get back at him for is leaving you behind at the ranch. And that probably has more to do with your bruised ego than breaking the law. Come on, Lieutenant, don't you need, what do they call it—probable cause? Well, then tell me what that is."

Harris remained silent, either because he was as surprised as Damon to get what amounted to a tongue-lashing or because he was in awe of this young woman showing maturity well beyond her years.

Damon wondered if this strength of character came from training horses, making them bend to her will. If so, he could only admire her more.

The silent standoff went on for a few more seconds. Finally Harris said, with a hint of sarcasm, the only defense he had left, "Ok, Miss Fischer, whatever you call yourself now, there is no sense dragging this any further. My only concern is about you. All I wanted to do when I followed Damon out to your home was to protect you. At the time I thought he was cooperating with me but he was only playing detective, like Sam Spade or Phillip Marlowe—who knows for sure. My goal is to keep you safe until we find out who killed Beth Rand. All I am asking is that you let me put you in a safe house. We have a comfortable apartment in Wayzata, ten minutes from the Schloss." He waited for a response and when she did not answer he said, "Well, how about it?"

Amy looked at Damon. "What do you think?" she asked.

"Lieutenant," Damon said, "Please, give us until tomorrow. This has been a big day. Amy met Sarah just before we came out on the lake. Everything went incredibly well, if you can imagine meeting your grandmother for the first time, and Sarah is gathering the family for dinner tonight to meet Amy. Let her have that opportunity, won't you? And then tomorrow, I promise, I will bring her to your office. Will you agree to that?"

Harris pushed the brim of his hat up and wiped his forehead with back of his hand. Damon noticed for the first time that the officer was sweating.

"So you want to make a deal."

Damon shrugged. "Call it a compromise."

"Are you going anywhere after the family dinner? I have to know. I'm through chasing you."

"Amy is spending the night at the Schloss. She will be in Beth's old room and I will be in the guest room right next door."

"If you need my help, the closest I can be to the Schloss is right here, on the lake."

"Why would I need your help?"

Harris looked skyward in frustration. "You are at the scene of a crime, remember?"

Damon dismissed the warning. "We'll be fine," he said. "What could possibly happen?"

26

If there were a word to describe the rest of the day that word would be whirlwind, although at any given moment there was no sense of it, only in retrospect. After Harris returned to the patrol boat and sped off, Damon and Amy stayed on the lake for awhile, touring random bays and inlets, looking at real estate and waving at people dangling feet from their docks, sunning on towels, sitting in lawn chairs, not to mention other boaters leisurely spending time on Lake Minnetonka on a pleasant, sunny summer day.

But this was just a prelude to the pressure-filled evening that lay ahead. Returning to the dock, anxiety was also returning for Damon and especially for Amy. They tied up *Das Boot* and walked across the lawn to the terrace doors. Phillip must have seen them coming, either that or he divined their presence, and met them in the Great Hall to escort Amy to her rendezvous with Sarah. Damon waited for Phillip to come back down before he went to his room; well, not exactly *his* room, the guest room to be precise, but being that he was its regular occupant one could readily assume that the room was now his.

"Phillip," Damon said as the butler joined him. "Have you seen Arvid?"

"He returned Sunday afternoon, Mr. Damon."

"Did he say where he was?"

"No, sir, but he seemed the worst for wear."

"What do you mean?"

"He was nursing quite a hangover. He has not made an appearance since."

"Probably holing up."

"That was my impression as well, sir."

Damon showered and walked out of the classic white–and-black tiled bathroom—tossed his towel across the antique quilt and lay on it, letting the breeze from the window dry him off. He didn't realize how exhausted he was and fell asleep only to awaken half an hour later shivering. He yanked the quilt over his body until he warmed up. As he lay quietly, his thought processes revived and he wondered how Amy was doing next door in Beth's old room, how she was managing with Sarah, what she was going to wear. He would find out soon enough.

He got up and stretched his cramped muscles, bending and twisting, lifting his arms over his head and reaching for the ceiling. His body felt older than its years and he let his mind ponder for a moment about getting old, when muscles atrophy, lungs wheeze, brain cells shrink...

He caught himself. The last thing he should do is indulge in self-pity. He shook off the bad vibes and went to the closet to select fresh clothes, enough of wearing two-day-old underwear. He was glad now he had not taken his clothes when he fled the Schloss in anger yesterday.

He studied his meager wardrobe hanging in the closet. When Sara suggested Amy wear something of Beth's at dinner, the implication was not lost on Damon. Better that he dress up, not down, and so he donned tan slacks, a pale blue shirt open at the neck, and a tan linen jacket—as dressy as he could make it. At Schloss Fischer the cocktail hour began at six. Damon knew from experience that Sarah arrived late in order to make a grand entrance. And this time it was going to be the grandest of all, introducing her newly discovered granddaughter—like a coming out party for a debutante, a prescient thought if there ever was one.

He was dressed and ready ten minutes early but rather than spend the time in his room pacing the floor he decided to go downstairs and fortify himself with a drink. Not only that, but also have an opportunity to get the collective pulse of the family members. Damon could only speculate, but he did not think anyone yet knew Amy's special relationship—except for the discrete Phillip and the indiscrete Arvid. There had to be a lot of curiosity when they were suddenly invited to dinner for what Patti Azquith would call "breaking news."

Damon was feeling better, growing more confident as he walked past Beth's—rather Amy's—closed door and down the grand staircase. He had the advantage because he knew the reason for the special dinner. In fact he was the instigator, the guy in charge, no longer the guy taking orders. It was refreshing to see the tables turned. Even Arvid does not yet know that his long-lost daughter was meeting her family for the first time, something he could not negotiate but Damon could, and did.

Damon planned to study their reactions, the looks on their faces. Maybe there will be a slip of the tongue, something incriminating that he can pass on to Harris. Someone was guilty of murder and wouldn't it be great if Damon was the one who broke the case?

He walked past the front entryway and looked out at the portico. Under it was CT-Two's fancy Land Rover and behind it a luxury sedan he recognized as Jon Love's Jaguar XKE. Interesting, he thought, that Sarah invited her lawyer to a family dinner to introduce Amy, certainly a dark implication for Fischer heirs who probably expected a larger share of the financial pie now that Beth was dead.

Anyway, Damon's loaner was gone. Del probably parked the embarrassment behind the garage where it would be out of sight, just like his Buick. Well, who cares? Status isn't what you own, status is what you know before anyone else.

Entering the Venetian Room, Damon joined 'the usual suspects,' to paraphrase Captain Louis Renault, Claude Rains' character in Casablanca—and there was Jon Love standing by the bar mixing a drink. Damon approached the cuddly bear of a man who wore a sport coat of muted plaid, making him look even chubbier.

"Jon," Damon said, "haven't seen you since the funeral."

He turned, holding a scotch and soda. "Great hat," he replied. "The Lady Sarah invited me to dinner. Are you as surprised as I am by my presence?"

Damon smiled as he prepared a gin and tonic, his back to the room. "Sarah never does anything halfway."

"I have a feeling that this is a major event," Jon continued, "as in capital M and capital E. Otherwise I wouldn't be here. What do you make of it?"

"I guess we'll have to wait and see," Damon said noncommittally, but he remembered Jon wondering who would be heir apparent now that Beth was gone. Damon realized that the only reason for Jon to be present was to meet that heir apparent, namely, Amy, Jon's new client, which probably meant a change in Sarah's will. That should stir up some anxiety, Damon thought. He turned to observe two clusters of family members, joined together in their comfort zones—CT-Two with his wife, Ruth, and CT's brother Richard on one side of the room, Crystal and Arvid with Irene leaning on her cane on the other.

Damon turned his attention to the doorway to see Ellen arrive pushing her father in his wheelchair. Dolores was a step behind, her faded beauty a distant memory of her career as a chorus girl. No one talked about her past, of course, nor was it to be mentioned in the family history, but Damon had to laugh privately seeing this as a minor embarrassment compared to everything that had developed since Beth died. He realized also that there could really be no truthful family history any longer. If the family wanted something whitewashed, they'd have to find another writer. So it looked as if his days at the Schloss were indeed drawing to a close, perhaps tonight. Fine with him. He was more than ready to return to the Art Center and resume his job. Time to get in touch with Troy and tell him to give Maggie Bovin her walking papers.

Ellen guided her father to the sideboard where Dolores helped Edmond make his drink, which he held with both bony hands, better to control his tremor. Ellen poured plain quinine water into a lowball glass and sipped it without ice. Her choice seemed to fit her personality, he thought—unimaginative, plain, unadorned. What will this prim and proper person do when she meets a Fischer whose very origin brings shame to the family? Will Ellen accept Amy or will she project the unnatural, willful act of incest onto Amy herself, branding her like Hester Prynne, and judging her to be forever unacceptable? Damon could not imagine Ellen ever accepting Amy for that reason.

He looked them over, the Fischer clan, and wondered who among them had the most to lose with Beth dead, according to Jon Love's provocative comment at the funeral. CT-Two was jealous of the preferential treatment Sarah always gave Beth, but was that reason enough to kill her? Besides, Beth died intestate—who expected her to die so young—which made moot a financial motive. Why Beth died had to be connected somehow to the incestuous relationship between Elizabeth and Arvid. Who knew about this? Arvid, certainly, the perpetrator, and Sarah who hushed it up. Henry must have known as well since he was the recipient of those anguished letters from Elizabeth. There is also Irene, Arvin's mother. What role, if any, did she play in this scenario? What about Phillip, the loyal servant who heard things but said nothing? Even if he was aware, what was his role except keeper of the secret?

My god, what a tangled mess.

Arvid joined him and said in a low voice. "Did Amy get in touch with you?"

When Arvid said that, Damon knew he had no clue as to the reason for the dinner. He nodded. "Saturday at the Art Center."

"Did you tell her I'm her father?"

"She knows." And a lot more than that, Damon thought. He wondered how this evil man could have a clear conscience knowing that Amy's mother, Elizabeth, was his first cousin.

"By the way, where were you Saturday? I called you from the Art Center and Phillip said you were coming into town to see me but you didn't. What happened?"

Arvid leaned in and lowered his voice. "I used you as an excuse. I didn't want anyone to know where I was going."

"Where were you going?"

"To see Jon Love."

"Jon Love?" Damon asked, surprised.

"Shhh...I don't want anyone to know." He looked around nervously. "I can't talk about this now. I'll tell you later."

Arvid walked off, leaving Damon alone to puzzle over what was said. He must have looked like a lost soul because Richard spotted him and came over. "Cheers," he said, raising his glass.

Damon returned the gesture and sipped.

"I got back from the Club an hour ago and Phillip said that we all had to show up for dinner. I have a date tonight. Damned inconvenient. Wonder what the fuss is all about."

"Fuss?"

"Something is up. You can feel it in the air. I noticed that *Das Boot* was not tied up in her usual berth. Someone took her out. That surprised the hell out of me. Sarah never lets anyone use it since Beth died."

"Oh, I took her out for awhile."

Richard arched his brows in surprise. "Alone?"

Damon realized he had said too much. "Just for a spin. I didn't pay attention to what post I tied her to."

"That only deepens the mystery, Damon. Granny let you use *Das Boot*. What am I missing?"

"Why don't you ask her? She'll be here any moment." *And so will the answer to your question,* Damon said to himself.

The atmosphere in the room was one of nervous anticipation. Everyone sensed that Sarah was going to make a major announcement, like the evening she told the family that Damon would move into CT's old office. That was bad enough, but what was coming up was a bolt of lightning by comparison.

Attention shifted to the doorway and the room fell silent. Damon turned expecting to see Sarah and Amy but it was Madie and Mrs. Stockton who arrived. Madie was greeted with an inordinate amount of fussy attention, exaggerated greetings reserved more for children than adults. And why not, Madie was very childlike and what she wore proved the point, a frilly pastel pink dress puffed out at the hem with several layers of white lace. Across her front was a white organdy apron tied in back with a large bow. And she wore white gloves. If she had a staff and a few sheep, she would look like Little Bo Peep, who in children's books was slender and cute, not formless and plain like Madie. The whole ensemble was glaringly inappropriate but everyone oohed and aahed as though programed. Damon could not help but wonder how Beth would have reacted.

He always believed that Madie, though simple-minded, had another side, that of an idiot savant who was cleverer than she was given credit for. Perhaps she dressed in this manner to upstage her grandmother. Damon had the uncanny feeling that Madie knew something major was coming up and wanted, in her own odd-duck way, to participate.

Standing quietly beside Madie, Mrs. Stockton was beaming as though enjoying the attention vicariously. She was an enigma to Damon, a person who got attention simply by avoiding it, a contradiction but nevertheless accurate. Mrs. Stockton had no personality, no *raison d'etre* for her existence other than taking care of Madie. As if to prove the point, she wore a severe dress—the only way to describe it—a one-piece black frock with a low hem and sleeves down to the wrists as though she were defying summer.

It was ironic, with the cloying attention being paid Madie, that Damon was the first to see Sarah and Amy making their grand entrance. The moment was brief however because the shock waves came quickly and persistently. A stunned silence hung over the room. There were no audible sounds, but there was no doubt that Amy's appearance with Sarah leaning on her arm sent shockwaves through the group.

It was not only the sudden appearance of an attractive stranger who bore an uncanny resemblance to Beth, but also what she was wearing—one of Beth's dresses. And not just any dress in her extensive wardrobe. This one everyone recognized—even Damon who saw it the night months ago when Beth put it on in the privacy of the guest bedroom. She meant to seduce him and it worked—the gown Beth wore for her coming out party, the debutante ball at the Lafayette Club when she turned eighteen.

That Sarah chose this particular dress was intended to convey a strong message to the family—Amy is someone special, someone deemed important enough to wear Beth's coming-out costume. It was as though this young woman herself was coming out, not as a debutante but as successor to the throne, if you will, the throne Beth was destined to occupy had she not died.

Looks of confusion spread through the group. However, since this mystery woman was in the company of Sarah, everyone learned from childhood that one did not speak unless spoken to, and waited with polite anticipation for Sarah to explain everything.

Nevertheless, there was a whisper loud enough to be heard by all: "Who is she? Why is she wearing Beth's gown?"

If anyone knew the answer it was Arvid, whom Damon was keeping a close eye on. Arvid stood frozen in place, keeping his emotions, which had to be running rampant, in check. But Damon gave him credit at least for not shouting, "My daughter, Amy!" or some such reaction as one would expect in a soap opera.

Even though Damon was prepared to be surprised, he was not prepared for the impact of Amy's beauty. Up till now he saw her as a cowgirl, attractive in a boyish way, as though she could pitch hay as easily as any male, only sexier, but now the impact of her femininity came through, and he realized that she was strikingly beautiful— no, breathtakingly beautiful, and none of this was lost on anyone else.

The silk dress that caused the stir would look stunning even hanging in a closet. It was a slender style reminiscent of the twenties, stopping at mid-calf with an uneven hemline that dipped and rose like a wave. The gown was blue, as blue as a lagoon, a blue that defied description, deep yet shimmery, a color that subtly changed as Amy walked, her arm extended so that Sarah could hold it. The grandmother who was not comfortable being upstaged did not seem to mind.

Sarah was also finely attired. Damon had never seen her in anything other than one of her flowered caftans, but now she was wearing what a diplomat's wife would reserve for state occasions, including a diamond-studded broach and necklace. And, who knows, as a young girl, Sarah may have worn something similar to grand affairs in Europe. After all, her father was ambassador to Austria during the Coolidge administration.

"Everyone!" Sarah announced as the pair came to a stop mid-room. "This is Amy Jacobsson, a long-lost relative I want you to meet."

The word relative not to mention the phrase, long-lost, startling and unexpected, created a low rumble of murmurs like 5.1 on the Richter scale, not enough to run out of the building but nevertheless unnerving. The only one not so affected was Arvid who, now that Amy was introduced, was smiling as only a proud father could. Damon scanned the others. CT-Two planted his feet as though warding off a blow. Next to him Ruth drained her glass, sensing a fissure in the Fischer hierarchy. Richard had the look of someone still taking in the information and not able to process it, as if his twin sister had been resurrected. Either that or life was playing a cruel trick on him. Henry, hiding in back as was his wont, peeked around Arvid's taller head, curious but not enough to reveal what was going on inside his own. Ellen gripped the handles of her father's wheelchair, draining the color from her knuckles. And Irene, standing in the rear next to Henry, was dividing her attention between Ellen and Amy as though comparing the two.

But the most interesting reaction was from Madie who stared as if she had seen a ghost. Among the family members, Beth was closest to Madie and perhaps she was seeing Amy as an apparition, fascinating yet frightening. Perhaps having Madie come to the Venetian Room was a mistake. Too bad no one thought about this in advance. Beth would have.

"I don't get this Granny," CT-Two said. "Whose relative?"

"Yours."

He chuckled nervously. "I know all of them, Granny, unless you have been holding out on me."

"To my regret, CT, I have been holding out on you. As an infant Amy was given up for adoption, a secret I have kept from the family for almost 30 years, but the time has come to correct this mistake. I do not look back upon my long-ago decision with pride, however my hope is that by bringing Amy to her rightful place within the family I have redeemed myself, at least to some extent."

The high-toned speech took everyone by surprise. Except for Arvid, the collective look from the Fischers was one of confusion, even resentment.

Damon was impressed that Amy continued to maintain her composure in what was becoming a hostile atmosphere. Nevertheless he felt enough concern to walk over and stand by her opposite Sarah. Amy touched his arm in a gesture of appreciation.

CT was the first to find his voice. "If you kept this from us all these years, Granny, what changed your mind?"

"I did not change my mind, it was done for me. And once you understand everything I'm sure you will accept Amy as I have, without reservation, and love her as you did Beth."

"Beth?" CT stormed "You bring a stranger into our home and you want us to compare her to Beth?"

"Shut up, CT!" Arvid shouted. Everyone turned to see who was so brazen as to shout like that—no one ever raised his voice in Schloss Fischer.

CT made a big show of turning slowly, mimicking what he thought was an air of superiority. "What right do you have talking to me like that?"

"I have every right," Arvid replied, pausing for emphasis, "because Amy is my daughter."

The room stilled. Not even ice tinkled in a cocktail glass. Arvid and Amy traded long stares, examining one another for the first time, father and daughter.

CT emptied his glass before responding. "I was wondering whose kid she was. She has to be the reason you disappeared, Arvid. And who did you knock up? Clearly someone who, if found out, would create a big scandal. Is that why Granny sent you packing?"

"For god's sake, CT," Ruth said, trying to quell her husband's outburst. She looked apologetically at Sarah. "Sorry, Granny, he's had too much to drink."

"I haven't had enough!" CT said and headed to the

sideboard for replenishment.

The atmosphere in the room was now like a burbling volcano, capable of erupting at any moment.

Sarah straightened her arthritic frame as far as she was able, an aged tigress gathering up her waning energy, and patted Amy on her arm. "My apologies, my dear, for assuming my family had better manners." She sighed. "I suppose it was too much to ask, introducing you in this manner. But CT, you are correct. I was responsible for all that happened." Then Sarah went on to explain how she arranged, both monetarily and legally, to have the Jacobssons raise Amy as their daughter—not that far away really, on a horse farm in Rogers.

"At that time I thought I was doing the right thing. I see now it was a mistake." Sarah looked at Amy, her eyes begging forgiveness.

This remarkable apology caused a moment of group reflection. Could she actually be mellowing in her old age? They had never before witnessed a mea culpa from a woman who never forgave anyone, least of all herself. This introspective pause gave Arvid the opening he was looking for, a moment of sympathy, of compassion even, a pathway to compress a quarter of a century into a few short steps. He approached the daughter he had never before seen, not even in infancy, another remarkable moment in an evening filled with them, and kindled speculation whether or not they would embrace. Alas, it was not to be. A reunion of this magnitude demanded privacy, not an audience of staring onlookers. The two stood a foot apart like awkward teenagers on their first date.

"I'm sorry we had to meet like this in front of everybody," Arvid said, bending his lanky frame in a gesture of welcome. "I'm very happy that Damon brought you to the Schloss."

The tenderness ended abruptly as CT's voice exploded like a gunshot aimed at Damon. "So *you* are behind this? While digging through our private records, you learned about the adoption, right? It fit perfectly in your a plan to weasel your way into the family, just the way you were using Beth."

CT's harsh accusation bounced around the room like a bat.

"Your imagination is working overtime, CT," Damon said.

"Really? You were sleeping with Beth to make her pregnant so she would have to marry you to avoid a scandal. And now that Beth is dead you'll probably try the same thing with this girl—marry a Fischer and take control." CT looked at his grandmother. "Can't you see what he is doing, Granny?"

"All I see, CT, is someone acting in a way unbecoming of the name Fischer. If you are so concerned about control, try it on yourself."

But CT was not to be denied his moment. "Look at them Granny! Arvid and his daughter are puppets and Damon is the puppeteer."

"Stop talking nonsense!"

The forceful comment stilled the room. Everyone turned toward the source: Ellen, unbelievably, standing next to her father's wheelchair, fingers to her mouth. Edmond reached out and put his arm around her waist, an instinctive reaction to support Ellen in case she fainted but he could not help her even if she did. Crystal came over and stood by just in case.

Ellen's face turned crimson as everyone stared at her. Having undivided attention was more than she could handle. Always the shrinking violet, she now had made herself the blue ribbon rose.

CT stared at his cousin. "If you want to know the truth, Ellen, I *am* blaming Arvid for everything that has happened since he came back. Beth dies, Damon takes over CT's office, and then this strange woman shows up and claims she is my cousin. Do you think all of this is a coincidence?"

Damon watched for reactions to CT's damning

words. What caught his attention was the look on Madie's face. She was actually grinning—what he might imagine spectators in the Coliseum would do watching gladiators fight to the death. Mrs. Stockton even let her lips part in a smile of satisfaction as though pleased that her charge was having a good time even though it was at someone else's expense.

The whole thing was surreal. Damon began to wonder whether bringing Amy into this maelstrom was a good idea after all.

Crystal was rubbing Ellen's back soothingly. "This has been an emotional time," she said. "We all need to take a step back."

"But CT has a point, Granny," Richard dared to say. "The way you came in and made a big show of introducing her," he pointed with his head, clearly not willing or able to call Amy by her name. "It looks to me like you want her to be the new Beth. And you don't even know her!"

There were nods of agreement.

"This character assassination has got to stop!" Sarah shouted, and it took all of her energy. "I have to sit down."

Just about everyone rushed for a chair, wanting to be the first to help the old lady out. But it was Amy, who pulled a chair over for Sarah to sit on.

"Thank you my dear," the old woman said, almost whispering.

Rather than accepting Sarah's appreciation, Amy came over and stood next to Damon, separating herself from Sarah as well as the Fischer clan, a symbolic move to express her irritation. It was clear she had had enough. "I know how hard you tried to make this work, Granny." She looked around at the group, meeting their eyes with her own. "You all act as though I'm contagious. Well, if you were to ask me, I'd say you are the ones who are contagious, and whatever the disease you have—jealousy, fear, anger—whatever it is, I don't want to catch it."

Clearly Amy no longer gave a damn whether or not she was a Fischer. She turned her attention back to Sarah. "I should change back into my regular clothes and go back to my horses. They are much nicer to be with."

The insult struck home. Sheepish looks, some downcast, pervaded the room. CT swallowed what was left of his drink but Damon could tell the flush on his cheeks was more than just booze.

"Please don't leave," Ellen said, stepping away from her father's wheelchair. Damon was amazed to see her come forward, totally out of character, and giving voice to what everyone else was thinking "This is all so sudden, none of us has had a chance to take it in. We tend to be a critical family, defensive, over-protective, even mean, and I know how that feels. I've taken the brunt of criticism often enough. You are a fighter, Amy. I can see that. I wish I had been more like you."

Seeing Ellen stand up for herself like this was such a surprise it served to take the attention off Amy and concentrate it on Ellen, the last thing she wanted. The stares of surprise, certainly not criticism, drove her from the room. She headed for the terrace, leaving her father in his wheelchair and everyone else in a state of shock, including Damon. What shocked him more, however, was seeing Arvid, after a moment's hesitation, chase after her. Through the window, Damon saw him embrace Ellen, say something to her and together they walked away toward the dock and out of sight. Damon wished he could eavesdrop. He had never before noticed any interaction between them. Interesting, he thought, quite interesting.

With Arvid gone, Damon took the opportunity to approach Jon, who had kept himself discretely in the background, observing the family histrionics like someone watching a performance on a thrust stage, close to the action but not part of it.

"Jon," Damon said, "can I talk to you?"

"Gladly," Jon said, "I could use a break from the action." Damon followed him to the bar where the two refreshed their drinks. Jon turned to observe the family standing quietly, the atmosphere subdued now, waiting for a sign from Sarah.

"Arvid just told me he came to see you Saturday," Damon said in a low voice so as not to be overheard.

Jon nodded. "Family matters." He looked around, not wanting to say more. "Remember at the funeral when I told you to find the person who had the most to lose? Look at them. They have broken into factions, intent on self-destruction."

"That's the problem. They all look like losers."

Just then, Sarah pulled herself to her feet.

"I refuse to let this evening completely go to ruin," she announced with renewed determination. "I am going to have dinner and, if I have to, dine alone." Without help Sarah started walking across the floor to the adjoining dining room.

For another moment everyone remained frozen, as if each was wondering, who among us is going to help Granny? None of them seemed willing to take on that responsibility—with one exception, surprising everyone: Amy.

"I will join you," she said and took Sarah by the arm. As they walked toward the dining room, one by one, the rest of the family followed suit, creating a shuffling image of a chain gang, less the chains, walking in lockstep. Bringing up the rear was Ellen's father, Edmond, whose wheelchair was duly taken over by Arvid's wife, Crystal.

Phillip stood by the door as they filed through.

"Phillip," Sarah said as she walked by him, "please go out to the dock and tell Arvid and Ellen that dinner is being served."

27

"What changed your mind?" Damon asked Amy, as they sat alone on the terrace following dinner, watching the sun laying itself to rest behind the western horizon.

He was recalling her complete turnaround by joining Sarah and the others at dinner. Sitting around together at the dinner table, served by Karl and Hettie with Phillip in the wings brought a semblance of normality to the clan. A truce, if you will, meaning that no one had changed his or her mind but, for the time being, put down their weapons to do battle later. They made the effort to enjoy dinner and each other, even welcoming the newcomer in their midst without rancor. Idle talk prevailed—How was your tennis match today, Richard? Anything new at the office, CT? What makes Arabians different from other horses, Amy?

Damon was looking out at the large expanse of immaculately manicured lawn when Amy answered him: "I didn't want to be the one who ruined Granny's evening. I didn't want the others to feel they had won."

"They didn't."

"I'm not so sure. Just because dinner went well doesn't mean they like me."

"They will have to like you."

"Tolerate maybe, but not like me."

"Except Ellen, surprisingly. She admires you. Remember she said she wished she had been more like you when she was young?"

Amy nodded. "Ellen seems so trapped, taking care of her father like that. They have all the money in the world, so why does she devote her life to taking care of him? She acts like a servant. By the way, what happened to Edmond's wife? Did she die?"

"All I know is that she left Edmond about the time Ellen was born. I don't know anything more, whether or not she is even alive."

"The family is one great big riddle, isn't it?"

"Jon said that if I find out who has the most to lose, I will find out who killed Beth or, as he put it, did her in, but the more I dig the more confused I get."

They fell silent for a time. Finally Amy said, "Maybe I can help you."

"How?"

"Help you with your research."

Damon smiled at the thought of Amy joining forces with him. "Lieutenant Harris would have cardiac arrest."

"Not if we solve the crime."

Damon was intrigued. If nothing else, this would keep her close to him. However, as he looked at her wearing a dress once worn by Beth, a wave of déjà vu washed over him.

"He doesn't think it's even safe for you to be here."

"At least you can show me what you are working on."

"Ok," he said, thinking there was no harm in that. "Follow me."

Damon closed the door to CT's office, now his workplace. He didn't want anyone coming down the hall and finding Amy there with him. It would certainly ruffle feathers.

The rectangular conference table in the center of the room, under the antique rococo chandelier, held the records Damon was examining. Amy began leafing through them as one would casually, not looking for anything in particular. She came across a photo album and opened it. She stopped to look at a page.

"Here is Sarah when she was young. The man with her, is that CT?"

Damon was sitting at the big roll-top desk looking at his lined pad filled with notes. "If his eyes are burning that is CT."

"They are burning, all right."

"He did not suffer fools gladly, or anyone else for that matter."

Amy kept turning pages. "Who is this?"

Damon got up and joined her. "That's Beth."

"Pretty."

Damon fell silent for a moment. "Yes, she was."

"You were...close, weren't you?"

He might as well admit what everyone else knew. "Yes."

"Were you in love with her?"

"Sarah hoped we were," he said without answering directly. "Her wish was that we would end up together. She imagined Beth and me carrying on her legacy."

"How did you feel about that?"

"Uncomfortable."

"You are more comfortable in a gallery filled with abstract art, aren't you?'

Damon laughed. "Much easier than figuring out the Fischers." He went back to his notes. "Are you interested in going over some of this stuff?" he asked.

"I'm having more fun looking at these old photos."

For a time, all was quiet except the dry sound of

old paper being handled. Every now and then Amy slanted a page so the chandelier lights did not reflect off it. "Are there pictures of Elizabeth?"

"There are some loose photos that I haven't been able to identify. She might be in one of those, but otherwise Elizabeth remains a mystery."

"You said Beth looked a lot like her."

"That's what I was told."

"She was my mother. What do you know about her?"

"I have letters she wrote to Henry when she was pregnant. Let me find them." Damon sorted through one of his stacks. "Here they are." He handed them to Amy. "Elizabeth wrote these when she was sent away to have an abortion, but Henry convinced Sarah otherwise."

Damon went back to the roll top desk while Amy slowly read the letters, holding each as though she was handling ancient parchment. "What a sad story," she said after reading them. "If it weren't for Henry I wouldn't be here."

"Maybe that's why Sarah is so solicitous of you. She must feel guilty and is trying to make amends."

Amy shook her head in dismay. "I wonder why there are no photos of Elizabeth like there are of everyone else. Is it because of what she did? She shamed the Fischers so badly they wanted to eradicate her from the face of the earth by destroying any photographs of her?"

"I wouldn't put it past them," Damon said from the roll top desk. He was silent for moment, then got up and rejoined Amy at the conference table. "Wait a second, don't put them away yet."

He looked through the letters as though examining them for fingerprints.

"What are you looking for?"

"I just had a thought, probably a wild one but let me check it out." Damon pulled over a stack of files and began going through them. He selected a manila folder whose label read Transactions. "CT invested in property in northern Minnesota and toward the end of his life he started selling it off. He once owned practically all of Backus. Sometimes he would turn a plot of land over to the family with a quitclaim deed so he could avoid paying taxes on the sale. He spread it around, a building here, forty acres there. Signatures were required, of course, witnessed by a notary public. CT was pretty shrewd."

Damon leafed through several documents and then pulled one out and removed the paper clip. "Here it is, a parcel of land CT gave to Ellen in 1927." He laid one of Ellen's letters next to it. "Check them out."

Amy bent closer. "What am I looking for?"

"Compare Ellen's signature on the deed with the handwriting on the letter."

"Looks the same."

"Exactly. Elizabeth did not write those letters, Ellen did. All this time, I just assumed that E stood for Elizabeth. It didn't. It stood for Ellen."

"You mean Ellen wrote the letters?"

"The handwriting matches."

"Then who is my true mother, Ellen or Elizabeth?"

Damon shook his head in doubt. "I don't know."

"If it is Ellen, why didn't she tell me?" Amy's words were laced with frustration and disappointment.

"She may have, in her own way," Damon replied, "when she called you a fighter and wished she was like you when she was young."

"So you think that was her way of saying, I'm your mom?"

"That she said as much as she did is remarkable."

"Someone owes me the truth and I won't be satisfied till I hear it."

28

It was nearing midnight when they finally wrapped up, so absorbed in the collection of memorabilia and Damon's pages of notes that they did not realize how late it was.

Damon pulled the cover of CT's roll top desk down, the wood slats, dry and aged, making angry noises as if resenting being moved at all.

"Now you know as much as I do about the Fischers," he said, as he opened the door and shut the room lights.

"Spooky," Amy said softly, looking out into the gloom.

"The Fischers or the Schloss?"

"Both."

They stepped into the carpeted hallway. Low glows of illumination filtered from sconces on the wall. They stopped at Beth's, now Amy's, bedroom.

"Whose room is that?" Amy asked in the same soft voice, pointing to the door across from hers.

"Madie's."

"She's right across the hall from me?"

"That's the way Beth wanted it."

Amy put her hand on the gilded doorknob but did

not turn it, becoming thoughtful. "You said she collects stuffed animals."

"The place is packed with them. I saw them the night when I was looking for Beth, the night she died."

"I'd love to see them."

"Now?"

"Why not? We could do what you did, just look in."

"What if she wakes up?"

"You took that chance the last time, didn't you?" she said. "I'm dying to see her room."

"Don't use that word."

"Ok, but this is the only time we can do it." She was filled with the excitement of doing something daring.

Even though cautious, Damon was as intrigued as she was, not to see Madie's childish obsession again but rather to share the experience with Amy, a moment that would bond them in a common secret and tighten his relationship with her.

"All right but be careful."

Slowly he turned the knob as he did the night Beth died, and pushed the paneled oak door inward, just far enough to look in. He remembered that she slept like the dead, an unfortunate simile he realized as he heard the heavy snoring—everything was as it was the night Beth died, except for Amy. He got the jitters thinking about it.

As their eyes focused in the semi-dark they saw stuffed animals of every size, color and description: big ears, floppy ears, bug eyes, flat eyes, bulbous noses, little noses, lumpy paws, round bellies, furry bodies—dozens and dozens of stuffed creatures sitting on shelves, overflowing the dresser top and the window ledge, leaning against the wainscoting, sitting on the floor in groupings.

As Amy stared in awe at this scene of super indulgence, a large shapeless mass shifted on the bed and the snoring stopped. They held their breath, concerned Madie would awaken, see their shadowy forms in the doorway and, in all likelihood, let out a scream that would arouse the entire household. Damon drew back into the hallway but Amy, transfixed, stayed where she was as Madie slowly roused herself, looked toward the door and stared at Amy. As the seconds ticked Damon expected the worst but Madie simply said, "Beth, is that you?"

Realizing she had to play the role in order not to frighten Madie, Amy answered, "Yes," and withdrew from the doorway.

Damon kept his hand on the knob until Madie settled back down on the mattress and her snoring recommenced. Then he closed the door.

"Whew, that was close," Amy whispered as they stepped across the hallway to her bedroom. She looked at Damon, a bit shaken. "Come in for a minute, will you?"

They stepped inside. Amy flipped the wall switch that turned on the bed lamps and twin floor lamps flanking the fireplace, creating a ghostly glow. She looked around and shivered.

"Are you all right?"

"She thought I was Beth."

"It was an awkward moment but you handled it well."

"I had to answer her, reassure her so she wouldn't yell out or something. But it was so weird, pretending to be Beth. I hope her spirit wasn't watching."

"You've been through a lot."

"It's been an adventure, believe me." Amy stood close to Damon, needing reassurance. "You were probably right, we should not have peeked into her room."

"It's done now. My guess is she won't remember, and if she does she will probably recall it as a dream."

"I hope so." She leaned into him, still shaken.

Damon put his arms around her waist. Holding her this way, it was perfectly natural to take the next step and he did. He pulled her body toward his. As tall as she was, he barely had to bend his head to reach her lips with his. She did not resist. In fact, she was more than cooperative and they stood this way, clinging to one another, kissing one another, creating expectations for one another that lasted a long time but not as long as Damon wished. Finally they separated and stared into each other's eyes, as though they had crossed from one dimension to another in their relationship.

"I didn't expect this to happen," she said.

"At all?"

"Not so soon."

"I'm glad it did."

"So am I."

They stopped talking, searching for what to say next, what to do next.

"I think we better say goodnight," she said.

"There is no curtain between us," Damon replied, referring not to 'It Happened One Night' but the night it happened to them.

"There is a wall," she said.

Damon pointed with his head. "And a door."

Amy looked. "I thought that was a closet."

"It connects the two bedrooms."

"Yours and mine?"

He nodded.

Amy was thoughtful for a bit. "So that is the door you and Beth…"

"Yes" Damon interrupted.

"Your room or hers?"

"Mine."

Amy didn't say anything but he knew what she was thinking.

"As long as we were in my room," he said, "the family looked the other way."

"What about you and me?"

"They would look the other way as well."

"Is that an invitation?"

Damon stirred, the pleasant feeling he was sleeping with disrupted. He rolled to his right and extended his arm expecting his fingers to touch Amy's shoulder. Instead they met only a folded-back coverlet and her mashed pillow. He pulled himself up and leaned against his own pillow, puzzled and a little alarmed. He checked the dial on the illuminated clock on the nightstand—four thirty-five, not long to sunup. He turned sideways and let his feet hang over the edge of the nineteenth century antique bed, one of CT's acquisitions when he furnished the house nearly a century ago. But Damon's mind was not on that but rather on where Amy was, and it only served to stir up memories of the night he was similarly awakened when Beth got out of bed, put on sweatpants and shirt as she explained to a sleepy Damon that she would be gone only a few minutes, long enough to make sure Madie was resting comfortably.

He shook his mind back to the present, chastising himself for letting his imagination run rampant. Amy must have gone back to her own room, not wanting the rising sun to find her in bed with Damon, daylight being the kiss of death for clandestine romance. Now why did he think of that?

He got up and went to the door separating their rooms and opened it. The half-light of a slowly gathering dawn revealed an unmade bed—and the dress Amy wore at dinner lying across it, the beginning of their trail of love-making. Her suitcase was on the floor by the bed, the top open and leaning against the mattress. Amy must have dressed and gone out, the only explanation that made sense. But where did she go?

He returned to his room, his own clothing draped over the back of a Windsor chair by the expanse of windows. He put on his shirt and trousers and walked barefoot into the hallway, glancing right and left before proceeding to CT's office, thinking that Amy, unable to sleep, returned to look again at the photographs that had so haunted her. He went inside, but it was dark and still. Then he padded down the wide staircase to the Great Hall, and walked through the grand rooms CT had proudly decorated to replicate his Austrian heritage. But now, in the pre-dawn dimness, the spaces were curiously melancholy, and Damon realized that human presence defines a room, illuminates its character and expands its dimensions, like the stage in a darkened theatre—devoid of feeling until actors bring it to life.

Not finding Amy anywhere and growing more worried by the second, he returned to the Great Hall and went outside to the terrace. He stood on the cold flagstone, taking in the expanse of property that CT had grabbed in one of his numerous land deals, Breckett's Point, pristine and private, one of the best locations anywhere on lake Minnetonka, a perquisite of the Fischer fortune. He took in the slowly emerging outlines of trees, shrubs, flowerbeds and, beyond, the boathouse and the Chris-Craft tied to the dock. He stopped, wondering where to search next, when he heard a splash. He tensed, the sound drawing him like a dragline back to the night Beth died. The memory of pulling her lifeless body from the lake spurred him to action. He took off across the broad lawn, the dewy grass underfoot, as he ran pell-mell toward the lake. He rounded the boathouse and jumped onto the dock whose boards, weathered gray, were slippery and he nearly slid into the water himself when he saw Amy sitting at the end of the dock, her back to him.

She turned and waved. "Good morning." She had taken off her shoes and was splashing with her feet.

He reached her breathless. "My god, I was looking all over for you. What are you doing here?"

"I'm an early bird. Back home I get up with the horses, so I decided to come down to the lake. It's beautiful. You were sleeping so soundly I didn't want to wake you. I'm sorry. I thought I'd be back before you woke up."

Damon's breathing returned to normal. He was in his bare feet anyway, and so he rolled up his pants to his knees and sat down next to her. They splashed together and watched the sun come up.

*****

Damon and Amy were at breakfast in the Venetian Room, serving themselves from the buffet. Richard showed up on his way to the Club for a cup of coffee and a croissant, but otherwise they had the place to themselves. Damon thought it was a sinful extravagance to prepare a full buffet for so few people. That's the way the Fischers were, never do anything by halves.

They were on their second cup of coffee when Phillip came in. "Mr. Damon," he said, "there is a phone call for you."

"Shall I take it here?"

"I think you would be better off taking it in the Great Hall."

Damon excused himself and walked to the telephone next to the main entrance. "Good morning," he said rather than hello to reflect how wonderful he felt.

"This is Harris."

Damon felt his heart pump a stroke faster. Why would Harris call him this early in the morning? To make sure he was still alive?

"So what can I do for you?"

"Just pay attention. I have news about Arvid Campbell."

"What about him?"

"Do you want it in the past or present tense?"

Damon was losing patience. Clearly Harris was toying with him. "What are you talking about? He was at dinner last night when everyone met Amy."

"That was last night. This is now. Campbell is in the county morgue."

"*What?*" Damon said, reeling like someone who had walked into a wall.

Harris segued, "Early this morning, Campbell was spotted by a fisherman trolling close to shore. He was lying face down with a rope around his neck. Crows were picking at his body. Lots of little holes poked into him."

"Jesus, Lieutenant, do you have to be so graphic?"

"You're the art guy, I thought you liked description," he replied caustically. "Tell Sarah Rand the party is over. I am no longer walking on eggshells to please that old shrew. I am coming over this afternoon with deputies to get statements from everybody. I want to find out where they were when Campbell was killed."

Damon went to the pantry and found Phillip sitting at the table where the help ate their meals. He was having a cup of coffee.

"That was Harris."

Phillip nodded. "I knew that, sir."

"He called about Arvid." Damon stopped, anticipating a reaction of some kind, a look of curiosity at least, but Phillip only stirred his coffee.

Finally Damon said, "His body was found along the shore this morning by a fisherman. He was strangled."

Phillip slowly set his spoon on the saucer. "I was

afraid something bad happened. Mr. Campbell went out for a walk after dinner. And that is the last I saw him."

He looked up at Damon, his eyes filled with profound sadness. The protected world he had known for the last thirty-five years was collapsing around him.

*****

Damon rejoined Amy in the Venetian Room. He poured himself a fresh cup of coffee. His fingers trembled, clattering the cup on the saucer.

"What's the matter?"

He sat down next to her. "Harris called."

"I can see from your face that he didn't have good news. Is he going to arrest you after all?"

"I wish that was it." He turned to face her. "Arvid was found dead this morning. A fisherman spotted him."

"Arvid?" she asked in disbelief. "Dead?"

"He was strangled."

"Oh my god."

No words came for a while, the shock was too great. They were both unable to give voice to what was going through their minds, that madness was running rampant on Breckett's Point.

Presently, Amy shook herself as though coming out of a trance. She began to speak, softly, slowly.

"I should feel some emotion other than fear shouldn't I?" she asked. "He was my father, but I never knew him. He was nothing to me until a few days ago, and now he's dead. How do you reconcile something like that? Shouldn't I be crying, shouldn't I feel grief? Even guilt? Damon, I don't feel anything."

He put his arm around her shoulders to comfort her but she did not bend her body toward him, still struggling with her unique quandary.

"We were going to meet this morning after breakfast, just the two of us, and talk. What if he was planning to make amends? What if he was hoping to redeem himself, ask forgiveness? I wish I could have had a conversation with him other than sitting around a dinner table with a crowd of people. But now I will never know what he would have said."

"I know this is not easy for you, Amy, but we have to get ready. Harris is on his way over and all hell will break loose. Before he shows up I have to tell Sarah. Do you want to come with me?"

Amy thought it over, then shook her head. "You better go alone. I'll wait for you here."

Damon took Sarah's private elevator, hidden behind the fake bookcase, to her apartment. She was expecting him; Phillip had called ahead. This was the first time he had been to her private residence, the floor above the library. The elevator opened to a small vestibule and he emerged from that into a world he'd never seen before, the world of a person fading from life. He could not help but be reminded of Norma Desmond's house in Sunset Boulevard.

The apartment was heavy laden, the only way Damon could describe it, with the *accoutrements* typical of the Victorian era—carved tables, pedestals, cabinets, chairs, ottomans, wall hangings, and thick drapes drawn against the rising sun. Sarah had only two floor lamps on. They were made of heavy brass with opaque shades, providing the only illumination except for a gooseneck lamp on a table next to the easy chair Sarah occupied. The focused light from the lamp made her look like a figure in a chiaroscuro painting.

"Sit down," she said.

Damon sat across from her in a high-backed throne chair with a cushion of brocaded silk which should have been in a period room at the Art Institute. It creaked when he settled into it.

Sarah remained in remote silence for a time, letting Damon survey her apartment a bit further. He noticed on the wall behind her a stunning group of miniature landscape paintings dating from the Renaissance. Which Fischer is going to inherit those, he wondered?

"You have some news—bad news or you wouldn't have come up here."

"It's about Arvid." Damon knew that mincing words with Sarah only angered her and so he was direct. "He's dead, killed sometime last night. He went out for a walk, following the shoreline apparently, and was found early this morning by a fisherman."

He expected to see her react with shock but she simply sighed.

"I'm sorry," he said.

"For whom? Arvid? He was no good. What I am concerned about is more scandal—screaming headlines, snoopy television crews, neighbors worrying about plunging property values—they will now all have their day."

"That is why you hired me," Damon said wryly, "to keep this from happening. But I haven't done my job."

'I am not firing you if that's what you are implying. I need you more than ever now."

"The only way to stop it, Mrs. Rand is to find out who killed Beth and now Arvid. Someone in the family is responsible."

"We don't know that!" she snapped. "Anyone who has a grudge against the Fischers, and they are legion, could have done it."

"Lieutenant Harris doesn't believe that and neither do I. After Beth died he came to see me at the Museum. He asked me to report to him if I saw or heard anything that might help him."

Sarah sat as if frozen in place. "You have been an informant to the police?"

"He said I owed you no loyalty because you would not hesitate to incriminate me if it would protect the family."

"My god, do you believe that?"

"I don't know what to believe. But you don't have to worry. I haven't been any help to Harris. In fact, I keep undercutting him. He is upset with me."

Sarah's eyes narrowed. "Can I still trust you?"

"Can anyone be trusted?" He waited for her to answer but she remained silent. "Mrs. Rand, who are you protecting?" The question was direct, blunt and gratuitous, providing sufficient reason for her to end not only this conversation but also his relationship with the family—including his job at the Museum—even if she did say she needed him more than ever. If that truly is the case, then maybe she will listen to him.

"This time Lieutenant Harris means business. He told me he is going to interview everyone in the Schloss, including you. He is assigning extra officers to take statements. He gave you two options, doing it in the Schloss or taking everyone, including the servants, to police headquarters in Wayzata. If you think the publicity is bad now, wait till the television cameras shoot videos of the entire family walking into the station."

"He can't do that."

"Yes he can, and he will. He's coming to see you." Damon checked his watch. "In fact he'll be here within the hour."

Sarah seemed wasted, as though her body was losing mass. "I will not talk to him."

"You have no choice."

""I will only talk to you, Damon."

"Mrs. Rand," he said sharply, "this nonsense has got to stop."

"Nonsense? If you only knew." She became reflective and finally said, "The time has come to tell you something I have not shared with anyone, not a soul." Her voice dropped nearly to a whisper. To hear her better, Damon pulled his chair closer until their knees almost touched.

"What is it?" he asked.

"The Curse of the Big Water."

She is being overly dramatic, Damon thought, like a Gothic novel. "What Curse," he asked, not taking her seriously.

"Minnetonka means Big Water in the Dakotah language," she explained. "Imagine the lake when they lived here—without mansions, noisy boats, water skis."

"What has that got to do with..."

Sarah raised her hands to interrupt him. "CT was like the Big Water, it matched his ego, large and seemingly endless, which held the family together. After he died, without his enormous presence, the family fell into disarray. Bad business decisions were made. We even had to close the museum during the Depression. You know this from your research."

He nodded. "But you don't learn much from business ledgers."

Sarah rearranged the folds on her caftan as if she were girding her loins for battle. "That is why I must tell you about a decision that had nothing to do with running a business yet affected the family far more. That is why I call it The Curse."

Damon sat so still even the antique chair did not creak.

"This decision, or perhaps I should call it a change of mind, occurred when Ellen was in a clinic to abort an unwanted child. There are letters she wrote during those months, letters now in your possession I understand. Henry gave them to you."

Damon nodded. "At first I thought they were written by Elizabeth, but on a hunch I looked up a quit-claim deed for property CT gave Ellen, and her signature matched the handwriting on those letters."

She smiled. "Good detective work. You should take over the investigation from that Lieutenant."

Damon ignored the backhanded compliment. "But I was mistaken thinking all along that Elizabeth was Amy's mother."

"You were *not* mistaken."

"But Ellen is Amy's mother isn't she? She wrote those letters pleading with Henry to let her have her baby…"

Sarah held up a hand, the joints purple and swollen with arthritis. "She wrote Henry because she knew he had strong feelings about abortion and that between the two of them they could convince me to change my mind." Sarah's sigh went deep in her chest. "I did so reluctantly, the biggest mistake of my life."

"But everything turned out all right, didn't it? Look at Amy."

"I am not talking about Amy. Ellen gave birth to Madie."

Damon was confused. "But Mrs. Rand, Arvid is Amy's father, not Madie's."

"He is both Amy's father *and* Madie's father."

So that is what Henry meant when he said, God help us all.

"On the day she was born I could tell Madie was abnormal. She was remote. She did not respond to touching. And she was slow to develop, awkward, unable to connect thoughts." Sarah sighed deeply. "That is why I kept her hidden, away from public view, and the shame."

"Is that why Arvid left town?"

"He left town because I banished him from the Schloss. I could have had him put in jail but the scandal would have been even worse, exposing us to ridicule. I thought I was rid of him forever, but then Beth died unexpectedly and he came to her funeral."

"But he stayed, he stayed to find Amy."

"Yes, he needed to confirm that he had a child who was normal to make up for the one who was not. A daughter he could point to with pride."

"At least there is some good news."

"How can any of this be good news?"

"Look at Amy. She is everything you saw in Beth."

Sarah finally managed to smile.

"You wanted to find her, too, didn't you?"

"What do you mean?"

"Arvid did not act alone. He had help."

"Help? Whose help?"

"Yours, Mrs. Rand."

"How can you say that?"

"You already knew the detective Arvid used to find Amy. You had hired him to do a background check on Elroy Jacobssen before you let him adopt Amy."

"Did he tell you that?"

Damon nodded. "You set Arvid up with Rankin who pretended to find Amy when you knew all along where she was."

"Why would I do that?" she said huffily, but there was no steam in her statement.

"Because you secretly wanted to bring Amy back after Beth died and used Arvid as your cover, which he happily agreed to. You did it for the same reason Arvid wanted to find her: A Fischer you could point to with pride. Beth is dead and Madie is incompetent. Only Amy is left to restore the Fischer name."

31

Damon left Sarah staring into space, no doubt reflecting on The Curse as she called it. She found some relief unburdening herself to Damon, but he had a strong feeling that this was not the whole story.

He returned to the Great Hall and called Harris. "I talked to Sarah."

"What did you find out?"

"Plenty."

"Meaning?"

"I can't tell you over the phone. But she doesn't want to be questioned."

"I need a statement from everyone and that includes Mrs. Rand."

"She needs more time." Sarah needed more than time, she needed forever, but if there was any possibility of finding the killer, or killers, Damon decided, Sarah was the key, but he would not yet expose her unhappy story to Harris. What Damon heard just now was a preamble, a preface, a preview of coming attractions as one reads on a movie screen. Sarah was the principal character in the sad tale of The Curse; whether she tells the rest of it remains to be seen, but at least this was a start.

"Ok, I'll give her more time," Harris said, "but I want to see everyone else. How do you want to set this up? Your place or mine?"

"Not the police station if that's what you mean."

"That's what I mean. We will come out to the Schloss at two."

"We?"

"Three deputies. Do you think I'm doing this alone?"

"I guess not."

"I'm glad we got that settled. What I plan to do is split my crew up into different rooms. I'll use the library. I like it there, that's where I met the old dame. I need a list, and that means everyone, including the help."

"You've got Sarah."

"For later."

"Her daughter-in-law Dolores Rand, her grandson Richard, Beth's twin, and CT-Two, her other grandson, and his wife Ruth and their kids."

"Leave the guy's wife and kids out for now."

"All right. Then there is Henry, the rock polisher, Sarah's other brother, Edmond, and Ellen, Sarah's niece."

"Ok."

"Then there's Irene Campbell, Sarah's other sister, and her daughter-in-law, Crystal."

"Arvid Campbell's wife or, should I say, widow?"

"Correct."

"Anyone else?"

"The help."

"Include them."

"Do you want to interview Amy?"

"Whoever was in the Schloss last night."

"What about Jon Love?"

"Who's that?"

"The dinner party I told you about, to introduce Amy to the family? Sarah's lawyer and financial advisor, whom she calls her barrister, was also there."

"Call him and ask him to come out. It's easier for us

to get the interviews done in one day but we can also see him at his office. I have to make sure we don't miss anyone." Harris hesitated. "What about that goofy dame?"

"Madie?"

"Yeah."

"She's bashful."

"I have to interview her even if she grunts."

"She doesn't go anywhere without Mrs. Stockton."

"These are private statements, Damon. No one else can be in the room. Even if Madie doesn't say anything, I can study her reactions to questions, the look on her face, the way she holds her body."

"What about me? Don't you want my statement?"

"After all the shit you've given me?" Harris was ready to hang up.

"Just a minute, Lieutenant, I have an idea."

Harris sighed audibly. "Oh, oh. What now?"

"You said you are going to use the library."

"I want to sit at that table by the window, where I saw Mrs. Rand. I like symmetry."

"I like symmetry, too. Let me listen in on Madie."

"What are you talking about?" Harris replied impatiently. "I told you, no one but her and me."

"I won't really be in the room. There is an elevator hidden behind a fake bookcase Mrs. Rand uses. I can stand in there."

"Are you serious?"

"Remember when we first met by the Marini sculpture at the Fischer? You asked me to be your eyes and ears."

"This is different."

"Not that much. I might pick up things you'd miss since you don't know her at all."

"There's the little matter of police procedure, but so far you haven't let that get in your way."

"No one will know but you and me."

"What are you getting out of this?"

The Curse, Damon thought. Madie was the Curse.

Harris remained silent on the other end of the line, thinking over Damon's request. "I don't know why I am doing this. I shouldn't even trust you, but I have to admit you are resourceful. You have a detective's instincts, I'll give you that. But whatever you hear—if she says anything at all—you cannot repeat it, do you understand?"

"I understand."

"And you better be there before we arrive. If you make a sound and she hears you, my ass will be forever in the ringer. I can get suspended without pay if this comes out."

"It won't," Damon said, crossing his fingers.

*****

Damon notified Phillip to call Jon Love and break the news about Arvid. "Tell him that Lieutenant Harris wants him to make a statement. See if he can drive out this afternoon."

Then he rejoined Amy in the Venetian room. She was on her third cup of coffee.

"I thought you'd never come back. Tell me what happened with Sarah."

He sat next to her and retraced Sarah's incredible story about Arvid's sins and Sarah's efforts to cover them up—"The Curse of the Big Water as she calls it."

Amy listened intently, her eyes barely blinking and behind them Damon knew there had to be a myriad of questions crowding her brain.

"Madie and I have the same father?" she asked.

Damon nodded. "And Ellen wrote those letters I mistakenly thought were from Elizabeth. Sarah confirmed that Elizabeth was your mother after all. I don't want to sound as if I am minimizing the terrible things Arvid did to his own family but at least it should be a comfort to know that your mother and father were cousins, not directly related."

"Does that make me normal?"

"As normal as I am."

"That might even be worse!" Her kidding relieved the tension, and they even managed to laugh, the sound in stark contrast to the foreboding atmosphere engulfing the rococo palace of CT Fischer.

"I have to get ready," he said, touching his fingers to her lips in a vicarious kiss. "Harris is coming this afternoon with deputies to take statements."

"What do you want me to do?"

"Ask Phillip to call Sarah and see if you can keep her company. She was pretty broken up when I left her."

Damon called a meeting of the family in the Great Hall to brief them before Harris arrived with his deputies. The word spread fast that Arvid had been murdered. At least the terrible news served to coalesce the family with a common concern—fear—and they showed up promptly, including Mrs. Stockton but not Madie. Damon did not expect to see Crystal, Arvid's widow, but she arrived, stoic, calm. Sarah sent word through Phillip that she would remain in her apartment. She had company. Amy was with her.

No one seemed to mind that Damon was taking charge—let him handle the grisly details. It was as if the mantle of authority had been yielded to the PR man from the Art Center, the outsider now running the show.

The Great Hall was like a spread-out living room, with everyone sitting on sofas and easy chairs grouped around a coffee table large enough to be a helicopter pad. CT chose to stand, probably because he looked more dominant than he did sitting down. Mrs. Stockton stood, too, her back against the wall. She was unhappy having to be present; she did not like leaving Madie alone. Ellen sat on the arm of one of the sofas next to Edmond in his wheel chair. Irene sat in an adjoining chair, her legs and arms folded as if warding off a chill, but it was summer.

"Why do we have to suffer through some kind of interrogation this afternoon, Soldier?" CT-Two asked when they were settled.

"Not interrogation," Damon replied stiffly. Someday he would bop that little dictator in the face. "You are only being asked to make a statement. An officer will record what you say. This will be typed up and presented to you for your signature. It's routine."

"What will we be asked?"

"Your whereabouts after Arvid left the Schloss, if you saw or heard anything, that sort of thing. Routine as I said."

"You, too?" Richard asked. "Are you going to give a statement?

"He didn't say."

"He didn't say? Does that mean you are working for him instead of us?"

"I am not working for anyone." Damon looked at the expressions on their faces, especially CT's, showing nothing but sour grapes. The time had come, he decided impulsively, to be rid of this rat's nest of sickness and deceit. "And that includes you. After today I am leaving."

His sudden and unexpected announcement, more like a dismissal of the family, caught everyone by surprise. They all stared, first at Damon and then at each other.

Henry spoke up. "Damon you can't be serious."

"I guess I've had enough."

"But you can't leave us alone."

"Last night everyone wanted to see me go."

"Think it over. Don't make a hasty decision. We want you here."

Almost everyone nodded agreement. Everyone, that is, except CT-Two.

Ellen raised her hand like a student in class. "May I say something?" she asked, and then continued. "The time has come to put away our petty grievances and act like a real family. Ever since Damon arrived, I have felt more comfortable than I have in a long time. He has brought a sense of calm authority that has been lacking since Beth died. Granny is tired, worn out, you all know that, and she

THE CURSE OF THE BIG WATER

was the one who held us together. I don't see anyone in this room, other than Damon, who has the will to see us through this difficult time. If he leaves, then what? Who will face the press, who will keep the police at bay?" Ellen looked around and each time her eyes locked on a relative, that relative looked down.

Nevertheless there were a few comments muttered so low that they could not be understood, a last vestige of resistance it appeared, but not strong enough to overthrow the newly reigning monarch.

After staring down members of her family, Ellen looked at Damon. "Please reconsider, at least until this horrible business..." she came to an impasse. Then she shook her head. "First Beth and now Arvid. When will it end, how will it end?"

The question was like a plea for resolution, for a return to normality, and forced Damon to reconsider. Among those gathered in the Great Hall who else but he could seek an answer to that question.

Looking over the attentive faces, he wondered, who among you has, as Jon Love put it, the most to lose? CT-Two was jealous, with feelings of inferiority he barely masked, but what did he have to lose with Beth, and now Arvid dead? Beth was Sarah's favorite, groomed to step in when Sarah died. With her out of the way, CT-Two had a clear path, except of course for Damon. Maybe that is why he was attacked. CT did not have powerful hands, but he could have hired a hit man. A garrote is a common method of execution in the crime world.

What about Richard? His Mercedes had a damaged headlight, evidence however circumstantial, that he ran down that detective, Jacob Rankin. What did Richard have to lose by that? He didn't have a care in the world but, then, the person you least suspect...

Damon believed he could write off Henry, as Henry appeared to have written him off. He could also eliminate Edmond, in his wheel chair debilitated by a stroke. And Irene? Her life was wrapped up in the Art Center. What about Dolores and Crystal? None of the women was physically capable of killing, yet all were capable of killing by proxy.

Consider Ellen, sitting on the sofa arm, her hand on the back of Edmond's wheelchair, looking down at her lap, a tragic figure whose appeal convinced Damon to stay on—did she have an ulterior motive? She had a deep grudge, deep enough to have Arvid killed, but certainly not Beth. This made Damon wonder if there could be more than one person involved, two murders for two different reasons. But why was he also a target, first in his car and then by the lake?

His eyes met those of Mrs. Stockton, proper and stiff in a plain gray dress, her long skinny arms hanging by her side. Her stare was icy cold, unforgiving. What was her connection other than caring for Madie—a thankless job. Who would want to do that unless there was a prize, similar to what Sarah promised not only Damon but also Del: "I will remember you financially and otherwise."

The common denominator has to be Sarah, rich as Croesus. Behind her failing health, she was the fierce protector of the family name with unquestioned loyalty to her dead father—a man far from the glowing hero everyone wanted Damon to write about. CT was as ruthless as the robber barons of his time and left an inheritance amassed by greed and blind ambition. It was a legacy for his descendants to inherit, and they did so with pleasure, particularly Sarah. If only he could get her to finish the family narrative.

If anyone could get Sarah to finish her narrative it was Amy. As he thought about her, Damon wondered what she would have been like if she had grown up in the clutches of the Schloss instead of a horse farm, with its fresh air, smell of manure and hay, and the sense of freedom and openness. That was nature at its best and most honest, he thought. She was a woman of the earth, while the others were of the money pit.

Sarah recognized that Amy was the only one with

the qualities and strength to restore honor and reputation to the Fischer clan. But for Amy to succeed, Sarah had to cooperate by baring all, revealing ugly truths beyond the one she revealed to Damon in the privacy of her dark chambers.

Sarah, a locked door to the past; Amy, a key to the future.

Damon cleared his throat. "Maybe I was a bit hasty. No one wants to clear the air as much as I do. So let's make a deal—give your statements to the police and I will help in any way I can."

There were audible sighs of relief and nods of heads.

"Ok," he said, relieved to have their cooperation. "Let's have lunch."

As they began to leave the Great Hall, Mrs. Stockton came over to Damon. "May I talk to you for a moment, Mr. Petroulis? In private?"

They walked into the adjoining Chinese room, adorned in Chinoiserie decor—dragon-shaped floor lamps of porcelain, their shades like miniature pagodas, embossed wallpaper lush with roses, vines, and palm fronds, and chairs upholstered in traditional Chinese brocade.

Damon motioned her to one of the chairs.

"No thank you, I prefer to stand."

Damon wondered if she really could bend her body, she was so rigidly erect. "I'll stand, too."

She was rubbing her hands. "I understand Madie is to be interviewed."

"That's right."

"With the detective?"

Damon nodded. "Lieutenant Harris."

"I won't allow it."

"You have no choice, Mrs. Stockton. The police are running the show."

"What can she possibly add? She stays in her room.

And when we go out I'm with her. How could she know anything about Mr. Campbell's murder?"

"Who said it was murder?"

If she was startled by his challenge, it never showed. She deflected the question by saying "That is what everyone is calling it."

"Well, then, that makes it more important for the police to interview her. Not saying anything would suggest she is hiding something. You don't want that do you?"

"Then I have to be with her."

"The Lieutenant was adamant about that, too. It would appear you are coaching her, like having a lawyer sitting next to you at a trial."

"She is not on trial."

"I didn't mean it that way, Mrs. Stockton," Damon replied, feeling uncomfortable trying to reason with her. She was like a trial lawyer herself looking for ways to catch him in a semantic error.

She turned and walked out of the room, her hips so stiff they seemed to be laced in a corset.

32

Everything went more smoothly than Damon could have hoped. Not exactly like sheep but certainly orderly, the nine family members reported when notified, three each in the Venetian, White and Red Rooms where Harris's deputies had set up shop. The round of interviews began at one pm with Phillip acting as runner-messenger, notifying who was next. After they finished, the staff, including Mrs. Stockton, were questioned one at a time, with Phillip taking the final turn.

Harris decided to meet with Madie during the time Mrs. Stockton was being interviewed in order to separate the two. Her anger and distrust at being blindsided like this was clearly evident when she dropped Madie at the doorway, her eyes like poison darts, the paper-thin skin on her cheeks sucked in to reveal the outlines of her teeth.

Damon had hidden himself in the narrow space between the bookcase and the door to the elevator. He could easily see through the one-way mirror Sarah had installed in order to survey the library, giving her the advantage of knowing who was there before she made her grand entrance. But he could not hear, and so he left the

fake bookcase cabinet door open an inch. He was ready—
nervous but ready.

Madie came in wearing her little-girl-costume-of-
the-day, a pastel blue pinafore with ruffles at the hem, over
a white blouse with puffed sleeves. Her accessories were
also white: her gloves, sunhat, coin purse and Mary Jane
shoes. The ensemble was in glaring contrast to the
thickness of her body. In fact, Damon could not imagine
Madie putting on her clothes, more like being stuffed into
them.

She sat primly on the edge of the chair, her purse on
her lap, and pulled her skirt over her knees, as though she
had been coached.

On the table was a portable Panasonic cassette
recorder with a small microphone and a wire leading to a
socket under the window. It looked pretty formidable
even to Damon and he wondered how well Madie would
handle this, but she was so calm and self-possessed that he
figured Mrs. Stockton must have given her a Miltown.

Damon waited tensely as Harris turned on the
cassette and asked:

"What is your name?"

"Madie Campbell."

"Speak into the microphone please."

She leaned forward. "Madie Campbell."

Her voice was tinny as though coming from an old
gramophone rather than her throat. Except for hearing her
say "Beth, is that you?" when he and Amy peeked into her
room, this was the only time Damon heard her speak. He
never saw her without Mrs. Stockton and that is probably
why—imagine being in the company of someone as
controlling as Rasputin was with the son of Czar Nicholas.
In all likelihood you'd keep your mouth shut, too. It was
downright eerie. Damon was surprised though that Madie,
except for the way she dressed, seemed as normal as
anyone else.

"Does Madie stand for Madeline?"

"Yes."

"Where do you live?"

"Schloss Fischer."

Harris smiled paternally, a rare expression from the tough cop image he always portrayed, making Damon wonder if he had a family of his own—a wife and children, maybe even grandchildren. He'd have to ask him.

"Now, Madie, I'd like to ask you a few questions about where you were and what you were doing since last Friday, all right?"

Madie nodded.

"Did you leave the mansion?"

She shook her head.

"Not even with Mrs. Stockton in the backyard, down to the dock, out on the boat?"

Madie pressed her knees together and tightened her hold on her little white purse. "I don't like the water."

"Does the water make you afraid?"

Madie remained silent.

"Since you didn't reply can I say for the record that you did not answer?"

"What does that mean?"

"Because the tape machine only listens, it does not see." Even Harris was taken in by the little girl effect Madie was using, reacting as if he were talking to a child or, if not a child, someone mentally retarded.

Silence.

Harris changed the subject, "Do you always stay in your room?"

She nodded

"Please answer."

"Yes."

"Does Mrs. Stockton stay with you?"

"She has her own room."

"But she goes with you when you leave your room, right?"

She nodded and then remembered to answer, "Yes."

"Do you go for a ride?"

"Unless I have to go to the doctor."

"I mean go shopping, go to a movie, visit friends."

Madie stared as though Harris had lost his mind. "I don't have friends."

Harris thought a moment, looking for questions to ask. "What do you like to do, Madie?"

Madie looked past Harris out the window. In the distance beyond the lawn the roof of the boathouse was visible. "I watch television."

"Really?" Harris asked as if this was exceptional. "What do you watch?"

She shrugged.

"Do you have any favorites?"

"I like to watch people."

"People? You mean actors?"

"Oh, no," she said. "All they do is pretend. I like to watch real people."

"Real people?" Harris asked. "Like who?"

Madie reflected a moment. "People giving the news like the reporter on Channel 4."

"Channel 4?"

"She is on at twelve o'clock. She is pretty and I like her voice."

"What is her name?"

"Patti."

Damon tensed. Did Madie mean Patti Azquith?

"I can't remember her last name," Madie said, "but Mr. Petroulis would know."

"Why would he know?"

"He was on her show. He talked to her. I don't think he likes her very much."

Jesus! Damon realized. Madie had seen him being interviewed at the gate, heard all the damning things he said, how Azquith baited him into saying more than he intended, giving away private information about the Fischers whom Patti labeled the Family Without a Future, as well as the patronizing things he said about Madie, describing her as plain looking, even calling her a Poor Little Rich Girl. He recalled how anguished he felt, hoping no one in the family had seen him. Madie heard all of it.

"Well, we can always ask him, can't we?" Harris said, boredom setting in. He shut off the recorder. The interview was a formality anyway, not that the detective expected to hear anything useful from Madie but that he had to close the circle, as it were, and get interviews from all the Fischers,

"I guess that's it, Madie, but I want to caution you that if anything new turns up, I may ask you more questions. I don't think you'd mind though because you did so well this time, cooperating and being a good witness."

Madie rose from the chair smiling pleasantly and pulled her dress down around her hips. She reached behind and yanked at the fabric, one gloved hand at a time as Damon stared through the crack in the bookcase door. The reach for her was difficult because of the thickness of her shoulders. She was ungainly, graceless and awkward, especially as she tried to grip the fabric with her pudgy fingers. Those fingers...

Damon opened the door wider so he could watch her as she walked out. When she was gone, he opened the bookcase all the way and stepped into the library.

Harris looked over at Damon as he was unplugging the tape recorder and winding up the cord. "Well that was a waste of time."

"I'm not so sure," Damon said, looking at Madie's retreating figure waddle away. He began to follow her.

"Where are you going?"

"To talk to Madie."

"If you think you can have better luck than I did, be my guest."

Damon caught up with her in the Great Hall. She was sitting in a straight-back chair waiting for Mrs. Stockton, stiff and proper.

"Hello, Madie," Damon said, approaching her casually as though he was just walking past and stopped to have a brief conversation.

Her body arched as she tightened the grip on her purse.

"Kind of warm isn't it?" he said and fanned his face as though to exaggerate the temperature.

She pretended he wasn't there, toying instead with the strap of her purse, twisting and untwisting it.

"Those gloves must make your hands pretty hot."

She pushed her thick thighs together.

"Wouldn't you like to take them off? I'm sure you would be more comfortable."

She began to squirm.

"I'll bet you use nail polish. Working at the Art Center, I see women wearing the latest fashion and, you know, not one of them wears gloves. That's old-fashioned now." Damon made a face to show how passé gloves really were. "Nail polish is all the rage now. And not just red but blue and green, even black! Really weird colors."

She gripped her hands together even tighter.

Damon drew close and stood over her. "What color do you use?"

He bent over and put his fingers on one of her hands to pull the glove off when a low growl gargled from her throat, like the warning a dog makes when threatened, an odd sound that made Damon pause for a moment but then he tried again to pull the glove off. Suddenly, the sound erupted in a crescendo of such volume it had to rattle the rafters of the Schloss—if indeed there were any—the continuous full-throated howl of a trapped animal, so unexpected and so unearthly that Damon jumped back, the hackles on his neck tingling. He watched hypnotized as the horrific sound contorted Madie's face, twisting her mouth, exposing her teeth, dribbling spit from the tip of her extended tongue. The girl-child had turned into what Damon could only describe as a monster, a werewolf under a full moon.

He shuddered. He was witnessing a scene that had no reference to anything human. In his entire life up to this moment and whatever years that lay ahead, he would never witness anything as nightmarish as this, and it would forever be seared in his memory no matter how feverishly he might try to erase it.

Madie's howl echoed and re-echoed throughout the Schloss like a hurricane rattling the windows with its frightening intrusion, and interrupting the interviews going on in various rooms.

The first person to rush in was Mrs. Stockton, her face ashen white, her lips blood red, her eyes black orbs of rage.

"What have you done to her?" she shrieked and rushed to Madie's side. She dropped to her knees and embraced the formless body, pulling it to her barren bosom.

"Madie, Madie," she said again and again, the two rocking as one. "You are safe now, I'm here."

Madie's features slowly melted back to the persona of a little girl and the sounds from her mouth turned to snuffles punctuated by a lifting of the shoulders.

Like people rushing to get the last seat in a theater, everyone converged on the Great Hall. At first there was confusion, milling around, with looks of concern, fear even, and then the focus fell on Madie and Mrs. Stockton, seeing not what Damon had witnessed but rather two women huddled together. Where had that awful cry come from? they seemed to be asking as they gathered in a semicircle around Madie and Mrs. Stockton, still intertwined as in a Renaissance painting of Mary and the Christ Child.

Damon looked around like a teacher taking attendance. Richard and CT-Two stood side-by-side, more curious than fearful. Henry lingered at the doorway, looking in before proceeding into the room. He pressed himself against the wall trying not to be noticed. Crystal came with Irene who appeared to be in a daze. Still missing were Ellen and Edmond. Standing in back as servants who knew their places, which they did, were Karl and Hettie, Phillip and Delmar. Jon Love was there, too, having arrived shortly after Harris and his deputies set up shop. Jon aligned himself next to the servants, as though he also knew his place. There was an embarrassed look on his face, like that of a voyeur who was witnessing a lot more than he bargained for. Damon was surprised to see the chauffeur in his livery, wearing his flared pants and black boots. Damon presumed if Del was going to be interviewed by uniformed men he wanted to be in uniform as well, not looking like a nondescript civilian. A proud man, all right.

Snatches of words filtered above the general mayhem. "What happened?" "Is Madie all right?" "Did she fall?" "Is she hurt?"

Damon was still looking for Ellen and Edmond when Harris came in. He pushed his way to the front, intent on creating order.

"What is going on?"

Mrs. Stockton looked up. "Madie screamed and I ran in here and found him standing over her." She pointed an accusing finger at Damon, bony and trembling with fury.

Harris glared at Damon. "You went chasing after her. What in hell happened?" He pulled his fingers through his gray hair in frustration.

Before Damon could answer, a voice rang out, "Stand aside, please!" It was the authoritative, commanding voice of Sarah Rand, likely making her last grand entrance.

Amy was next to her, a head taller, holding the old woman by the arm. The two standing together created an undeniable image of unity and power. Whether she accepted her new role or not, Amy no doubt radiated the same prediction of strength, command and vision as Sarah in her youth that would have made CT proud.

Watching them, Damon began to understand it all, the inadvertent coming together of seemingly unrelated pieces, seeing the whole for the first time.

The crowd separated to allow Sarah to observe

Madie sitting in the chair and Mrs. Stockton on her knees. Madie was trembling.

"Can't you see she is suffering from all this attention? Take her upstairs, Mrs. Stockton."

Damon stepped forward. "Not yet, Mrs. Rand."

Sarah gave Damon a hard stare, not happy to be countermanded. "What are you telling me, young man?"

"I want to look at her hands."

Stillness fell over the group. In their entire lives, no Fischer had ever heard anyone face up to Sarah until now, as though they were witnessing history, the moment had the strong implication of a changing of the guard. Besides, they also were curious, wanting to see Madie's hands, like archaeologists anticipating the opening of an Egyptian tomb that had been sealed for millennia.

But not Mrs. Stockton, who stared terror-stricken. "Please Mr. Petroulis, let her be."

"If she has nothing to hide why are you so reluctant?"

Sarah sighed audibly, a signal that she was through fighting. "Damon is right, Mrs. Stockton." She nodded at Madie. "Take off your gloves, dear. I'm sure you will be more comfortable, and so will we all."

The atmosphere in the room was electric with anticipation. No one moved, no one blinked. All eyes were locked on Madie's hands, curious why Damon wanted to see them.

Madie stared admiringly at her white satin gloves for a moment and then with slow deliberation removed one at a time, loosening them by pulling on each finger. She tucked the gloves into her little purse and laid her hands primly on her lap.

Now exposed, her hands were pulpy but muscular under their fleshiness. What grabbed Damon's attention most were her knuckles. They had deep scratches running across them, now scabbed over. It confirmed his worst suspicions.

"Oh," Dolores noticed, "Madie hurt herself."

"It's nothing," Mrs. Stockton said.

Nothing? Damon thought, far from it.

"Are we done now, Damon?" Sarah Rand asked. "Can Madie return to her room?"

He nodded.

"Take her upstairs, will you, Mrs. Stockton?"

Mrs. Stockton helped Madie to her feet. With her arm around the stocky torso, she led Madie to the grand staircase, disappearing after they turned at the landing.

"So what were you looking for, Damon?" Richard asked.

"Those scratches."

"So she scratched her hands," Richard said huffily, "so what? Madie likes to pick roses from the garden."

"Thorns didn't make those scratches, Richard, my fingernails did."

There was a sharp intake of breath. Damon didn't notice whose it was.

"What are you talking about?" Richard asked.

"I made those scratches trying to defend myself." Damon touched his throat in recollection. "Down by the boathouse on the night Madie tried to strangle me."

33

For a second, even less than that—a split-second—there was at first shocked silence not unlike what happens at an airshow when a plane crashes, followed by sheer bedlam. Lieutenant Harris remained unmoved. He had no emotional stake in any of this and he was also a cop, so he assumed his authority by raising his hands, but it had little effect to calm the cries of bewilderment.

"No! No!" "How can you even think that?" "Sheer lunacy!" "You've done it this time, Soldier!"

Damon stood in the middle of this maelstrom of invective, denial and outrage. Amy, though not joining in the chorus of naysayers, nevertheless appeared perplexed, wanting to believe Damon yet not able to accept it as fact. Maybe you are wrong her eyes were telling him.

Not everyone reacted similarly, Damon realized, as he scanned the room. Henry covered his face in his hands, no doubt recalling that those very hands, hardened by stone polishing, were once also suspected, wrongly as it turned out. Sarah remained encased in stony rectitude. Irene was looking sharply at Sarah, as though expecting more from her. Dolores exchanged glances with her son, Richard, looking like they'd rather be anyplace but here.

CT-Two just looked angry.

Everyone was accounted for except Ellen and Edmond. Where were they?

"Settle down!" Harris shouted above the commotion, repeating himself several times until finally the condemnation spent itself. "Everyone take a seat!" He waited until the family found places to sit down. Amy helped Sarah to the sofa and sat next to her. Phillip, Del, Karl and Hettie remained standing, unsure that they were invited to join their employers as if they were guests.

Harris saw them hesitate. "That means, you, too."

Reluctantly the quartet of servants drew chairs together and sat along the wall, lined up like patients in a waiting room.

"What about him?" CT threw an accusing stare at Damon.

"In a minute." Harris motioned Damon to follow him into the foyer. He closed the pair of glass-paneled doors behind him with a snick of the lock. "What in hell were you doing," he snapped at Damon, "scaring that kid half to death."

"Half to death is what she did to me, Lieutenant. Those scratches on her hands prove it."

"So you tried to take her gloves off and that is when she went ballistic?"

"Yes, and I think she wore those gloves with her fairy tale get-up so she could hide the scratches and no one would suspect anything."

"She isn't clever enough for that."

"But Mrs. Stockton is. I'll bet a month's salary she played a part, even if it was only to protect Madie."

"But what would be Madie's motive? If she attacked you, then she had to attack Beth, the only scenario that fits, and it would be hard to prove unless she confessed. But why do you think she went after you?"

"She saw me on Channel 4 when I was interviewed by Patti Azquith. I said some pretty harsh things that may have upset her enough to attack me."

"That may explain her revenge on you, but why would she kill Beth?"

Damon shrugged. "Jealousy maybe. She resented the fact that Beth and I were sleeping together. It was no secret. In a perverted way she felt displaced. She lost Beth's attention and we both became targets of her anger. But you'd need a psychiatrist to figure out what was going on in her head. There is a textbook I read in college about the psychology of insanity. Madie would be a perfect case study of a conflicted mind."

Harris shook his head. "She's nuts all right but I need more proof than scratches on her hands. And what about Campbell? The MO is the same, strangled with a rope by the lakeshore. Madie is strong enough to take care of a man, especially if he is taken by surprise. Look at you, you are a big guy and she almost did you in."

Damon's eyes widened. "Lieutenant, those are the same words Jon Love used at the funeral: 'Did her in.' He said, 'Find out who has the most to lose and you will find out who did her in.'"

"Most to lose? What did he mean by that?"

"If you are a proud person and lose your reputation, what is left?"

"Are you talking about Sarah Rand?"

Damon nodded.

"The perfect suspect. I'd rather grill a gorilla."

"If you let me handle it, I think I can get her to open up. She's been hiding a family scandal for decades. What she calls The Curse, and it's eating on her just like her cancer. She wants to clean the slate before she dies, but she needs some prodding."

"Get the old lady to confess?"

"That is exactly the word you don't want to use, Lieutenant. If we can characterize this at all it would be to reveal a secret regarding the family. Forget official procedures where she will feel threatened and defensive. Surrounded by her family, it will be easier for her to open up. I think Sarah really wants to tell her story. She can't be the only one who knows it. So if I handle this right, maybe I can get others to open up. I don't know who, but someone might say something, like group therapy."

"You think that will work?"

"It's worth a try."

"I don't know why I always give in to you."

*****

Damon and Harris returned to the Great Hall. The cavernous room became quiet as they approached, everyone curious about the private conversation they just had, but no one spoke, waiting in anticipation for the two to set the agenda.

This time Damon sat down without waiting for another challenge from CT, pulling one of the straight chairs over to the center of what had become a semi-circle of family members facing him, like a thrust stage with Damon the thespian. Harris stood to one side—the understudy to complete the metaphor. It was Damon's show, but if Harris needed to take over, he was right there.

Damon glanced at Amy on the sofa next to Sarah. He wished there had been an opportunity to talk to her in private so he could explain what he planned to do, but this was not to be. He hoped she would understand if he had to be a bit hard on Sarah.

He took a deep breath and began. "I know you are all angry at me for upsetting Madie, but there was no other way to see her hands." He looked at Beth's twin. "Richard, you said that Madie scratched herself picking roses but you saw the scratches. They were deep and long, a thorn would never create those marks. Those were defensive scratches made by a person who was fighting for his life. I was that person."

No one said a word.

"I know she attacked me but what I don't know is, did Madie attack Beth? There has been a concerted effort to cover up her murder, impede police investigation, and try to convince authorities that Beth died accidentally or even committed suicide. But you don't believe that for a second, do you, Mrs. Rand?"

The unexpected question aimed at Sarah caught her off guard. She drew back slightly, even sideways, pushing herself toward Amy as though Amy would protect her.

"Would they Mrs. Rand?" Damon repeated.

"Damon, please!" Amy said,

Sarah laid a hand on Amy's arm. "Thank you, my dear, for trying to protect me, but Damon asked a fair question, and I should answer it. All right, Damon, there is no reason any longer to be still, is there? My life is almost over. I hope there is enough time to atone. I've never before believed I would have to do that."

Sarah paused, not for effect but rather to collect her thoughts.

"Shall I begin at the beginning?" she asked rhetorically, and then reflected a moment. "Just when *was* the beginning. Was it when Father died? When Alfred and I married? When I gave birth to Elizabeth?" Sarah turned in the direction of her younger sister. "Or, Irene, was the beginning when you gave birth to Arvid? You were in your teens then, still unformed, a Fischer who did not yet understand or appreciate what it meant to bear that name. It didn't matter to you who fathered your child. You didn't care a whit for the future of the Fischer dynasty. You let us down, Irene, by producing a son unworthy of carrying our name and doing so scandalously, coupling in the back seat of an open car. But you always were a maverick, weren't you, an irresponsible maverick who grew up to forsake her father's art collection and the museum he built. Not only did you sell off his beautiful treasures you also turned his elegant architecture into a plain box and filled it with tasteless art."

Damon fully expected Irene to jump up and storm out, but she did neither. She simply stared into space as though she had heard all this before. But Damon clearly had not, and it jarred him. What he loved most, the world of modern art, the benefactor of Fischer Art Center loved least.

Sarah read the look on his face. "My apologies to you, Damon, but my personal taste in no way diminishes my support of the Museum and your work there. I hope you believe that."

"Thank you," he replied but he wasn't sure any longer what to believe.

Sarah returned to the difficult matter at hand. "This is the beginning of a rather sordid tale. I hope you are all ready to hear the rest of it."

"Hear what Granny?" Richard asked, worried that his cozy little world was about to crash around him.

"You and CT know nothing of this. You are not part of a conspiracy the rest of us share. What I have to say will impact your lives from here on. I hope you are strong enough to handle it." The tone in her voice strongly implied that she was not very confident they were.

"At least on the surface our lives appeared normal. Irene married the Museum's curator, Daryl Campbell, who adopted Arvid. And so I thought finally that everything was in hand, but Arvid was not the model nephew I naively expected him to be. A wolf in sheep's clothing, if I may use that tired expression, but it fits. I can only be blunt because I have become so desensitized I no longer have any feelings, except remorse and regret. Arvid did the unthinkable. He raped Elizabeth."

Crystal spoke up, the first time she said anything. "My god, Sarah, that isn't true! He did not rape Elizabeth. They had an affair."

"Is that what he told you? It doesn't surprise me. You married him for his family connection, I know you did, and now you have to take the bad with the good. Live with it my dear, what I am telling you is the truth."

Amy leaned forward. "Is that why I'm here?" she asked. "Why I'm in the world at all? Because of rape?"

"Amy, if there is any comfort, Elizabeth would have raised you with all the love a mother could give, but she died giving you life."

Tears formed in Amy's eyes. "Is that why I was given up for adoption?"

"Not because we didn't want you, Amy. I was only thinking of your welfare. I made sure you were given to loving parents, the best outcome any of us could hope for. If Arvid did anything decent in his otherwise deceitful life, he helped bring you back to us." Sarah looked down at her lap. "But, no matter what good he might have done, he will also be remembered for a dreadful..."

A cry of despair cut the air. Everyone turned in the direction of the sudden outburst. It was Irene, her eyes wide with anger. "Sarah!" she shouted. "Don't say anymore!

Sarah stared at her sister who was having a hard time composing herself. "Irene, you have to accept the inevitable. There is no possible way I can keep this a secret any longer. If you can't bear it, then leave. No one is keeping you here."

Irene blew her nose into a tissue. "I will not leave, Sarah, which is what you really want, isn't it, shaming me in front of everyone so I will burst into tears and run out of the room? If I have to accept the inevitable, well then, sister dear, so do you! You will sit there and listen to my side of the story. You accused me of being too young to appreciate what it meant to be a Fischer. But how could I possibly appreciate what it meant if I was constantly ignored by Papa? He gave you all of his attention, all of his love—I in shadow, you in limelight. It was as if I did not exist, in fact he did *not* want me to exist! He blamed me for mother's death because she died when I was born."

"That is nonsense, Irene," Sarah interjected but she was cut off in mid-sentence.

"Nonsense? I was not only unwanted I was *hated*— If I hadn't been born she would have lived. Save the child, right? So when you ask me what it meant to be a Fischer I will tell you: being a Fischer meant rejection, anger, guilt. That is the way I grew up, a girl in revolt, lashing out, being angry without knowing why. Even as an adult, I never lost my resentment. So don't bother to question why I auctioned off Papa's collection and reopened the museum as a modern art center—even if it was a good business decision. At least Papa would have been proud of me for that, but I also derived tremendous satisfaction to see his collection sold off because it was his proudest achievement, what I had to destroy in order to make me feel whole!" Irene allowed herself a small smile. "What would he say if he knew what I did to his precious collection—exactly what you said, Sarah, because you are just like him."

The shocking testimony forced Damon to study Irene more closely, having essentially ignored her as a factor in the family history. Wow, was he wrong. But his relationship with her had been strictly professional, seeing her at board meetings, but never examining her until this moment as a flawed human with bitter feelings and regrets and lost opportunities. While she had the facial bones of her older sister, she lacked the steeliness that sculpted Sarah's features. But now, though, Irene's face flashed from the release of pent-up frustrations and suppressed emotions.

Sarah remained silent, not so much that she was taken aback, which she must be to some degree, but because she thought it best to let her sister vent her grievances. If there ever was time to do it, the time was now.

"As you pictured me, Sarah, I was not a model child. I admit, but let me say in my own defense, I found the affection I did not get from Papa in a boy who was more than willing to be my teenage lover. I was wild, wasn't I Sarah? Don't wince, sounds strange coming from me doesn't it? As you said, we can't keep secrets any longer." she laughed now, bitter and sardonic, "I was out of control, a teenager intent on embarrassing Papa and you, too, Sarah."

"Perhaps you should let me continue the narrative,

Irene," Sarah said, her patience wearing thin. "You have become much too emotional."

"Let me finish!" Irene thundered. "I won't let you paint my son as an evil person. Like me, Arvid was a lonely, troubled child feeling as abandoned as I was, trying to find his place in an unforgiving world."

"I respectfully disagree with you, Irene," Sarah interrupting firmly. She scanned the group to make sure everyone was back paying attention to her. She needn't have bothered. "Because of your son, a horrible evil descended upon us," she said. "Elizabeth was not his only victim..." she hesitated, fighting back a rising temper.

My god Damon thought, can this get any worse? Indeed it could.

"Your son was a predator," Sarah stated. "His victims were innocent and vulnerable. His perversion knew no limits. He even seduced his own sister."

34

The silence in the Great Hall was deafening—a contradiction of terms, but this was the only way Damon could describe the atmosphere. No one moved, even breathing was held in check as the bomb Sarah dropped on them blew up in their faces.

The first to respond was Richard. "Who are you talking about Granny? Arvid didn't have a sister."

"Yes he did, Richard, and this is the hardest part I have to tell you..."

Irene began sobbing again, but Sarah was unmoved by her sister's vulnerability. Instead she bore down, staring hard at Irene. "It was bad enough, wasn't it, Irene, that your fling with a teenage boy produced Arvid. But when that same boy got you pregnant again..."

Irene wiped her cheeks, fissured from old age. "I wanted to get even and I succeeded."

Sarah shook her head in dismay. "Unfortunately you did, consorting with rich teenagers like yourself, driving around in fancy cars with no adult supervision—the flapper of Lake Minnetonka. You may have hated CT, but you still inherited his impulsive nature, compounding it manyfold. But you did not inherit his common sense. Regardless, the damage was done. In the space of three years you had two children out of wedlock, first Arvid and then Ellen."

Richard and CT exchanged puzzled looks. "What are you talking about Granny?" Richard asked. "Ellen is Edmond's daughter, not Irene's."

"That is what I wanted you to believe. I made a pact with the devil, agreed to by Irene, Edmond and Henry. Our reputation was at stake. How would CT feel had he been alive?"

"CT! Always CT! Can't we just forget him?" Surprisingly the man after whom CT was named cried out.

"Hush," Sarah admonished. "You don't know what you are saying. How can you even think for a moment we could let the outside world learn that under our roof an act of incest was committed—a curse on all of us."

So that is what Sarah meant by the Curse of the Big Water, and it sent goose bumps up Damon's arms to his cheeks. Condemnation was built into its very utterance. Now he understood why Ellen and Edmond were absent. The denunciation would have been too much to bear.

Crystal began crying, her body racked with the heavy sobs of shock, sorrow and betrayal.

"Yes, I made a pact with the devil," Sarah continued amid the ruination she had created. "Edmond's wife was paid handsomely for her silence and a divorce settlement. It was a simple process for Edmond to adopt Ellen so it would appear as though she and Arvid were not blood relatives. I did this because she insisted on having her child. I could not ignore the real possibility that her unholy pregnancy would result in a congenital disorder at least or a mental deformity at most. I wanted Ellen to have an abortion—do not take the risk, I told her. But she wrote passionate letters to Henry begging to save her child, and he argued with equal passion to preserve Madie's life. I relented."

Henry looked up at the mention of his name but said nothing, keeping his thoughts to himself.

"When Madie was born I could see what a horrible mistake I made—vacant eyes, an expressionless face devoid of emotion. She was the devil's answer to incest, an evil sin whose penalty was eternal damnation. A terrible curse descended upon the family, and my worst fears were answered when Beth was killed."

"Are you saying that Madie killed Beth? But why would she do that?" The voice was out of place in the protected bosom of the Fischer clan. Everyone turned to find the source. It was Lieutenant Harris speaking up, no doubt thinking about motive.

Sarah attempted a smile. "Can my answer be the statement you planned to tape?"

Harris held up his microphone. No one had noticed, in the turmoil before order was restored, that he had brought the tape recorder from the library. "If you say so I will turn it on."

"You may. I no longer have anything to hide. And you have your job to do."

Amazing, Damon thought. Sarah was finally cooperating with Lieutenant Harris, the officer she so deeply resented having around.

She turned to face his direction so her voice would be captured by the mike. "You can well imagine, Lieutenant, how many doctors I consulted over the years, including psychiatrists, who told me that Madie was emotionally unstable, with the mind of a child. She was unpredictable, with unbridled jealousy and paranoia. They all cautioned that we institutionalize her because there was no way to predict her moods. But with medication and Mrs. Stockton watching over her, I thought she could live in the Schloss away from prying eyes. However, things began to unravel when Damon came into our midst. None of us understood that his presence would be a threat to Madie. I should have seen it but I was blinded by the relationship he and Beth had, holding the promise of a new generation of Fischers." Sarah gave Damon an appreciative nod of her head.

This was too much for CT. "You risked everything bringing that damned Greek here and now we are all paying for it!" he shouted, his fists clenched.

"Shut up, CT! Can't you see the tape recorder is running?" Richard shouted back. "You should have more judgment."

Richard was finally showing some backbone. Even Sarah was pleased. CT-Two leaned back, his cheeks flushed more from embarrassment than anger. It was the first time in Damon's memory that Richard stood up to his older brother, and that was fine with Damon.

CT's outburst interrupted the flow of Sarah's narrative sufficiently to lose her train of thought, and there was a feeling that she needed a jump-start. Damon stepped in. It was natural, instinctive and he felt comfortable taking over. "I'm truly sorry that I was a factor in Madie's undoing, Mrs. Rand..."

"Stop calling me Mrs. Rand, Damon. From now on I'd prefer that you call me Sarah."

There were murmurs and one sharp intake of breath but no objections. A seismic shift was taking place, a shift of power, a bloodless coup. Sarah asking to be called by her first name put them on equal terms. Damon was no longer an outsider, he was an insider, more than that, *the* insider.

"That is very generous of you."

"Generous?" Sarah replied, laying it on thickly, "no more than you deserve, Damon." There was more hand wringing, even gnashing of teeth. Was she paying him compliments because she really meant it, or because she wanted to remind her heirs that getting the job of leading the family was not a matter of assigning it, but rather earning it. Take it away from Damon if you have the guts, she was saying. If you want it you have to fight for it.

But all of this was down the line, somewhere in the future, and he wasn't ready yet to commit himself. In the meantime there was work to do.

"I know Madie attacked me, whether you want to believe me or not," Damon said. "She saw me on TV making unflattering comments about her, which Patti

Azquith exaggerated. This made her angry enough to seek revenge and that night she jumped me by the boathouse. But what was her motive for killing Beth? Sarah, you said things started to unravel when I got between Beth and Madie, like the alienation of affections in a divorce suit. That being the case, why wouldn't Madie go after me instead of Beth? When she finally did go after me, it was for an entirely different reason. It just doesn't make sense somehow."

Damon shifted gears. "I've never seen Madie without Mrs. Stockton. I don't know anything about her. There is nothing in the family records except her signature on a payment ledger that dates back to Madie's birth. Just who is she?"

"I will fill you in, Damon," Sarah said. "Mrs. Stockton was a registered nurse at the clinic where Ellen stayed. She became very attached to Ellen, and also took up Ellen's cause to bear the child. And so, after Madie was born, I asked her if she would live with us and take care of her. In a way I was calling her bluff to see if indeed her conviction against abortions was more than mere talk. Well, we have the answer to that. She has been with us ever since."

"Just for the sake of argument," Damon said, "what if Mrs. Stockton knew what Madie was doing?"

"Does she share Madie's bedroom?" Harris asked.

Sarah shook here head. "She has her own room, next to Madie's."

"Well, then, if she has her own room, isn't it possible that Madie could sneak out without Mrs. Stockton being aware?" Harris sounded like a trial lawyer, not pleased that Damon was undercutting his case against Madie.

"There is a connecting door," Damon said, "like the one between my bedroom and Beth's. We don't know if that door is kept open, or how often Mrs. Stockton checks on Madie."

The implication of what Damon was suggesting

began to sink in. "Just what are you implying?" Sarah asked.

"How was Madie able to sneak out of her room, disappear for half an hour and go back to bed as if nothing happened—not once but twice? What if Madie was the puppet and Mrs. Stockton the puppet master?"

The question hung in the air, held aloft by sighs of relief, everyone thinking: Damon is onto something, something that would lift the stigma of Beth's unfortunate death from their shoulders.

Irene cried out, "Are you saying Madie is innocent?" She began to laugh, releasing pent up tension. Her declaration was met with collective nods. It was far easier to blame Mrs. Stockton than a member of the family.

Harris stepped forward. "Before you all go off half-cocked, making assumptions without any tangible proof or motive, I have to listen to Mrs. Stockton's statement, and I can't do that till after I get back to the office." Harris was clearly annoyed that Damon was, as always it seemed to him, gumming up the works when Harris expected to wrap up the investigation and finally close the file on The Curse of the Big Water.

Damon was not to be deterred, however, helped in no small measure by Sarah's endorsement of his status at the Schloss. "But this makes more sense than Madie wandering off by herself, doesn't it? Mrs. Stockton has absolute control over her. Look how agitated she became when you told her she couldn't be present during Madie's statement."

"Ok, ok!" Harris was frustrated. "Let me just once do the police work will you?"

"Sorry Lieutenant."

"Not half as sorry as I am."

An atmosphere of finality took over the Great Hall, suggesting that the meeting was over and it was all right to leave and get on with the day. They began to rise from their seats.

"Just a minute everybody, we are not through here!" Harris called out. "There's still some unfinished business we have to talk about."

Glances of frustration were exchanged as everyone sat down again.

"I'd sure like to get to the Club," Richard said. "I have a tennis match at three." He was ready to go, wearing white duck trousers and a navy blazer with the Club crest sewn on the pocket.

"Unfortunately this involves you, Mr. Rand."

"What are you driving at?"

"Driving is exactly what I want to talk to you about. There was a hit and run in an alley off University Avenue in Minneapolis on the eighth of June. A private detective named James Rankin was killed."

Amy became attentive. "Is that the man Arvid hired to find me?"

"That's the one," Harris said.

"What has that got to do with me?" Richard snapped. He crossed one leg over the other trying to appear nonchalant.

"You drive a Mercedes convertible, right? The day after Rankin was killed, Damon saw a cracked headlight and bent trim on your left fender."

"Damon?" Richard asked suspiciously.

"I was in the garage when you pulled in. You were coming back from the Club. You were in your tennis clothes."

"I didn't see you." Richard turned to look at Delmar. The chauffeur shifted his weight from one leg to the other. "You let him in?"

"No, sir," Del said. "He must have sneaked in."

Richard worked to suppress his growing anger. "The car is perfectly fine," he said to Harris. "Go look at it if you don't believe me."

"I will, Mr. Rand. Our forensics people can easily tell if a car has been repaired."

"Really?" Richard snapped his fingers. "Oh, that's

right, I almost forgot. I had lunch at the Club and when I was pulling out I scraped a light pole in the parking lot." He laughed nervously. "One too many, you know?"

"Did the Mercedes dealer repair your car?"

"No, Del fixed it. He's good at that." Then he stared angrily at Damon. "You were spying on me? I can't believe you would stab me in the back like that!"

"Don't blame Damon, Mr. Rand. He was helping me and I have to follow every lead no matter where it goes." Harris turned to Del. "Can you confirm that you fixed the car for Mr. Rand?"

Del nodded. "A simple job, really, I had to order a whole headlight assembly. You know," he laughed, "it's a Mercedes, cost three hundred dollars."

Damon and Amy exchanged brief glances. That was close to a week's salary but to the Fischers it was small change.

"What did you do with the damaged part?"

"I'm a packrat." Del stopped short when he noticed Richard motioning with his head.

"So you still have the headlight?" Harris asked.

Del looked down at the shine on his boots as if he were checking to see if they were scuffed.

"Easy enough to find out." Harris walked to the door and called for one of his deputies waiting in the hall to search the garage.

Richard jumped up. "Wait a minute, don't you need a warrant?"

"If there is a likelihood that evidence was tampered with, I can move right away."

Del looked at Richard helplessly. "I'm sorry Mr. Rand, I know you wanted me to throw it away."

Harris smiled, as would any detective who sensed that he was beginning to crack his case. "If your car was involved in that hit and run, you have some explaining to do, Mr. Rand."

Richard buried his face in his hands. It was difficult to hear him through his fingers. "It was an accident."

Dolores rushed to her son and sat next to him, putting her arms around his shoulders. She looked at Harris. "He didn't mean to do it."

"What do you know about this?" Harris demanded.

Her cheeks glistened from tears. "He was doing what any Fischer would do. He was protecting the family."

"Dolores, don't say anything more!" It was Henry speaking up for the first time, his voice tired and worn as if he were bearing the burden for the whole family.

Harris looked around. "You all knew, didn't you?" He shook his head as though he'd lost faith in human nature.

"You are right, Lieutenant," Henry admitted. "We all are complicit." He rubbed his worn hands together. "Ironic, isn't it, that what held us together all these years was Arvid's sin."

"You made Arvid the scapegoat just to save your own hide!" Crystal shouted suddenly. "I can understand why he didn't want to have anything to do with you."

"Keep quiet!" Dolores shouted back. "You are not a Fischer."

"Because I married Arvid I am stained as well, is that what you mean?"

Harris came forward, his hands raised as though he was protecting himself from a mob. "All right, all right, stop arguing! You all are guilty of conspiracy as far as I'm concerned. One person killed Rankin, even if he was doing something you all wanted done anyway."

There was silence, remarkable in its completeness. Damon looked at the Fischers, sitting mutely, red-faced and speechless.

Sarah was the first to find her voice. "You are an impressionable young man, Richard. The vitriol with which we spoke of Arvid spilled over and affected you as well."

Richard dropped his hands and stared at his grandmother. "I just wanted to give that detective a warning."

Harris asked in a soft, fatherly voice. "Are you willing to tell me what happened?"

Richard sighed deeply and pressed his fingertips together, oddly reminding Damon of Durer's famous etching of the praying hands. Maybe he really was praying, at that. Killing someone, whether or not he meant to, was a serious crime.

"Arvid told us he was searching for Amy. We didn't know anything about her. She was a mystery, finding her was a threat."

"But Amy was his daughter. Didn't you think he had the right to find her?"

Richard looked at Amy. "Now that I've met you, I don't understand what all the fuss was about." He smiled lamely. "But that doesn't excuse my behavior. I just wanted to scare the detective, not hurt him or, heaven forbid, kill him. I threatened him on the phone a couple of times and then I decided to confront him. I sat across the street in my car watching his office one night, and when he came out I followed him in my car to the alley. He turned and saw me and drew his gun. He was going to shoot me! I speeded up to get out of there and swerved into him. It was an accident, I'm telling you it was an accident!" Richard finally broke down and began to cry. Tears of remorse fell down his cheeks. Dolores rocked him back and forth as though comforting a baby.

It was a scene from the Theatre of the Absurd— human existence losing purpose or meaning, and a form of madness taking over. How did it come to this, Damon wondered.

"Nevertheless, Mr. Rand," Harris said, "I will have to arrest you. I'm not doing this with any satisfaction, I hope you understand, but your admission gives me no choice."

"Am I'm going to jail?"

"Not if Mrs. Rand has anything to say about it." Harris looked at Sarah. "I'm sure your lawyers will have him out in no time."

Sarah remained mute, staring not at anyone but into space as if she were watching a documentary of her life, its successes and failures, but with the emphasis most likely on the latter. Amy was watching the old woman with deep concern, clearly feeling her distress. It was a strange alliance, Damon thought, a young woman who had been banished in infancy was now the one Sarah depended on. And it was about time, too, because all her life Sarah stubbornly rejected assistance from anyone, a proud individual who needed no one to help her. But now the time had come when indeed she needed someone to oversee her and, whether one can call it fate or not, that person was Amy.

"And then what?" Richard asked, obviously concerned about his fate.

"I can't answer that. I'm only the arresting officer."

Anxiety furrowed eyebrows, as though they all expected Harris to put Richard in handcuffs and march him out of the Schloss. The moment gave Damon an opening to create even greater alarm. It was now or never.

"You also cut my brake line, didn't you, Richard?"

The statement, tossed without preamble into the conversation, was as unexpected as a rock through a window.

"What are you talking about?" Richard asked, fear now replacing concern. This was new information.

"Last Friday, someone cut my brake line, two of them in fact. I nearly smashed into a car when I was driving back to my apartment. I am lucky to be standing here."

Bewilderment etched Richard's face. "I didn't touch your car, I don't even know what you drive. More than that, I don't know how to cut a brake line!"

The cry of innocence echoed throughout the Great Hall, creating what amounted to a family cabal. Shouts of anger increased in intensity, denouncing Damon's accusation.

Harris again stepped into the growing furor, this

time supporting the Fischers. "Let me handle this," he said to Damon, his voice overflowing with frustration. "You can't accuse someone of a crime with absolutely no proof."

He glanced apologetically at Richard. "Sorry, Mr. Rand, you have enough on your plate to worry about."

Damon's own frustration grew. "Well, someone around here knows how to cut a brake line." He stared accusingly at Del. "A mechanic would know, right, Del?"

"First you accuse my brother," CT-Two growled, "and then you accuse a man who works for us, as though you will stop at nothing to bring us down, even if it means destroying the reputation of one of our most loyal employees. You heard the Lieutenant, Soldier, leave it alone!"

"If you ever tried to brake your car and nothing happens, you would have a hard time leaving it alone!" Damon shot back. "And stop calling me Soldier!"

There was a silence so brittle one felt the Schloss itself might crack.

Del rose from his chair and stood straight and tall, imposing in his uniform. "I know cars, Mr. Petroulis, I won't deny that. And I also admit I repaired Mr. Richard's Mercedes, but I am telling you the truth right now. I did not cut your brake lines."

"Then who did?" Damon said of no one in particular but rather out of futility.

"How about you?"

Damon looked in the direction of the accuser. It was CT-Two in a cocky pose, daring to take Damon on in a fight to the finish.

"Are you suggesting that I cut my own lines?" Damon asked. "Why would I do that?"

"To get attention. '*Someone is out to get me!*'" CT mocked in a falsetto. "Just like that crap about Madie."

"That is totally absurd," Damon fired back.

"Stop squabbling like a couple of teenagers!" Harris called out wearily. He gave Damon a dirty look.

"This is not part of my investigation but I will make it so if you two keep arguing. I will take you both in for fingerprints and then I'll dust Damon's car to see who cut those lines, and that will settle it. Are you willing to do that, Damon?"

"Sure," he said confidently. He had to keep from smiling. There were no prints. They were destroyed when Jim repaired the brake lines at the garage. Harris was playing a game of high-stakes poker. He was more daring than Damon had given him credit for.

"What about you, Mr. Rand?"

CT acted like a ground hog ready to disappear into his hole. "Never mind," he said presently.

Damon was willing to bet a year's salary that it was CT who crawled under his car when it was parked behind the garage and cut the lines. He hated Damon enough to do that. But Harris clearly he had no interest and no lawful reason to pursue this further.

"All right, then," Harris said, ready to wrap things up, "are we finished here?"

"I have a question, Lieutenant," Irene said. "What about Madie? Are you going to arrest her?"

"Before I decide that, Mrs. Campbell, I will have a talk with Mrs. Stockton."

Phillip came forward. He had said nothing till now, a private man who kept his thoughts and opinions to himself.

"Shall I ask Mrs. Stockton to come down, Lieutenant?"

"Yes, please. Have her meet me in the library." Harris looked around at the group. "You all can leave now."

The room began to empty. The last to leave was Sarah holding Amy by the arm.

Amy looked over her shoulder. "I want to make sure Granny is comfortable." They walked off.

Damon and Harris were now alone. He could tell that the officer was really tired. Harris was not young and this was a day even someone Damon's age would have found exhausting.

"I don't think I'd like your job."

"There were times I thought you really wanted it, like when you brought up those goddamned brake lines."

Damon smiled. "Thanks for bailing me out."

"I wasn't bailing you out, I was trying to save my investigation."

"But you took a chance. Suppose CT went along and you had to admit there were no prints?"

"When you spend your life interrogating people, you can read minds pretty well."

"You're sure he did it?"

Harris shrugged. "I really don't care."

"I ought to forget about it, then?"

"You are still in one piece, aren't you?"

Damon nodded. Harris was right. Forget about it. "Ok, back to Mrs. Stockton."

"She was never out of my mind," Harris said.

"What about my theory that she is a suspect?"

"Intriguing, but in my business you dump theories in the waste basket. Inserting Mrs. Stockton into the mix just gums up the works, clouds things. A prosecutor wants a clear-cut case. That's how you convince juries, and that's what I need to deliver, a suspect who can be charged and convicted. That's what my job is about. Sometimes we make mistakes, but we let the court system sort that stuff out."

"Sounds cold-blooded to me."

"It works most of the time."

Even that bit of justification did not make Damon feel better. Lady Justice was not just blind she was also deaf and dumb. He became silent, thinking that the road to justice was filled with potholes.

The late afternoon sun cast long shadows through the west-facing windows when Damon's thoughts were suddenly interrupted by a shout from upstairs that slashed the air like a knife ripping a heavy curtain.

It was Phillip looking over the second floor railing. "Lieutenant, come quickly! Something terrible has happened!"

His words echoed in the stairwell as Harris and Damon ran up to the second floor where they found the butler, ashen white, pointing a trembling finger in the direction of Madie's room.

"I knocked on Mrs. Stockton's door several times," he said, panting heavily, his words tumbling one over another. "When she didn't answer I went to Madie's room. The door was ajar and so I looked in..." His face was filled with horror as he led them down the hall.

Damon and Harris walked into the menagerie of stuffed animals. Madie lay across her bed wedged between a jumbo green giraffe and a gray kangaroo. Her arms were wrapped around the kangaroo. Mrs. Stockton was on the floor next to the bed, kneeling against it, her head slumped forward. There was a heavy stillness in the air.

Harris rushed over muttering "Jesus Christ" under his breath. He leaned over Madie. A knotted rope around her neck was turning her face purple. Her eyes bulged and her tongue stuck out. He felt for a pulse but it was already too late. He shook his head in frustration, then he bent down and turned Mrs. Stockton onto her back, straightening out her folded legs. Her face was lax but there was labored breathing. "She's still alive." Harris looked up at Phillip standing next to him. He was in such a nervous state Damon thought he was going to faint.

"Pull yourself together, Phillip! Run downstairs and call emergency!"

Phillip left them and Harris started pulling Mrs. Stockton to her feet, grunting from the effort.

"Aren't you going to give her CPR?"

"Not with a drug overdose. I don't know what she has in her but it's obvious she strangled Madie and then took enough drugs to kill herself, too. Well, she got half the job done. If we're lucky that will be it. Take her other side and help me walk her."

Damon held the limp figure under the arm and together the two men walked back and forth across the room, dodging stuffed animals, trying to keep Mrs. Stockton's legs from dragging. "We have to keep moving," Harris said between breaths. "Her system is shutting down. We have to counter that, wake her up if we can, make her irritated."

Damon was surprised how much effort it took to keep an unconscious person upright. "She wants to die," he said.

"Not if I can help it," Harris said. "I want to talk to her. Keep walking."

Another minute of exertion went by and Damon began to feel resistance. Mrs. Stockton began to pull on his arm, trying to free herself.

"Good," Harris said, "she's waking up."

Just as he said that Mrs. Stockton lurched convulsively and threw up, spewing vomit on a life-size panda bear sitting in a wing chair, its paws resting on the curved arms. The shiny glass eyes of the stuffed animal clouded over from the poisonous contents of Mrs. Stockton's stomach, but it didn't matter, they were as blank and unseeing as Madie's eyes.

35

At noon Damon walked into the Sculpture Courtyard and sat on the bench by the Marini Horse and Rider. The skylight above his head revealed gray clouds announcing the beginning of fall. He was alone and would remain so until Lieutenant Harris showed up. It was Monday, the traditional closing day of museums all over the world, and they would have the place to themselves. Damon was early for the meeting, their last in the Courtyard with the officer because, as Harris put it on the telephone, "Let's end up where we began. As you know, I like symmetry."

Given the turmoil that had engulfed Damon during the summer, symmetry was the last word that came to mind. The cataclysmic afternoon when he and Harris entered Madie's bedroom was the crushing blow that shattered the Fischer image, crumbling it to dust. Burned in his memory was the image of Madie lying on her bed, hugging her make-believe kangaroo in a death embrace, choreographed by a mad woman who had put an end to Madie's life with a rope around her neck. The Fischer's diligently honed reputation, the mantle of power, the perpetuation of a family dynasty was torn to shreds.

Amid the chaos, the first to arrive was an ambulance

with lights blinking and siren blaring, not only jarring the bucolic nature of Breckett's point, but also announcing for all within earshot that there was an emergency at Schloss Fischer. A neighbor would have assumed that, finally, the old lady, Sarah Rand, had had a stroke. Certainly that was a reasonable if not expected assumption, but the person who was wheeled out on a stretcher was the loyal nurse and caretaker of Madie, the rigid and crusty woman hardly anyone ever saw or talked to. It was enough to start tongues wagging.

And then, as far as Sarah was concerned, the impossible happened—Schloss Fischer was overrun with law enforcement personnel: men in black with Forensics printed on their shirts, the Medical Examiner with his black bag and plastic gloves, a police photographer taking dozens of pictures of Madie lying on her deathbed before being covered in a gray blankct and moved on a gurney to a van waiting in the drive.

On the heels of the police, television trucks from three channels pulled up at the gate and set up their equipment. Reporters vied with one another for interviews with anyone who came close to a microphone, even people driving by in their cars, wondering what all the action was about. Tom, Patti Azquith's cameraman from Channel 4 followed the ambulance up the drive, and pushed his way into the Great hall before he was stopped and escorted out, but not before he got a lot of sordid footage for Patti, unfortunately, to make the most of.

Sarah remained in seclusion. Amy showed up at the front entrance along with Damon and Harris to wait for Sarah's private physician to arrive. After hearing the gruesome news about Madie, Sarah had collapsed. Phillip, the only calm, clear-headed person left called her physician, Dr. Hayward, whose arrival was missed by Damon because of the crowds teeming in and out of the Schloss, but he did catch sight of Richard getting into a squad car on his way to the county jail. CT was with him and leaned into the back seat, probably assuring his brother that he would be out in minutes, free on bond.

Damon was standing in the doorway concentrating on the squad car carrying Richard away when he sensed an imposing presence sidle up to him.

"Great hat."

It was Jon Love. In the turmoil Damon had totally forgotten that Jon had come to make a statement to the police. He smiled wryly. "We seem to run into each other under unusual circumstances, don't we, funerals and crime scenes."

"I hope this is the end of it. How did your interview go?"

"Painless. The officer just wanted to verify where I was when Arvid was killed. I told him I was home in bed."

"That's what we all need to do, put everything to bed."

"Not quite. I haven't told you yet about my meeting with Arvid on Saturday."

"So Arvid was with you. I was wondering where the hell he was. Phillip told me he was coming into town to see me but he never showed up."

"He did not want anyone to know."

"Why not?"

"I will tell you. As you know, Sarah has been my client a long time, long enough to learn where all the bodies are buried, if you will kindly excuse the pun. I've handled Sara's personal finances ever since her father died. Her will is in my office, under lock and key of course."

No question Jon Love had a unique position with the family. His success had to do with his lawyerly and financial acumen but also with his disarming personality, his charm, his charisma, as well as an innate skill in observing the human condition. He was not so different from the Greek chorus of ancient drama, which stood apart from the action on stage, observing and, when needed, commenting.

"Is that what he came to see you about, Sarah's

will?"

Jon nodded. "An astute deduction, Damon."

"You said her will was under lock and key. Weren't you breaking Sarah's trust, if not the law, showing Arvid the will?"

"I wasn't showing him the will, my friend, I was adding to it."

"What do you mean?"

"Arvid delivered a codocil replacing Beth Rand's name with that of Amy Jacobsson. The young lady you are so obviously attracted to is the chief beneficiary of Sarah's estate."

Damon whistled softly. Even though he knew this was a distinct possibility the news was still startling. "So Sarah is passing the torch."

"As well as the pocketbook, my friend."

"But why would she entrust Arvid with bringing you a change to her will?"

"She did not want anyone in the family to know about it. This was not an overnight decision. After Beth died Sarah decided to bring Amy into the open. Sarah used Arvid to do her dirty work."

"That also explains the connection to the detective, Jacob Ratner," Damon said. "Sarah used Arvid as a cover to find Amy and bring her home, home to the Schloss, that is. My god, how devious she was."

"Arvid and I talked about this over double martinis at the Minneapolis Club that night. Arvid got so plastered I brought him to my apartment. I could not let him drive home in that condition."

"So that's where he was."

Jon nodded. "Recovering from a massive hangover. But at least he cleared out the garbage in his soul. He desperately needed to talk to someone."

"You were his father confessor."

Jon made a small bow of fake humility "He explained to me how his unholy relationship with Ellen developed. They grew up pretty much shunned by the family, lonely and isolated. They had no one else but each other. Eventually they became lovers. He cried talking about it. I don't think he ever lost his love for her. Sarah separated them, as you know, kicking him out of the nest and turning Ellen over to Edmond as the ersatz daughter. They never saw one another again until Arvid came home for Beth's funeral. It must have been quite difficult to be in the same room and yet keep a discreet distance."

"That night at dinner, remember? Ellen ran outside after her emotional outburst and Arvid followed her. How sad that was the only time they were alone together. At least they had a few minutes of privacy." Damon became thoughtful for a moment. "But none of this excuses his behavior with Elizabeth."

Jon shrugged. "Well, to be honest, Damon, we wouldn't have had Amy, then, would we?"

*****

There was no funeral for Madie. She was taken to the morgue where her body was claimed three days later after the autopsy, a perfunctory exercise since it came as no surprise that she died of asphyxiation caused by strangulation. Her body was cremated, and her ashes scattered, without ceremony, on Lake Minnetonka by Phillip leaning over the side of the Chris-Craft. It was as if she had never existed. In a perverted way she never had.

As for Arvid, Crystal insisted that he be given a proper burial, but not a single member of the family attended his funeral at the Welander-Quist mortuary on Hennepin Avenue, nor the burial service at Sunset Memorial Cemetery on St. Anthony Boulevard north of Minneapolis. The further away the better.

These unpleasant recollections, clattering in Damon's mind like so many marbles rolling around, kept him occupied till Harris showed up. He joined Damon on the bench, his suit as rumpled as ever, and Damon wondered idly if he ever had it pressed. But no matter, he was not part of the art world where fashion was keenly observed and religiously followed in order to stay current with the latest trend.

"It's been awhile," he said to Damon, exhaling as he sat.

"Nearly a month."

Harris spread his arms. "Are you happy to be around modern art again?"

"I'm glad to be back, but my job description has changed. The woman who took over when I was assigned to the Schloss is now PR Director."

"What do you do?"

"Planning and Development."

"Sounds fancy, must be a promotion."

"Not really, it's a deal I made with my boss. I told him if he wants me to stay I have to do something else, and I presented him with a proposal to help the Fischers restore their battered image."

"What would that be?"

"A new Fischer Art Center."

"Really?" Harris asked, raising a bushy eyebrow.

"The plan is to tear this old building down and replace it with a new museum, a modern showpiece for modern art. What CT built represents a past everyone wants to bury and a new museum will help erase the bad memories."

"Did your boss like the idea?"

"Enough to fund a feasibility study, which I am heading up."

"Good for you. Sounds like you are getting your life back together. So how are things between you and the Horse Girl?"

Damon made a noncommittal shrug. "She is busy taking care of Sarah. I don't think Amy has left her side since Madie died. They have really bonded."

"What about the horse farm? Has she given that

up?"

"Amy is not someone who forgets her roots. Her relationship with Elroy and Doris can only be better with Arvid dead, and it doesn't hurt that the stigma associated with her birth is buried along with him. By caring for Sarah, she is no doubt relieving pressure on the Fischer family and helping regain some stability in the Schloss."

"So how does that affect your relationship?"

"I told her once that the only time we'll see each other is at Board meetings, on opposite sides of the conference table. And that looks truer by the day."

"You spent the night together when I was looking all over the county for you. Two people that close don't just hang it up."

"We move in different circles now. I don't fit in with the Fischer elite. That's not my style or my desire."

Harris looked kindly at Damon. "If you want my advice—not that you ever took it—keep your options open. A gal like her comes once in a lifetime."

Damon did not have to be reminded. "Right now, she doesn't need me to complicate her life more than it is. Besides, I need time away from the Schloss. The place haunts me, makes me feel strange."

"That's a good word for it, strange. Like that Stockton woman."

Harris changed the subject. Good, Damon thought. He was more than ready to shift attention away from him and his relationship with Amy. "So what have you learned?" he asked.

"Getting anything out of her was harder than pulling teeth. She has nearly driven me crazy." Harris stopped and looked at Damon apologetically. "I didn't come here to complain, but she is one tough cookie. We've had her at Minneapolis General since the day she OD'd. She's in the psycho ward, which is locked off from the other floors."

"What did she take that nearly killed her?"

"Diazepam, an anxiety drug prescribed for Madie. There was enough in that bottle to tranquilize an elephant.

Stockton could have had seizures and cardiac arrest but we got to her in time. I could not have saved her without you. Walking her around made the difference. Because of that she threw up and dumped out the contents of her stomach."

The memory of that brown viscous fluid dripping off the face of Madie's panda bear turned his own stomach.

"If she hadn't thrown up she would have died," Harris continued.

"The opposite of poetic justice," Damon said. "She swallowed the pills to die but by throwing them up she lived. That didn't save Madie, though. Why did she kill her?"

"You don't have to be a psychiatrist to see that Stockton's world was crashing around her. She has a super ego and also a twisted one. She wanted to kill herself but she could not leave Madie behind, convinced that Madie could not possibly manage without her. So it was a murder-suicide. Stockton needed Madie more than Madie needed Stockton."

"What a sad figure."

"You were right about her." Harris managed a smile of admiration. "I had my doubts about her involvement, remember? You missed your calling. You should have been a detective."

"I was just working on a hunch. I didn't find anything about her in my research, except that she was a nurse at the clinic where Ellen was pregnant with Madie."

"She did a good job hiding her past," Harris said. "Her first name by the way is Mildred. She grew up in Rich Hill, Missouri. Her father was a Pentecostal preacher and when she was fifteen he knocked her up."

"Her own father?"

Harris nodded. "Déjà vu all over again, right?"

Damon tried to smile at Harris's small joke but his jaw was too tight.

"Pentecostals don't believe in abortion," Harris said,

"and Stockton was forced to have the kid. It died at birth but the experience left her pathologically fearful of men, clearly a factor in what happened at the Schloss."

"My god, how could Sarah ever allow that woman to take care of Madie?"

"As I said, Stockton was good at hiding her tracks. At some point she started referring to herself as Mrs. even though she never married, and yet no one ever followed up. It's amazing how much you assume when you don't want to dig too far, take things for granted and accept them as they are. There was nothing to suggest anything was wrong while she lived in the Schloss. She took good care of Madie, actually too good, monopolizing her in every way. I don't think the family minded, everything was fine until Arvid returned."

"Arvid..." Damon said.

Harris nodded. "The fly in the ointment. Whenever I mentioned his name she clammed up. So we had a woman psychologist who faked being a nurse take care of her. She took her time to win Stockton's trust, and Stockton finally started talking. She hated Arvid for what he did, raping his own sister, committing incest just like her father, a frightening parallel there. Arvid was Madie's father and anyone labeled father was an automatic threat no matter who he was. She was managing to hold on to her precarious mental state, but then you came along."

"I was just going to write a family history."

"Yeah, except that your relationship with Beth heated up. That was the tipping point. Remember Stockton's attitude toward sex—evil and disgusting. Imagine what was going through her mind knowing that right down the hall from her room you were screwing Beth. Someone engaged in something that dirty had no business getting close to Madie who would get contaminated, even sullied."

"That makes sense," Damon said. "The only one who ever took the time to be with Madie outside of Mrs. Stockton was Beth."

"Stockton was as obsessive as someone who can't stop washing her hands. She had to end the contamination. If she didn't her whole world would have collapsed."

"So it wasn't Madie after all."

"It was never Madie."

"Except when she tried to kill me."

"Because, as you claimed correctly, Madie saw her family ridiculed on TV. She was as steeped in the pride of being a Fischer as anyone, and after she saw you taking pot shots at the family, she acted out her anger by attacking you. She could have finished you off, but when you scratched her hands the sudden pain must have startled her, like coming out of a trance, and she backed off probably horrified to realize what she was doing."

"Do you think Stockton saw Madie leave her room and follow me?"

"She claims she didn't but I don't buy that. I can't imagine Madie leaving her room without Stockton knowing. She wouldn't have shed any tears if Madie had indeed killed you. And when she came back with her hands badly scratched, Stockton covered for her, making sure she wore gloves when she left her room."

"And Stockton also finished off Arvid."

"She followed him when he took a walk along the lakeshore, and strangled him with the same rope she used on Beth. She had to kill Arvid in order to complete the cycle of revenge. By killing Arvid she also symbolically killed her father. He embodied everything that was at war within herself, both real and imagined."

Damon thought about Sarah's Curse. It began when Arvid raped his own sister and ended when Mrs. Stockton killed him, the first and last chapters of a family history that Damon did not write, it was written for him.

"So," Harris said, reading his mind, "how is the family history doing?"

"You can read it with someone else's byline on the front page of the Minneapolis Star."

"Not exactly how you planned it."

"Not even close. Sarah depended on me to handle what the press said about her and the family. I let them all down."

"No you didn't. If you hadn't become involved none of this would have come out. The family was rotting from within and you exposed it for what it was. You ought to be proud of that. I couldn't have solved the murders without your help, as misguided as it was from time to time. You are persistent, stubborn, willing to take chances. Like I said you'd make a hell of an investigator."

"You are more than kind, Lieutenant."

"Forget the Lieutenant stuff, will you? It's time you called me by my first name."

"I thought that was your first name."

Harris laughed heartily.

They stood and he extended his hand. Damon shook it.

Harris looked around. "I think I could start liking modern art."

"Anytime you want a guided tour, let me know."

They parted waving to each other and Damon was alone again—alone except for his thoughts. He followed the flagstone path, walking past familiar bronzes, old friends. Harris did not settle his mind the way he had hoped. That an outsider was responsible for the cruel deaths was a relief, but it did not lessen the horror of the root cause, an unforgivable act of incest, the Curse of the Big Water that, a generation later, fed the flames of hatred, fear and, finally, revenge. Will he ever be able to put to rest the disturbing memories of a summer now drawing to a close? He was far from confident that he could.

On his way back to his office he walked past Donna sitting at her switchboard.

"Damon!" she called out, stopping him. "I was looking all over for you. I have a phone message. You weren't at your desk and Maggie didn't know where you were. Hiding from her?"

He forced a smile. Donna was incorrigible. "I was in the Sculpture Court, meditating."

"Well, meditate this." She handed him a note folded over.

"What is it?"

"Just read it, honey," she said.

Damon unfolded the note. It was from Amy. There were only four words:

Sarah died this morning.

Peter Georgas, author of Dark Blues, The Empty Canoe, and The Fifth Slug, earned a BA in Journalism from the University of Minnesota. Following a decade in advertising, he joined the staff of the Walker Art Center in Minneapolis as the museum's first full time publicist. Later, along with his family, he moved to Austria, where he was Director of the Salzburg Seminar. He and his wife now live in the Linden Hills neighborhood of Minneapolis.